A KING ENSNARED

J R TOMLIN

ALBANNACH PUBLISHING

❀ Created with Vellum

MAP

The World of King James I

CHAPTER 1

MARCH, 1402

A black and gray lizard disappeared into the jumble of a patch of bluebells. Kneeling next to them, James pushed back the stems. If he caught the lizard, he could find out if the stories were true that it would regrow its tail. The bushy leaves rustled further into the patch. James lunged, and his fingers brushed the cool, dry skin of his prey, but it slithered away. The scent of crushed leaves and moist earth drifted on the air.

The murmur of his royal father's voice and that of Bishop Wardlaw blended with the buzz of bees in the flowers. Sir David Fleming of Biggar stood listening to their words. James glanced to be sure that they were paying him no mind. Even seated, his father bent forward, leaning upon his staff. He was a tall man but gray. His hair, what little remained, was gray, and beneath his long, thin beard, his face was gray. Facing the two men, father's grizzled chancellor sat with his elbows on his knees, broad shoulders hunched slightly as he listened to the bishop talk to the king. A man-at-arms was lounging, propped up by the garden wall, eyes half-closed as

1

he drowsed in the sunshine. The bishop gestured as he leaned, so his mouth was next to the head of James's sire.

The man-at-arms at the gate smiled in James's direction and winked.

The bluebells rustled again. James spotted the lizard in the greenery and leapt. He seized the lizard, which was not much longer than his hand except for its tail. It wriggled as he lifted it carefully. If he grasped it by its tail, the thing might come off so it could escape, but he wanted to watch the tail regrow. It would be amazing to see. He chewed on his lip. He had a wooden box in his chamber. In that, he could be sure the lizard wouldn't run away.

The creature stilled as he clutched it to his chest, and he glanced around, still on his knees. If they noticed his leaving, they'd believe it if he said he was going to his books, for he liked reading. He didn't mind his lessons and the stories in his few books, but now he had better things to do. He looked down at the lizard's bright black eyes and laughed a little. He stood to brush at the dirt on his knees. His tutor would be displeased if he came to table covered in dirt again.

The man-at-arms gave James a half-grin and said softly, "Caught it, did you, my young lord?"

James grinned back at him. As he sidled past a rosebush toward the gate, a commotion came from the castle bailey yard—clattering hooves and shouting.

"I have news for the king," someone yelled.

Feet pounded. The man-at-arms jerked around and dropped a hand to his pike.

It was only William Giffart, his brother's squire, and a few men. As Giffart strode through the garden, his band of men-at-arms filled the gateway. James sighed. No escape now.

Giffart, his handsome face still and serious, had reached the king, so James might as well listen, he decided. Forbye, the knight might have news of Davey.

"Your Grace!" Giffart dropped to a knee next to the bench where the king sat.

It had been long since he'd heard news of his brother, and Giffart had accompanied Davey when he had been given as a prisoner to their uncle of Albany. Mayhap he was at last free to return home. James shook his head. He'd never understand why their father had allowed his brother to be taken prisoner. Davey was supposed to be Lieutenant of Scotland, so it made no sense. They said he was wild, but he never seemed so to James.

"Whisht, man," Fleming said. "The king must suffer no excitement."

"My lord, he must be told," Giffart gasped. "It is the Duke of Rothesay, Sir David." He paused, eyes wide and face flushed from a frantic ride. "He is dead."

As though his chest were wrapped in ice, James couldn't breathe. His fingers let go the lizard, and it dropped to the ground. He stared as it skittered away, shaking his head. It must be a lie. "No," he wheezed with what felt like the last air in his body. He dashed to grab Giffart, who just raised an arm to hold him off.

"Prince James!" Sir William leaned forward and grabbed James's arm. He hauled him back, but James dragged his feet. Sir William threw an arm around his chest and held him tight. "Tha' will not help, lad."

"It's a lie," James said, through a throat that seemed to be squeezed closed. "It must be. Davey can't be dead."

Giffart shook his head and turned back to the king. "Your Grace, I swear it. In the dungeon at Falkland Palace. I waited in the town, thinking the duke would let me join my lord after a time. But they say..." He wiped a hand across his mouth and ducked his gaze to the ground. "They say the Duke of Albany ordered Lord David starved to death."

James jerked against William's arm, grabbed it, and pushed, struggling to free himself.

His father raised his head and gazed past them at nothing at all, his face blank and still. Slowly, the king let his head sink until it rested in his hands. "He swore to me he meant Davey no harm." His voice wavered.

James plunged and broke free, shouting, "You must do something!"

Sir William grabbed him around the waist.

He lunged at his father, fists clenched, straining against the tall knight. "Do something. Make him—make him pay for hurting Davey!"

His father's mouth moved without sound.

"Mother would have done something!"

A sob ripped the king's thin voice. "My son…" He reached for the bishop's arm. "It was for Davey's own good to imprison him for a while, not to hurt him."

"For his good?" James shook from head to foot with an emotion he could not name. "You… You let them take him, and they killed him!"

"Prince James, be still," the bishop said sternly.

With Sir William holding him against his chest, James felt as though he were floating, and only the regard of the two men held him to earth.

The bishop rested his chin upon the palm of his hand. He rubbed his eyes with a finger and thumb, looking unbearably weary. "We must take the young lord to safety."

The king opened his mouth and shut it. "Miserere mei, Deus. Why did I trust him?" he choked out. Tears gleamed in his eyes and dripped down his lined cheeks into his beard. "Wha' should we do?"

"You must call a parliament," the bishop said. "Give James the earldom of Carrick as his regality, but do nae give him the dukedom of Rothesay, to leave his uncle in doubt to your intent. But by the time that is done, I shall have him safely awa' in St. Andrews Castle as his tutor. Even the Duke of Albany will not be in a hurry to attack me there."

The bishop was tugging on the king's arm, urging him to his feet. "William, see Prince James to his room. Some watered wine to calm him. Bide wi' him there."

"If he hurt James…" His father's voice broke. "By the Holy Rood, he might kill James, too, so he would be my heir…"

"You're supposed to be king." James shook his head, ashamed that his nose was dripping. He couldn't make them listen if he wept, but a sob shook him. "You will not even try. You are supposed to protect…" The rest wouldn't go past his closed throat, however hard he tried, as the though sobs he hadn't let out had scraped it raw.

"Enough, lad," the bishop said. "This is not your royal father's fault. For the nonce, it is you we must be concerned wi', and for a while, I can protect you."

Sir William tightened his grip, and James hunched, ashamed of the tears. "Lad, you must be strong."

"We must make plans, Your Grace," Sir William said. "We must see to the lad's safety."

The king leaned on the bishop's arm, and his staff quivered in his other hand. "Help me to my bed," he whispered.

James glared at his father's back. "Devil take him," he rasped out. "I hate him! He is no king."

William pressed a hand over James's mouth. "You must not say such things, my lord. It is only that he is a gentle man." He sighed. "Too gentle."

CHAPTER 2

FEBRUARY 1406

$\mathcal{J}$ames fastened his grip on the rough stone of the merlon and swung a leg through the crenel so that one foot dangled over the outer edge of the castle wall. Henry Percy stuck his head through the opening behind him.

"What do you think?" Percy asked.

An icy sea wind whipped James's hair around his face. "Don't shove so," James muttered and held on as he bent to peer down.

Since Henry's grandfather had fled for Wales the week before, at the threat of being traded to the English usurper, they'd both been forbidden to leave the safety of St. Andrews Castle by Bishop Wardlaw. Every gate was locked and guarded, but that did not mean there was no way out. Even if they couldn't ride, at least they could clamber over the rocks free of lessons and clerics' disapproving stares.

"One of the stones sticks out enough to stand on. Not too far to jump onto—halfway down." James chewed on his lip, trying to see what they might hold onto. The rocks below the walls of the castle that edged the gray, white-capped sea were fearsome if he slipped.

"Let me see." Henry pulled on his arm and slid into his place. He clung, white-fingered, to the merlon as he leaned far over. "I think my feet would almost reach it if I hold onto the edge," Henry said with a worried tone.

"We'd have to jump the rest of the way." James had jumped from high up, but those rocks were sharp and hard and further from that narrow perch than he was tall.

"You're afraid," Henry taunted. "I'm not afraid of anything." He swung his leg back onto the parapet walk to sit on the edge of the stone and frowned up at James.

"I am not! I'm not afeart of anything. My ancestor, the great Bruce, would have leapt down like a stag. And he beat the English as well." There was nothing that Henry Percy would do that he wouldn't. Henry might be a year older, and taller, but James knew he was stronger than Henry was.

"He did not!" Henry glowered. "No Scot can beat us."

"He did." James gave him a shove, and Henry shoved back, but it wasn't very hard. James grinned. "We have little time before the bishop sends someone looking for us."

"We should bring our cloaks. If we drop them over and—" A horn blew, wavering in the distance. Henry's eyes widened.

Henry didn't talk about his grandfather, the earl, who had fled Scotland to escape the Duke of Albany and the lord of Douglas. Henry's grandfather had led a rebellion against the English usurper, Henry the Fourth, when he overthrew King Richard. The rebellion failed. The Scottish nobles would gladly trade the Earl of Northumberland for their own relatives, captive in English hands. The bishop had been grim-faced at the threat to his guest, had sworn to keep the earl's grandson safe, and had seen the earl off secretly in the dead of night.

James raised his eyebrows at his companion and then

7

looked toward the road out of sight beyond the Sea Tower. For months, riders had galloped out at night, and the bishop's clerics had carried messages that had gone to ash on the hearth as he and Henry sat writing out their lessons. A week after the earl fled, the bishop had sent James's own esquire, William Giffart, on some secret mission they would not discuss.

"Come on," James said. He gripped Henry's wrist and jerked him to his feet. He whirled and dashed along the parapet walk and into the tower and through the far door.

The road to St. Andrews Castle was narrow and steep; it ran beside a steep drop to the rock-torn surf that threw spray high into the air. Men-at-arms, a hundred of them at least, came two abreast up the twisting, stony road. James let out a breath as he peered between the towering merlons. It was too few to be an attack. He chewed his nether lip. "Too few men to be Albany or Douglas. Forbye, they want your grandfather."

"They might be after you, though," Henry said. Everyone knew if James were dead, Albany would be the next King of the Scots.

Two banners flapped atop pikes. James recognized the white and black one. "That's the Earl of Orkney," he said and felt a flush of relief, but the second banner had wrapped itself around the pole at the head of the column. "And my mother's brother, mine uncle, Sir Walter!"

"What's the other?" Henry asked.

There were too many men-at-arms for it to be Giffart. Then the banner unsnarled itself and James made out the red and blue quartered banner of David Fleming of Biggar. "Sir David."

Henry shrugged. "Who?"

"My sire's chancellor. He must have come from Dundonald Castle." Sir David wouldn't have come for a minor matter. But what news would bring him all the way to St. Andrews?

Wood and metal creaked as the counter weights and pulleys raised the portcullis and lowered the drawbridge. James gulped a breath of air as though he'd been running hard, chest heaving. Whatever news Sir David brought, James was sure it would be dire. As dire as when Giffart had brought the news of Davey's death.

"Why would they come, do you think?"

"Let us to our lessons," James said and darted past Henry to clatter down the narrow stairs, leaping them two at a time. Hoof beats drummed behind them, crossing the drawbridge. "If we're there and quiet, we'll hear the news. He may be too busy to notice."

James ducked into a narrow side door with Henry on his heels. A gust of wind set the torches flickering as they hurried on tiptoe through the dimly lit stone passage. James hesitated at the door, but all was quiet within, so he pushed it open.

Henry snorted. "The bishop always sees what we're doing." He massaged the back of his head where he had received a slap from the bishop when he'd dozed off over morning lessons.

A small fire burned on the hearth. A long oaken table stacked with scrolls, parchments, and leather-bound books stretched near the length of the chamber. A single, heavy tall-backed chair was drawn up. The draft from the open door set tapers on the table fluttering.

James pushed the door closed behind them and scurried to the smaller table at the back of the room, where he and Henry spent long hours studying.

James's stool scraped on the floor as he pulled it out, plunked himself down, and hooked his feet around the legs of the stool. "Whisht." He lowered his voice to a whisper as he picked up his quill. "We can listen outside the door if he—"

Voices in the passage made him bend his head close over the parchment, where he was writing out Latin verbs before he'd fled his lessons. He dipped his quill in ink as the door opened.

"Bring wine and food for my guests," the bishop said to a servant as he entered. "My lords have had a weary journey."

The servants scurried like a covey of quail as they fetched wine, cakes, a faggot of wood to build up the fire. Pine logs on the hearth wafted a resinous scent. Men took the newcomers' cloaks, bowing and murmuring. All the bishop's servants were like that, solicitous and comforting, before they withdraw humbly out of sight.

The tall, long-limbed Earl of Orkney crossed the chamber to hold his hands out to the fire, his red hair catching the gleam of the flames. "Aye. Weary enough, and a wearier journey yet before us."

"Then they've agreed to receive him?" the bishop said. "I fear it is barely in time."

James, hair flopping in his eyes, peeked warily at the men, afraid his gaze would catch their attention. His bluff uncle, Walter Haliburton, dropped his eyelid in a wink but didn't give him away.

Fleming was a stocky man with a salt and pepper moustache and upright bearing. He blew out a gusty breath as he threw his gauntlets onto the table. His ruddy face was wind chapped and lined with fatigue. "Desperately past time. I would give a good deal if we had been able to act sooner."

The bishop jerked his head to look into James's face. His lips twitched, and his big chest shook with a low laugh. Even with streaks of gray in his hair, he was an impressive man, tall and beefy in a purplish black robe and fine white lace.

Inclining his head, he said in a mild tone, "A good try, lads. But you'll nae listen without being invited."

Henry dropped his quill and poked James's side with an elbow. He muttered, "Knew it wouldn't work."

James wiped the tip of his quill and laid it neatly next to the parchment. He stood and walked around the table as he studied Fleming's grim face, his heart hammering. "Wha' has happened?"

Fleming looked at Bishop Wardlaw. "He may as well hear now as later, Reverence."

Wardlaw nodded with a sigh. "Aye." He dropped a hand on Henry's shoulder. "Run along, lad. It's Scots business."

Henry gave the bishop a piteous look and was allowed to scoop up a cake. He ran out the door that Orkney closed quietly behind him.

James felt cold inside. "My father? Is he—"

"He lives, Prince James," Fleming said, his voice gravelly with emotion. "But he... I'm sorry, lad. He weakens by the day."

James's heart thudded like the hooves of a running horse. He stared at the stone wall hung with a tapestry—a hunt, and the stag lay bleeding. Moving a little in the draft, a long smear of crimson flowed from the arrow that had pierced its heart, at the feet of the hunters. Bleeding... but the colors swam together.

He hadn't seen his father since the terrible day at Stirling when he'd learned of his brother's murder. Now he never would, he thought. No more than he'd seen Davey after Albany took him prisoner.

James closed his eyes. "My uncle will slay me," he said. Would he lie bleeding at his uncle's feet or die starved in the dark? "As he did my brother."

"He must lay hands on you first," the Earl of Orkney said. "And we mean to see that he does not."

"How?" James shook his head. Even the near impregnable St. Andrews Castle would stand against his uncle's force for only so long once his father was dead.

"A ship awaits in Glasgow to leave for France," Fleming said. "I swear on my life, you'll reach it in safety."

Orkney turned his back to the fire. He swung the heavy chair around and pulled James by the arm to face him. "We'll travel in secret, but as long as the king lives, it is not as dire as it sounds. Letters have traveled to and fro between here and Paris. King Charles has agreed to receive you and you will be trained as befits a king. I shall head your household and see that a' is well."

"But—" James swallowed hard, and his words came out in a whisper. "They say that King Charles is daft."

The wind rattled the shutters at the narrow slit windows, and the flames of the wax tapers flickered before they stood straight. The bishop rubbed his forehead with the fingers of his large, beringed fingers. "It is true, I am afeart."

Orkney squeezed James's shoulder. "But those who govern his kingdom are not. Louis of Orléans, King Charles's brother, is most sane. You'll join his household as a squire, and I will be with you. You'll wait at the royal table, hear a' the talk of the nobles, and learn from it. There will be dozens of masters to see to your lessons. Orléans will see you trained and knighted, and you will return to claim the kingdom."

"My uncle will try to stop me." James felt empty and hollow, but he always felt so when he thought of his uncle. He took one of the cakes and bit into it; the honey taste filled his mouth, but he had to swallow past a stone in his throat. "If I am alive, he cannot be king."

"He may try to stop you," Sir David said. "But we will see you to Glasgow. Giffart sent word he has a ship awaiting you. From there, we can slip past the damned English pirates across the sea."

James said, "The Earl of Douglas holds Edinburgh. And they are allies."

Sir David grimaced. "Lothian is full of Douglas's ilk, no friends to me, but I shall see you past them."

"I am more concerned about secrecy to keep word from the English. If they knew Prince James was at sea, you may be sure they would try for such a rich prize." The bishop sipped his wine, his gaze distant. "So prepare, lad. You'll leave at first light before word can spread that your sire fails."

CHAPTER 3

*A*fter the bishop had sent him to his chamber, James lay for an hour or two, drifting half-asleep as he imagined thundering on his horse fast across snow-drifted braes. The sky outside his narrow window was still black when his chaplain looked in to say, "It is near time, my lord," and James went through his treasures: a dirk Davey had gifted him on his saint's day years ago, a gold ribbon and a much rubbed cameo of his lady mother's he had filched after she died, and a fist-sized piece of quartz that the bishop had let him take from his table of oddments. France was practically across the world. How could he remember his home?

During his musing, servants packed his clothes. There was thumping and shouting as the bishop ordered servants to pack gold plate for James's table and fine linens for his bedding, saying James must not give the appearance of a beggar to his French host. A servant laid out his armor and helped him to don it. He worked his shoulders, unaccustomed to the heavy weight. The bishop himself carried up his own fine copy of *La Chanson de Roland* to put into James's hand. Sir David said baggage would slow their flight, but the

Earl of Orkney only crossed his arms over his chest and scowled. The question in James's mind was: Wha' will my uncle do if he kens I am fleeing? If he tries to capture me, I shall kill him. I shall kill him. James's hands shook as he closed his bag and hurried down the narrow stairs.

Outside, icy rain trickled down James's neck, and his hair was in dripping strings. The bailey yard was filled with quiet confusion. Sumpter horses were being loaded with bags. Men-at-arms were leading horses from the stables to be saddled and talking in low voices as they looked at James from the corners of their eyes. Henry Percy stood near the keep door and gave James a little wave. James thought he wouldn't miss Percy much. They'd never truly been friends, just comrades for they were the only lads in the castle. The Earl of Orkney stood in the midst of the bustle watching, silent. Once he bent to a man-at-arms and gave a quiet order, so the man ran to lead James his horse. Sir David appeared out of the dreich, already ahorse.

James knelt at the bishop's feet, swallowing, clenching his shaking hands into fists. The bishop had been his only protection these last years, ofttimes stern, but James trusted him. The broad hand felt heavy on his head as the bishop prayed, "Sanctus Michael Archangelus te vigilet, et te custodiet ab omni periculo, et inimicos tuos ponet scabellum pedum tuorum." The hand fell on James's shoulder and squeezed. "Go wi' God, my prince. The saints protect and shield you whilst you are gone from us."

James stood and raised his chin to what he hoped was a proud angle. "May they shield and protect you as well, Excellence."

For a moment, the bishop looked grim, but he said, "We shall await your return."

Orkney gave the order to move out, the talk died, and they climbed into their saddles. Sir David sent half a dozen

15

scouts out first. Icy wind stung James's face as he rode between Orkney and Sir David in the vanguard of the column with his heavy cloak blowing in the blustery wind. They clattered down the incline of the stony road, past the gray-green sea that smashed itself furiously onto yellow sands. Then his chaplain rode with the sumpter horses and finally Robert Lauder with the rear guard. Two hundred men, all told.

After they clattered through the empty streets of St. Andrews town, Orkney wheeled his horse to lead them across country. They were climbing up from the coast into the high moorlands.

Beside James, Sir David gave the edge of his cloak a jerk, muttering a curse. "Falkland Castle is nearby. We should have traveled by night, as I said."

"This is the fastest way. The sooner we are awa', the less danger there is." Orkney loosened his sword in its scabbard, scanning the empty braes. "Send a man back wi' a command to keep in close order." He spurred his horse to a canter, and James eagerly nudged his horse to keep up.

After the weeks kept under close guard in St. Andrews, the horse between his legs and the wind in his face felt like freedom. They followed a narrow trail through woods that cut off some of the wind. It also cut off seeing if there were attackers waiting, and that made the skin between his shoulder blades twitch. The men behind were silent. James thought they were afraid, though no one would say so. He knew he had to learn not to be afraid. A king must not fear. He chewed his lip and wondered how one learned that lesson.

"The outriders will report if they spot anyone," Orkney said. He leaned forward in the saddle and sped up to a faster canter.

They rode in silence until James said, "How long until we're—"

Sir David finished for him. "We are safe when you set foot in Louis of Orléans household, nae before. Nightfall should see us out of Albany's reach, and within that of the Douglas, but they shall nae stop us nor have you."

A branch whipped at James's face as he passed. He rubbed at the sting. You sound nae too sure, he thought.

As the horses tired, they slowed to a walk, and James patted his mount's neck. He remembered suddenly how Davey had put him up on his first horse, laughing when James grasped at its mane. His gay and laughing brother. The weight in his chest made it hard to breathe when he thought of Davey locked in a black dungeon so crazed with hunger he'd gnaw off his fingers. It didn't help remembering the smiling face of his murderous uncle. He dropped his hand onto the hilt of his dirk and loosened it in its scabbard. A man needed a blade when he rode across Scotland, especially if he was sought by such enemies as his uncle, the Duke of Albany.

The sun had at last burned off the pewter clouds when their horses labored their way up the steep east face of Largo Law, their cloaks whipping around them. The harsh wet wind scoured James's face, but he gaped as they broached the top. He stared down at a vast chessboard of fields and green haughs and then the gray expanse of the never-ending Firth of Forth that faded into the far horizon.

Sir David muttered curses under his breath as they rode wearily down the south slope of the mound. They were much exposed to being spotted by their enemies.

"Douglas, hell mend him." Sir David hit his fist against his thigh. "He's more of a danger than even Albany." At least past its height, the south flank of Largo Law cut off some of the wind that had punished them.

When they came to the ford of the River Forth, a few beeches grew near the water and reeds filled the shallows. James looked anxiously around, but there was no sign of other riders. The river sloshed against the stony bank, burbling pleasantly, but black clouds boiled on the horizon.

Orkney held up a hand in command. "See to the horses, and we'll take a few hours rest."

James groaned in relief as he slid from the saddle. His legs wobbled, and he grasped the saddle. Well out from the camp, Orkney set a watch to ring their campfire.

"We're a large party," Orkney said as he sank to the ground with a sigh. "It will take luck to make our way through without being spotted."

"Ill weather is moving in," Sir David said. "I smell it on the wind. It may help cover our passage. But we pass close by Tantallon Castle before we turn west."

James tried to rub away the throbbing pain in his thighs. "I'm fair forfochen," he muttered, but he was ashamed for the hardened men around him to know how weary he was.

Robert Lauder held out a steaming bannock toward him. James broke it in two and chewed off a big bite, stomach grumbling. His hands were shaking with something, and he wasn't sure if it was the chill or hunger. "The Sinclairs are warders for Earl Archibald, aren't they?"

Orkney grunted in agreement. "I am nae afeart of Sinclair and their ilk. We're in more danger if word reaches the Earl of Douglas. He could bring out his whole army from Edinburgh." Orkney rubbed his face, shadows dancing over it from the fire and accentuating the dark circles under his eyes. "Finish that and rest, Prince James. We must ride before daybreak." He tossed over an apple that James caught with one hand.

CHAPTER 4

*S*leet slashed James's face as he spurred his horse across a narrow ford. A gust of wind caught his sodden cloak and set it slapping around him. Sir David was spurring his horse up the sloping rise from the ice rimed burn, its haunches bunching as it slipped on the slick ground, struggling. James slapped his horse's flank, determined to keep up. He was a good rider, but two days in the saddle with only a few hours rest had him stiff, with every muscle screaming. The ground was treacherous with ice and mud. The wind gusted again and whipped the sleet into his eyes. He thought of St. Andrews Castle, where the icy sleet would be coating everything until it glimmered, but within Henry Percy would be in the warm library bent over his books. James envied him at that moment. His wet cloak did no good against the cold, his shoulders and back ached from the weight of his armor, his legs burned with a fire he wasn't sure would ever go out, and his stomach grumbled.

Ahead, thin and wavering in the wind, an outrider blew his horn, sounding danger.

Sir David shouted, "Form up! On me!"

The horn sounded again, nearer.

As James spurred his horse to plunge up beside Sir David's dancing, snorting mount, the horn blared, harooooo, even closer. A line of oak and beech trees loomed blackly ahead.

Orkney pulled up and grabbed James's arm. "Bide beside me, lad!"

Then James could hear horses and shouts beyond the trees. A rider galloped through past the tree line bent close over his horse's withers. "Ware!" he shouted.

From behind the rider, James heard shouts of, "Douglas! Douglas!"

"Ride!" Orkney yelled as he slapped James's horse on the flank.

The horse surged to a gallop, nearly jerking James's arms loose. He bit back a gasp and used his reins to whip its shoulders. Mud showered in every direction from the pounding hooves all around him.

"A Fleming! A Fleming!" Sir David shouted. "To me!"

But the shouts mixed with the cries from behind them. "Douglas!"

Horns blared, and James wasn't sure which were theirs and which those of the Douglas warlords. A horse shrieked— a horrible sound. Hoof beats were like rolling thunder as they labored up a brae. Lather whipped into his face, mixing with the sleet.

"Pull up," Sir David said as they reached the top. "There is no way we can outrun them."

Bending and gasping for breath, James circled his dancing mount. "Then we fecht." He frowned down at the base of the hill where already hundreds of Douglas men-at-arms were forming a wide curved line. Twice their number. Perhaps three times. Mounted on the biggest horse James had ever seen, someone James thought must be the Douglas sat beneath the sodden banner. In the dim light, it looked almost gray, but James could make out the red heart it bore. Even from afar, Douglas looked nothing but a warrior in gleaming steel plate. He was pointing his men into position with a huge sword.

"I am no weakling," he said. "I can fecht."

"No," Orkney said. "You are the prize he seeks. And I'll nae chance tossing you into his hands."

Sir David gave a brusque nod. "I shall hold them here." He gave a look at Lauder, frowning. "We have few friends in Lothian but—"

Lauder offered Sir David his hand. "If you can hold our backs, I shall see Prince James safe to my Bass Rock Castle."

Sir David clasped Lauder's hand hard for a moment and gave a short nod.

James worked his dirk half out of its scabbard. He was sure he should put up some protest, should stay and fight his enemies, but the men paid him no mind. He couldn't think of the words that would convince them, though he told himself he wanted to.

"Aye, you are right, Lauder. It's our only chance." Orkney stood in his stirrups to shout, "Haliburton, wi' us." He pointed at one man-at-arms and then another, both burly men with scarred faces. "Keep close beside Prince James."

"Farewell and God keep you," David Fleming said, and he turned to one of his men. "Plant my banner. Dismount and form a schiltron." The men were throwing themselves from their saddles and running to make a circle, hoisting their pikes whilst three of them snatched up the horses' reins and led the snorting mounts away.

A horn blew at the base of the hill. There were shouts, and James looked over his shoulder. A column of horsemen moved toward them. The scrape of pikes being raised and the clatter of armor blended with curses and the hoof beats of oncoming horses.

One of the men-at-arms, the broader of the two, grabbed James's bridle. "We're awa'," the man grunted as he kneed his horse to follow the earl.

Orkney led them through the horses being hobbled, perhaps hoping they'd blend in, and their flight would go unnoticed. James had no time to think before they were cantering down the far slope. He could hear Sir David shouting commands.

Orkney set a faster pace, turning their little band toward the tree line that was a green-black mass in the distance. James's heart thundered in his chest in time to the fast hoof beats. A last glance over his shoulder and he saw rearing horses silhouetted against the setting sun. The circle of pikemen crumbled under the murderous charge. Men threw down their pikes to flee and were ridden down. Horsemen boiled on the top of the hill.

"Gallop!" Orkney shouted.

Screams roiled on the wind. James slammed his heels into his horse's flanks.

His dirk was in his hand, though he didn't remember drawing it. He'd die before he let them take him. Better dead than captured. He leaned forward in the saddle, urging the horse to a gallop between Lauder and the guard. The guardsman grunted. A lance stuck out from his back. He toppled slowly from the saddle.

James turned his dancing mount, raising his dirk, as the knight yanked his sword free from its scabbard. The man towered over him. The sword drew back in a lazy arc. James tried to take a last breath, his sight blurry, and the slash of his short dirk falling far short. Behind them were curses and shouts of pursuit.

In front of him, Orkney jerked his reins, and his horse

gave a fierce kick with its hind legs. The Douglas knight's horse screamed, the blow raking its neck. As the man fought his mount, Orkney hacked the man's arm through the elbow with a downward chop. "On!" Orkney yelled. The man-at-arms rode close, Orkney drawing up the rear as the trees closed around them. "Ride! Before more reach us."

They plunged into the stand of pines. A quick peek behind showed a horseman still hard on their heels.

"Faster," James yelled to his mount.

Orkney jumped a fallen oak and spurred between two pines and up a gentle slope. Their horses were laboring, hooves slipping in the dead leaves and ice. James was breathing almost as hard as his horse.

An armored hand clamped on his rein, and he slashed at it with the dirk he still clutched.

"Help me!" he shrieked as the man jerked on his reins.

His horse reared and came down hard. James catapulted out of the saddle. Dark sky, tree branches and Lauder hacking at the enemy knight somersaulted in his vision in a jumble. He managed to tuck his head by instinct. The ground smacked him hard, and a stone dug into his side. Winded and coughing, he rolled and scrambled away from thrashing hooves.

"Hell mend you!" Lauder shouted, above him.

The knight landed across James' legs and blood, warm and thick, splattered. James kicked, trying to free himself from the weight. He didn't recall Orkney dismounting, but the earl kicked the body off him and hauled him to his feet with both hands. "In one piece, lad?" he asked.

He took a deep breath as things settled, chest heaving, dizzy from the somersault, but nothing hurt worse than a fall in the practice yard. "Aye."

So Orkney boosted him back into the saddle, and Lauder grabbed the reins of the dead man's courser. James's side and arm throbbed from the fall, but he'd rather ride aching than wait for another of their pursuers. It was black as hell, and sleet pounded steadily on the canopy of branches, muffling the hoof beats and dripping icily down the backs of their necks. Orkney said they were heading east, although James wasn't sure how he could tell in the overcast night.

Once they were well away from the dead knight, the earl, in the lead, slowed to a walk along a meandering path. Lauder's horse stepped into a hole and went down on its haunches, Lauder cursing under his breath. He checked the horse's leg. They'd been lucky, and it wasn't lamed. James rode between Lauder and the nameless man-at-arms with Haliburton bringing up the rear. They were all expert horsemen, but the ground was icy and treacherous. A wolf howled in the distance, and the hair on the back of his neck stood up. Occasionally, he looked over his shoulder expecting to see their pursuers, but there was only the murk.

The Douglases were still seeking him, though, he knew. They must have spread out through the woods, but such a small party would not be easy to find. The sleet and rain might erase the trace of their passing.

After what seemed like hours, Orkney said, "If we are lucky, they'll think we headed west toward Glasgow and seek that way."

But they would be seeking. James never doubted it. If they catch me, they will kill the others and throw me in a dungeon, he thought, and then they will starve me to death as they did my brother. That way they could claim that he had not died at their hands. They were all kin. But a blade wasn't required to kill.

When they came to a narrow stream under the dark canopy of the forest, Orkney turned his horse's head and led them off the narrow rail to follow the water. The black night smelled of pine and river and cold. James sucked in his breath as the frigid water splashed onto his feet. He pulled his wet cloak closer around him, for all the good that did. The sleet had stopped. It started again when they came to another trail and climbed up the bank, scree spraying from under the horse's hooves.

Orkney scrubbed at his face before he said, "We'll rest the horses for a few minutes and water them before we move on."

James could have wept at the relief of sliding from the saddle. Shivering, he leaned his head on his horse's withers, warm and scratchy under his cheek.

Orkney patted his shoulder. "Braw lad." He put a flask into James's hands.

"Thank you." James took a drink and leaned his head back as the wine went warmly down his throat and curled in his stomach.

"It's nae so far to the coast." Lauder sank onto his haunches. "At Canty Bay, I keep a boat to reach the castle. They cannot touch you once we're there. It would need a larger army than even the Earl of Douglas has to take my fortress."

"They…" James cleared his throat. "They killed Sir David."

James couldn't make out Orkney's face in the gloom, but the earl bent his head with a long pause. "He was a good man."

"He died because he was helping me escape."

Orkney gave a deep sigh. "It's nae so simple as that, Prince James. He was behind Lord Percy fleeing, helped him out of Scotland. That made him an enemy of the Douglas." He shrugged. "He was doing his duty. Now I shall do mine, and we shall make it to Bass Rock."

"But we'll be trapped there."

Lauder snorted. "Wi' the wide sea for a bolt-hole? First, we must send word to William Giffart to bring the ship to us there, but you must not worry anent that. Leave it to us. You'll need your strength on the way, lad, so drink a wee bit more of that, and we'll rest for a short while."

"I wish we could build a fire." There was a hint of whine in James's voice, but he couldn't help it. He was cold, weary, and his empty stomach grumbled. He took another swallow of the wine before he handed the flask back to the earl.

The four of them sat, James drawing his legs up to his chest to wrap his arms around them. This was wrong, to be pursued only because he was the son of the king, for men to die for no reason except his uncle's greed. He laid his head on his knees and let his eyes close. When Orkney shook his shoulder, James realized he had drifted to sleep.

With a grunt, he used Orkney's hands to pull himself to his feet. A bruised body wouldn't keep him from riding. He climbed into the saddle and realized that the sleet had stopped. Perhaps at least they would dry as they rode.

The ground was thick with pine needles and leaves, a carpet of brown still wet from the rains. It squelched beneath the horses' hooves. Masses of pines and beeches that were bare of their leaves rose all around them.

The narrow, crooked path through the woods kept their pace to a walk. James couldn't help looking over his shoulder, wondering when the Douglas and his men would catch them. Something burst out of the branches of a pine. James ducked and grabbed for his dirk as a gray owl swooped over their heads. Haliburton gave him a wry smile and they rode on.

"We're nae far from Canty Bay," Lauder said. The trees were growing more widely spaced, and the ground slanted down to the sea. "It won't be safe until we are across the Forth so close to Tantallon Castle. So we should come up the coast from the south, as they're not like to spot us there."

Orkney grunted in agreement, and when they at last

rode out of the trees into a pale sun-washed noonday, he turned his horse's head south. They rode past moss-covered rocky outcroppings and crossed wave-swept strands. The air smelled of salt and seaweed, and James's stomach was so empty he was feared he would shame himself and throw up. All of their food had been on the lost pack horses.

It was black night with a sliver of moon and winking stars lighting the water as they clopped across the sand. The waters of the Forth rolled with slow thunder beside them onto the beach. The little village of Canty Bay was a line of black humps in the night.

"Whisht," Lauder said softly when they were a short walk from the first dark cot, too small to be even called a cottage. "Wait here." He swung from the saddle and strode along the beach and out of sight behind one of the cots.

Orkney moved in his saddle, leather creaking. Haliburton sighed softly. His mount snorted. James listened to the rumble of the waves. Then there were heavy footsteps, and Lauder strode back into sight with a brawny, dark shape behind him.

"Can they give me a meal and a corner for a few hours rest before I go?" Haliburton asked. "I'm in no fit state for my journey."

James frowned. "You're nae going wi' us?"

His uncle squeezed his shoulder. "Someone must take word to Giffart to bring the ship here."

"Oh." His heart thudded. It wasn't as though he often saw his uncle, but… soon there would be no one left whom he knew. And he would be alone. "I wish you could come," he whispered.

His uncle pulled him close in a brief hug against his barrel chest and released him. "We do wha' we must, my prince."

James blinked back the burning in his eyes.

Lauder pointed out onto the water. "There." A small craft was bobbing toward them.

"Come wi' me, my lord," the man with Lauder said and motioned to Lauder and the man-at-arms, who gathered up the reins to all their horses. Sir Walter clasped James to him one last time.

Two of the men in the boat were dragging it close upon the sands. Lauder clapped one on the shoulder and hurried them all through the surf. James was clambering over the gunwale when one of the men, stringy but strong, grasped his arms and hoisted him aboard. Lauder hefted himself beside James, and Orkney followed as though he were mounting a horse. James grabbed the edge as the boat lifted with a long roller. His stomach lurched.

He held on with a two-handed grasp hard enough that the wood cut into his fingers. Endless swells of black sea stretched beyond them. James swallowed, trying to still his racing heart. The four sailors pushed the boat back further into the water and leapt in. The ten-foot swells tossed them up before they swept down again. The four men pulled on their oars with a low chant. James was glad of a sturdy stomach, but the lurches in the dark left him dizzy. At the top of a swell, Lauder shouted, "There it is!"

James gaped at the monstrous knob of rock towering above the white foam of crashing seas. Tiny flickers of light at the top showed the watchtowers of the castle, home to the Lauders for time out of mind. James wanted to ask how in the name of the Holy Rood they would reach the top, but he was too busy holding on to be sure he wasn't thrown into the roiling sea. He hadn't breath for the question. Besides, the crash of the rollers was deafening.

The rowers took them past an outthrust spit of rock. They turned the bow of their tossing craft into a nook. The dizzying lift and drop of the rollers lessened, and after a minute the boat hit a bank. Again the two men in front jumped into the water and hauled. The pewter light of the moon lit a rocky shelf no more than two arm spans across. Lauder hopped off and turned. James realized, as he forced himself to his feet, that his legs were trembling. The two remaining sailors had him under his arms before he could protest and tossed him as though he were a bairn to Lauder, who lowered his feet onto the rock.

Orkney hopped out onto the narrow shelf with a quick laugh. "I'd nae care to do that every day."

Lauder's teeth gleamed in the faint light when he grinned. "Nae many do." He nodded to the sailor who blew a long note and then three short ones. A long answer from high above echoed off the rocks. "If you are nae expected, our greeting is a rain of stones."

"Should we wait for daylight to make the climb?" Orkney asked, sounding worried.

Lauder thrust his chin toward the eastern sky. Splashes of gold and a tint of rose had washed over the edge of the horizon. "We have light enough. I'll nae chance being caught in the open so close to safety."

James looked up. Directly above, outlined in dawn's light, he could see the bulk of Bass Rock Castle. It couldn't be more than a few hundred feet above them. From below, it looked white, but then a flock of birds took flight—a rustling cloud. Their harsh, grating krok-krok-krokkrok-krok-krok drowned out the wash of the sea—and exposed the brown of the stone castle. He flinched as a hundred of the birds swept close overhead. Before James was a tumble of boulders and stones and a defile so narrow only one man at a time could squeeze past.

The fishermen had already pushed off and were rowing once more into the towering rollers. Lauder led them through and up. The way was steep, littered with stones. It made a sharp turn onto a narrow ledge. He could see the tiny shelf where they'd landed and the sea straight below. An enemy intent on capturing the Bass Rock Castle would have to land a few men at a time and fight their way up whilst rocks poured down on them.

The day was growing light, the sun a golden coin half hidden by the horizon. James had never had a fear of heights, but his eyes kept closing. He jerked them open and shook his head hard. Scree slipped under his feet as he numbly followed Lauder, Orkney behind him. Lauder clambered over rocks that had fallen into the path and paused as James did the same. As they got higher, sharp gusts of wind tugged at his cloak and tossed his hair into his face. The trip now seemed to have stretched forever, and he felt that it might never end. Perhaps he would never again sleep more than a snatched nap on cold ground. His feet slipped on the loose rock. He gasped and threw his hand out. It smacked hard against the chill, rough stone.

Orkney caught him from behind. "Stay awake, lad."

James nodded. The drop on the other side was no more than a foot away. Had he been walking asleep, he wondered? He could have fallen over the edge to be smashed on the rock. He could see the Forth below them and the boulders where its huge swells crashed, tossing foam high into the air.

Lauder turned and smiled wearily. "Almost there." He held out his hand and pulled James onto the top of the precipice.

James took a deep breath at the sight of the castle perching on the edge of the cliff, but then he was coughing, a foul stink like nothing he'd ever smelled before burning his nose. His eyes watered. He hacked and hacked again. "Wha' is that?"

Lauder snorted a chuckle. "Bird shite. More gannets are here than a' the rest of Scotland together."

"Well, it stinks," James grumbled.

Lauder put his hand over his eyes and started laughing. After a moment, Orkney was laughing, too. James frowned at them, offended. Why were they laughing at him? But Lauder shook his head.

"Thanks be to the Virgin and the saints you're alive to smell the stink, lad." He gave James's shoulder a little push, and they trudged toward the open gate of the castle. "You'll become used to it."

Beyond the castle, cliffs rose another two hundred feet, seething with life, covered with a dense mat of birds—gannets and puffins and cormorants and more kinds of seabird than James had ever seen. But all James wanted was the castle, a crackling fire, and a bed.

CHAPTER 5

One of the dozen or so of Lauder's men at the castle
stood atop the gatehouse and waved as James sauntered out the gate. The March wind was chill, but James
didn't mind because the sun was bright in the pale morning
sky, with there was only a single wisp of thin cloud. He
huffed. Four weeks they had waited for news of a ship and
heard nothing except when young Robert Lauder, the elder
Lauder's heir, brought news that his uncle had reached
Glasgow and returned to his own house. Lothian crawled
with the Earl of Douglas's men seeking him, but here he was
safe and a climb up the cliffs called, as it did every day that a
gale didn't blow. Then Orkney said the prince was not
allowed to risk breaking his mucky neck, but he smiled when
he said it.

"Hoy, Prince James," Robert called from the bailey yard.
"Are you going up the rock?"

"Aye." He thrust his chin at the castle. "They do nothing
but throw dice. How can they sit a' day like that?"

Robert grinned. "Mind if I join you?" He was a young
man only four or five years James's elder, blue-eyed and

handsome and slender as a blade. Like James, he had changed to scuffed boots and plain hodden-grey breeches and tunic after he'd arrived the day before. In fact, James wore clothes outgrown by young Lauder since all he had left was the armor he'd worn in his flight. Even had James had others, fine clothing was wasted on the remote isle. Robert said he never bothered.

Lifting the bow he carried in his left hand, Robert grinned. "I want to see if the sheep have dropped any lambs, but with luck I can bring down a bird. They're nae bad eating. We'll roast it over a campfire. Keep us out of the way of the auld uns."

James held up a bag of oats he'd slung over his back. "We can make a bannock. Let's pick up some eggs from a nest. We'll have a right feast." With a whoop, he darted toward the zigzag climb, it couldn't really be called a path so steep and narrow it was—that led to the dizzying summit of Bass Rock. He clambered up the broken, crumbling, widely-spaced steps carved into the cliff, Robert on his heels.

Near the top, he snagged four bird eggs and dropped them into the bag with the oats. At the crest, James knelt for a moment and couldn't help smiling at the grassy smell. The peak of the rock was four or five acres of windblown grass and heather. A dozen sheep were grazing in the lee of an outcropping. They lifted their heads to look at the two of them before going back to chomping on the rich grass. A clump of thyme was sending up a sweet scent. James's hair blew in the early spring breeze, and his heart twisted a bit. He knew it was no place for a prince to learn what he must, but it would be a fine place to grow up for a lad who liked climbing and watching the birds and the clouds.

"When do you suppose the ship will come?" he asked as he glared at the towers of Tantallon Castle on the distant shore. Even from here he could make out the Douglas banner with its huge red heart flying above the ramparts. Damn the Douglases.

"Soon, I suppose." Robert smiled with a wry twist of his mouth. "Build a fire so it can burn down to coals. I only brought a couple of arrows, so I'll need some luck. I don't see any lambs yet, but I'd better take a closer look."

"There are no trees for wood," James said, but there were always sticks in the grass.

"I'm nae sure if the birds carry the sticks or if they blow or wha'. But you can always find some," Robert said.

He turned and walked slowly toward the sheep, not wanting to spook them, James supposed, though the creatures seemed placid enough. So James gathered up enough sticks to make a little fire and used his flint to start it. Then he took out the iron griddle with a wary glance at the sky. He hoped no bird shite would land in their food. There couldn't be so many birds all in one place anywhere else on earth, he was sure. He dumped oats in the middle, dropped in the lump of fat he'd brought and mixed it all with water from his flask, and then he pulled some leaves to cover it until the fire burned down. He wasn't picky anent a little dirt in his food, but bird shite was another thing entirely.

He was looking for another stick to stir the yolks of the eggs when Robert dropped a bird on the ground beside him. Robert dropped cross-legged onto the ground and started plucking his prize. James took out the eggs and cut a hole in one end. He paused for a moment, remembering that it was Davey who'd taught him to cook eggs in a campfire. They'd ridden out many a day before his older brother had been grown—James shook off the memory. It was too fine a day to think of that.

He looked up at the bright sky and the white birds sailing above their heads to dive as though dropped straight into the water. "Do you ken how they tell where the fish are?" It amazed him to watch them. Hundreds, no it must have been thousands of birds, swooping and diving and coming up with a fish in their bill.

"I suppose they can see the fish—though I cannot." Robert tossed the last handful of feathers into the air, and the wind spread them like snowflakes.

James smiled as he watched the white feathers spread and blow away on the wind.

Robert pulled out his dirk and made fast work of cleaning the bird. He stuffed it with a handful of thyme he pulled from a low bush, wrapped it in more leaves and used a forked stick to push it into the coals.

James carefully propped the four eggs against coals and dropped the griddle into the middle. He jumped to his feet and grinned at Robert. "I can beat you to that boulder," he said and took off running.

"Hey!" Robert shouted.

James heard his footfalls and stretched his legs. Robert was taller, which would only make victory sweeter. Hands shoved in the middle of his back, and Robert yelled as James toppled, yelping in surprise as he toppled. He caught himself and rolled. Robert hopped over him. He laughed and grabbed Robert's leg so that he fell flat. James threw himself on top of the older lad, straddled him and held him down, leaning a hand on each shoulder. "Lèse-majesté! Pushing a prince."

"No. Nae when the prince has a dirty face." Robert heaved and managed to throw James off, and they rolled across the grass. Robert raised his head and looked back toward the campfire. "And if you've made me burn my dinner, 'tis more than a push I shall give you."

"The food should be done," James said. He jumped to his feet and dashed back toward their fire. He pulled the eggs and bannock out whilst Robert did the same to the bird and they hurriedly split the food between them. The bannock was a bit burnt, but James still intended to eat it. He lay back on one elbow and spread his veritable feast on a bunch of thyme leaves. Robert stretched out nearby.

For long, comfortable minutes, they ripped the hot meat from the bones of the bird and stuffed themselves. "When I am king, you'll be my chancellor," James said.

"If you like." Robert shoved the last of the bannock, which took some fierce chewing, into his mouth. He slithered to the edge of the cliff and pointed down. "I love watching from here. There is nothing else like it."

James wiped the grease from his hands on a clump of thyme. He considered Robert's comment that his face was dirty, but decided he didn't care. He slithered to watch with his friend to stare down the four-hundred foot drop.

"Why do so many live here?" There were more birds soaring and diving than a man could possibly count.

Robert grunted an indifference to the question, so James just watched the display. When Robert picked up a rock and dropped it off the precipice, it bounced against the side once, twice, thrice and disappeared into the foam.

The Bass Rock stank, but James mostly didn't notice anymore, and up there so high the wind carried most of the smell away. Besides, it was worth putting up with the smell to watch the birds that rose in swooping clouds, scattered, and reformed to rest once again on the rocks.

James rolled over onto his back. He closed his eyes and let the mild warmth of the sun soak into his face. High on its cliff, with the supplies in the castle, the sheep in the field and the birds, why, Bass Rock Castle could withstand a siege for years and years. His enemies could never reach him here. Perhaps he could stay. Lauder could teach him in arms. He needn't ever leave for France. He dozed and smiled at the thought.

Robert's elbow poked James hard in the ribs, so he lazily

opened his eyes. Robert pointed down to the sea. "Someone is coming," he said.

Rolling onto his side, James followed Robert's gesture. A small boat was bobbing in the water, pulling into the shelter of the rocky spit. "Is it your father's?"

"We shall see. If it's not, they'll nae gain the castle." Robert jumped to his feet. "Come on."

James scrambled up and darted after his friend, who was already running for the cliff's edge. "If it were the Douglas, it would never be such a small boat."

"Aye, but they're searching for you everywhere." Robert held onto the edge and swung his legs over the precipice to drop a few feet and then hugged the cliff face as he worked his way down the path. "It might be someone spying the place out. Or mayhap news of your ship."

James saw all the lower cliff where the castle stood at a glance: a guard walking with a pike above the castle gate, a servant digging to plant in the kitchen garden, one of the castle dogs barking as it ran beneath an inner wall. He leapt along the narrow shelf, chivvying Robert, "You are so slow."

"Aye, well, I do nae want to fall."

"You won't. Hurry! If they drop rocks on enemies, I want to help."

The thin wail of a horn sounded. Robert held up his hand and stopped, frowning. He waited. "Did you hear more than one blaw?"

"I'm nae sure. Mayhap…"

Then clearly came an answering horn from the castle and Robert smiled. "Friends." He scrambled the rest of the way down, keeping one hand on the cliff face.

James sighed in impatience. It would be a terrible fall, so he didn't blame Robert. But a prince must be too proud to be afraid, so all the way down he kept his hands at his side. It didn't count if he sweated and bit his lip, but once at the foot of the cliff they dashed for the castle.

The great hall was damp and drafty, even with a fire roaring on the hearth. Through the narrow slit windows James heart the cries of the gannets. A flagon of wine, cups, and cards from a game the men had abandoned still lay on the long wooden table. A tall newcomer, brown hair shot with white and dressed for travel in armor, turned to look at James as he and Robert let the door slam behind them. He had a serious look to his gray eyes.

"Prince James," he said and a bowed.

James felt his face tighten. "Has something happened?"

Orkney smiled. "Nothing ill. It's news of the ship we're awaiting."

James opened his mouth to tell the earl that they wouldn't need it, that he could stay here, but Lauder cut in. "Since a' your possessions were lost in the flight, Sir Archibald Edmonstone brought fitting clothes for you to wear. You cannot arrive at the French court dressed like a churl."

Lauder gave a wry smile. "As long as we reach France, I'm nae worried wha' Prince James wears."

James opened his mouth again to protest, but Sir Archibald went on. "It is called the Maryenknyght. A cog carrying wool and hides home to Danzig, so we hope no one will think to look for the heir to the throne of Scotland on it."

Staying had been no more than a dream—foolishness. Such fancy was not for him, and even when he had dreamed, something within him had known it. He must go where he was sent and learn to be king. The burn behind his eyes made him squeeze them shut. He would not cry. He was a twelve years old—almost a man grown, by all the saints. "When will the ship come?" he asked.

"Tomorrow night. After nightfall, they'll anchor off the

west side of the Bass, well out of sight of Tantallon Castle, wi'
a light fore and aft to guide you."

"Guide me?"

"You, the earl, and Sir Archibald. My little skiff will take
you out," Lauder said. "Giffart will be waiting on board.
You'll nae be alone, lad."

"No," James said faintly.

CHAPTER 6

*T*he water lapped at their feet as they waited for the lights of the Maryenknyght to appear. Before them was the Firth of Forth, above, the sky, each so black you could not tell one from the other. The wind was up and clearing the clouds to show a thousand stars. James caught his cloak and pushed his hair out of his face. Four men sat in Lauder's skiff that rocked tied up to the stone shelf. The only sound was the endless crash of wave upon rock.

A distant light flashed in the blank darkness and then another behind it. They wavered, steadied. Orkney grunted. "Into the boat," he said. "Quietly. Noise carries over the water."

The wooden edge was wet and slimy to the touch when James grasped it and jumped aboard. It rocked under him. Sir Archibald and the earl followed more carefully. The men —James couldn't tell in the dark if they were the same as before—put their backs into their oars, rowing toward the flickers as they rose and fell. When he looked back, darkness lay black and thick around the base of Bass Rock. He couldn't see even the shapes of the friends he had left there.

The sea boomed against its cliffs, and his heart thudded. He'd not even have a last glimpse of Scotland—of home.

The oarlocks were muffled, so they moved in silence through the night alone on the Firth. The men bent, grunting, over the oars. Only the two specks of light broke the darkness. James hugged himself in the night chill and bit his lip. They rowed and rowed, and then James made out a shape in the flickering light of a small lamp fore and aft, a cog, her one sail furled. As they neared, he made out four or five men moving on the deck. Drawing alongside, one of the oarsmen cried out. A rope ladder dropped. One of the oarsmen grabbed it. "Up you go, laddie," he said.

The ladder was slick and rough as he swarmed up, his two companions close behind. He swung his leg over the side and two sailors boosted him. A rower hoisted up his little chest. There was faint splash from lowering oar blades, and when James looked down, the little skiff was already only a smear in the immensity of the dark sea.

William Giffart strode toward them. "My lords! Thanks be to the all saints." He motioned beside him toward an immense man, the moonlight glinting off his bald head. "Captain, these are the lords we awaited."

The captain sketched a bow, including the men behind James. "Captain Albrecht Giese of Gdansk, Eure Durchlauchtigkeiten. I welcome you aboard the Maryenknyght."

James looked at the earl, who nodded at the greeting. It sounded polite enough, although in no language James had ever heard. "Thank you, Captain," he said, but received no answer as Orkney cut in.

"Your ship is a welcome beneath our feet. We thank you. We would have Prince James safely in France as quickly as possible."

The captain grunted. "It will not be the quickest trip, but it will be safe, God willing. The biggest risk would be English pirates, who prey along their coast, but I assure you, I know how best to stay away from those vultures."

"But we have a truce." James looked over his shoulder at Orkney. "Why would they bother us?"

The captain grunted. "Because they're the English."

"A risk of your profession, I suppose," Orkney replied to the captain. "I'm sure it is as you say; you can stay out of their reach. But it has been a long and weary night. Is there a cabin for us?"

"I fear you will have to share a small space."

William motioned for them to go below. "I'll show you, my lord."

The sail cracked and snapped as it was raised. James turned to follow the earl.

The ship rocked under his feet as he went down the passage. The cabin was low and narrow. It smelled of salt water and hides. But a bed had been made on a shelf, one side piled high with blankets. More blankets were folded in a corner.

"Best you rest, lad," Orkney said. "The night is fair spent."

"Wha' about you?" James asked and frowned around the cabin, its ceiling so low that Orkney would bump his head on the thick beams if he wasn't wary.

"We must make do wi' blankets. It won't be a pleasure voyage, but we never thought that it would."

James sat to lever off his boots and stretched face down on the bed. Boards creaked, and the bed rocked beneath him with the movement of the ship. He cradled his head on a bent arm, closed his eyes, and felt the warmth when someone threw a blanket over him. Orkney's voice blended with William's and Sir Archibald's into a pleasant hum.

France... James wondered what it would be like there before sleep enfolded him.

CHAPTER 7

MARCH 1406

*J*ames scrambled up the slimy wooden ladder to the forecastle and leaned on the rail near the high bowsprit of the cog. The wind ruffled his hair. It washed away most of the stink from the hides and fleece in the hold. Watching the endless gray sea was the only entertainment he had, whilst the Earl of Orkney huddled with the captain, muttering anent English pirates and the English truce with Scotland. Sir Archibald Edmonstone crossed his muscular arms and watched the others, never saying a word.

William came up to stand beside James, chuckling. "They'll talk the pirates to death," he said.

Foam splashed into James's face, and he smiled at his esquire. William was cheerful company but didn't help the boredom of the journey. James sighed and scanned the horizon for something, anything, to break the monotony. He caught sight of a speck of white far to the right of the bow. "Wha's that?" He pointed.

"I'm nae sure." William frowned as high, white cliffs poked above the horizon. "But it isn't France."

The captain yelled a command. The sail creaked and snapped, the deck rocked beneath their feet, and the cog changed course. Foam splashed high around the bow as they plowed into the waves. The turn put the barren, treeless headland abeam to the cog, and James gaped at the first sight he'd ever had of England. "It's bare. Not a place I'd want to go."

Sir Archibald climbed the ladder to join them, forehead crinkled in a frown. "That's Flamborough Head, so the captain says. From here, we'll run straight south."

James stretched over the gunwale to better see the cliffs that sparkled in the bright sunlight. He grunted. "I suppose. And then more water. And waves. And water. And more water."

"It is boring," William agreed and yawned.

The sea spray stung James's eyes. He wiped them clear to take one last look at the land of their enemies. He turned his back, since the cliffs were no more interesting from a distance than was the sea, though the sailors' cursing had taught him some words that might be of use to him one day. The thought made him duck his head and grin. The knight looked askance at him, so he said, "How long until we reach France?"

"Depends on the weather. Two days... mayhap three," Sir Archibald said.

A sailor in the rigging shouted something that was carried away on the wind. The man pointed toward the rapidly disappearing coastline. The captain called out a command and the cog put about more to the east. Orkney strode to the rail. He grasped it, staring fixedly into the distance.

Sir Archibald looked down from the forecastle and called out, "Wha's to do?"

"They've spotted a sail. Just rounded the Head and moving this way."

The captain was shouting commands, and sailors swarmed the ropes. The deck lurched under James's feet as the ship changed course slightly. James narrowed his eyes and tried to pick out a ship in the shimmer of the sun on the sea. There was nothing. "It won't catch us." He looked at Sir Archibald. "Will it?"

"Probably just another merchant ship and nothing to do wi' us." But he was frowning fiercely as he glowered at the sea.

"It's matching our course," the watch shouted down.

James spotted a speck of white, almost like one of the gannets that swooped over the sea at Bass Rock. "Look," he said to William.

"It's gaining on us, then." William pinched the skin at his throat. "That is… worrying."

"I want to speak to the earl. And you need to go to the cabin, my lord." Sir Archibald prodded James toward the ladder. "That's the safest place for you."

James meekly climbed down the ladder with no intention of hiding in the cabin. He'd go mad wondering what was happening on deck. The captain was standing beside the helmsman, his mouth in a pinched line.

"This is not a place I would expect to sight another ship. It is why I chose this route." The captain frowned. "There are no ports near the Head."

A crewman in the crow's nest yelled down, "It changed course this way."

"Can you see what kind is the ship?" Captain Giese yelled up.

"A ballinger—under full sail and oars."

Orkney looked up at the sky and shook his head. "Too

long until dark." He shared a glance with the captain. "They will overtake us before we can escape in the dark."

"We have some lead, but they are light and making good speed. We're weighed down with cargo. If they are, as I fear, pursuing us—" The captain's mouth was drawn into a thin line as he spoke.

"Prince James," Orkney said, "you should go below."

"If they catch up to us, will we fight?" James asked, ignoring the order to leave.

"We must," Sir Archibald barked.

"Euer Hochwohlgeboren, on my ship the decision is mine." The captain made a commanding gesture and silenced them. "I will arm my men, but we must see more of what enemy we face."

"Captain," the watch yelled down, "they're gaining fast."

The ship was full of sound: the captain reeled off commands, swords and knives clanked, crewmen shouted encouragement, and waves slapped the hull as it plowed through the water. James hurried to the rail. A rippling wake spread out behind the Maryenknyght, but it seemed to move like a turtle. Foam curled around the high bow of the pursuing ship. Oars dipped and scooped, churning the water beneath a great square sail.

Orkney commanded William to bring their weapons, and soon the three were buckling on their swords, though none were in armor. When Sir Archibald said they should don it, Orkney scowled and asked if he would be pleased to swim in a suit of steel.

"I don't swim at all," the knight said.

"Then you can hold onto a piece of flotsam. In armor, you sink like a rock."

James looked at the earl in horror. "Do you think they will sink us?"

"Probably not, but it is best not to risk it."

Across the water, the ship was thick with men and bows who stirring as they neared. James heard the sound of a fast drumbeat in time with the stroking oars. No one was watching him as they stared at the oncoming ship, so James dashed up the ladder and knelt by the rail to have a better view of their pursuers. Shading his eyes against the sun, he peered at the ship. It was crowded with crewmen, many more than were on their own. Sunlight flashed on steel in their hands.

A shout went up from the ship behind, and arrows hissed like snakes over James's head. He flinched lower as the fearsome shower rained down. Men were scrambling to hide from it. A yard-long shaft thrummed down a foot behind James and embedded in the deck. James pressed his body as close to the rail as he could, breath coming as though he'd run for miles. He heard an anguished scream as someone tumbled from the crow's nest. James turned and ran for the ladder. An arrow pierced a crewman through the throat as another shrieked as he fell. Two lay moaning on the deck. Dimly, James heard cheers from the other ship.

"Douse the sail," the captain roared. "Throw down your swords." Men rushed for the lanyards and frantically lowered the sail. It creaked and thudded as it came down.

Orkney spun on a heel and strode to hammer his hand against the railing. "By'r Lady, hell mend them!"

A few more arrows thudded around them. Amidst the sounds of moans, weapons clattered to the deck. A shout came from the nearing ship: "Up oars." A grapnel clanged onto the railing. Another and another followed. There were shouts and grunts as ropes were hauled until the hulls thumped and the two ships were bound together. Men brandishing swords swarmed like ants over the railing. Archers aimed from the forecastle. A hand grabbed James's arm hard. He was wrenched off his feet and would have fallen, except he was trapped between Sir Archibald's back and the wooden bulkhead.

"Whisht! Stay still." The knight threw down his sword with a clank.

James craned his neck to see around his protector's back as Orkney raised his empty hands. Captain Giese stood grim faced.

The dozen remaining seamen of the Maryenknyght were herded together, the captain forced to join them, backed up with a sword to his throat held by a scar-faced pirate with a huge chest like a barrel of ale.

Then a spare, compact man jumped agilely over the railings to land, feet spread. He had black hair and eyes as hard and dark as obsidian. "I, Hugh-atte-Fen, claim this ship as my prize," he said.

"It is a ship of the Hanseatic League!" the captain shouted. Scar face slammed the flat of his sword into the captain's head, and the man went down to one knee, a gash on his temple leaking red.

"No longer," Hugh-atte-Fen said calmly. "However, you may have the skiff. If you are any seaman, you just may reach shore."

Orkney stepped forward and said, "Sir, we are merely passengers—with safe conduct from both the kings of Scotland and France. But if you would have ransom, I will agree to pay it for me and my few companions."

"And who might you be, sirrah?"

"I am Sir Henry Sinclair, Earl of Orkney, on the business of the King of Scotland with whom your own King Henry is in truce, I remind you."

The pirate shrugged. "Truces are of little moment to me, but one of your companions is another matter." His hard eyes darted from William to Sir Archibald and stopped as he looked at James. "The young man yon knight is trying so hard to hide. Now he is of some moment. I have sought him for days."

"For days? How?" Orkney exclaimed.

"I was sent word from London." Hugh-atte-Fen curled his lip in a sneering smile. "Lord James, Earl of Carrack, Prince of Scotland, if I mistake not."

James squared his shoulders, pushed his way from behind Sir Archibald and past William, who clutched at his arm. He wouldn't cower like a craven. Not for this Sassenach or any man on earth. If his stomach felt hard with fear, well, that was his own business.

He lifted his chin and looked the man in the eye, anger making his face flood with heat. "Aye. I am he."

Behind him, there was a splash as a skiff hit the water and muttering protests as the crew was driven into it. But he couldn't look away from Hugh-atte-Fen.

"Your servant, my lord." The pirate touched his breast as he made a deep bow. "And welcome to England."

CHAPTER 8

The bile-green Thames flowed in ripples around the ship. They sailed past a square, gray keep that rose like a growth above a dreary marsh. Was that the Tower of London where so many ended their lives, James wondered?

Orkney made a strangled sound in his throat. When James looked at him from the corner of his eye, the earl just shook his head and glanced toward scar-face. The man had his arms, thick as tree chests, crossed, but his sword was on his hip. His pig eyes never left them, and three other pirates had hands on their hilts as they stood guard.

Beyond the grim keep was a jumble of buildings that stretched out of sight on a reed-choked shore. The wind smelled of horse shit and sweat and smoke and rotting fish. All cities smelled, but not so strong it closed his throat.

Dozens of wharfs thrust into the water, and masts rose around them as thick as trees in a forest. Hugh-atte-Fen called out a command, and lines were thrown to the nearest. There were shouts, and the ship was hauled in and lashed to the quay.

James craned his neck from one side to the other. On the

shore, he made out nothing but a muddle of buildings with reeking chimneys, alleys, spires, and belfries hunched under a canopy of dark smoke that covered the sky. But the quays were all noise and confusion. Crates were being carried off ships. Wagons were being loaded, and men shouted, cursed, laughed. Everyone was in an uproar to be somewhere other than where they were.

"My lords." Hugh-atte-Fen swaggered in their direction and gave another of his taunting bows. "I must go ashore to arrange a greeting suitable to such lofty and honored guests. I shan't be long."

Orkney's lips were pressed together so hard they were white. "I would give much to know who in Scotland betrayed us," he whispered.

"Albany," Sir Archibald said. "He must have sent word to the English."

James opened his mouth to ask what would happen now, but scar-face shouted, "Shut your mouths."

The earl gave a narrow-eyed look at their captors and shook his head at James. Jams looked back at that grim tower and his heart tried to beat its way out of his chest. He gripped his fists so hard that his nails cut into his palms. It hurt but helped him to be quiet. His heart hammered. He couldn't return to Scotland, not until he was a man grown and able to fight his murderous uncle. But he couldn't stay in England— to be locked in a dungeon. He couldn't!

The sun was near its zenith, and sweat was dripping down James's back in the wet heat when Hugh-Atte-Fen strutted down the quay and up the gangplank, a score of men-at-arms, halberds over their shoulders, at his back. The man patted a fat purse hanging from his belt, his teeth flashing in a grin. "You have been profitable guests, my lords, so I wish you good luck with your new host."

"Enough chatter." The sergeant jerked his thumb toward

the gangplank. "We've orders to move you lot, and we've better things to do."

"Move us where?" Orkney demanded.

Sir Archibald crossed his arms, glowering.

The sergeant motioned, and the long weapons were lowered so that they bristled toward the two men.

Orkney rubbed his dark-circled eyes before he stepped forward. "Keep Lord James between the two of you," he said over his shoulder as he paced down the gangplank.

With William on one side and Sir Archibald on the other, James followed close behind. The men-at-arms formed a square around them.

The guards shoved their way between two wagons, where men were piling casks and crates. A broad-shouldered man didn't move out of the way, and a blow from the staff of a halberd knocked him to his knees. He shouted curses behind them as they marched past and into the warren of narrow streets.

The cacophony assaulted James like hammer blows. From everywhere seemed to come shouts, laughs, screams, bells tolling, distant hammering, horses whinnying, and it mixed with the clanking of their guards' armor. The street squelched with filth under his feet. The upper stories of the buildings jutted out, almost meeting overhead, letting through dim shafts of murky light. "Miserére mei, Deus…" James muttered under his breath.

The streets milled with crowds: a legless man yelled for alms, drunken soldiers staggered out the door of a public house, hawkers shouted their wares, and whores lounged in doorways making offers to their guards as they passed. Everywhere he looked, anywhere he looked, there were people. Vast seas of people, and no one he knew. Fiercely, he jammed his trembling hands into his armpits and kept trudging along. When a man carrying a barrel on his shoulder got in the way, two of the guards shoved him head first into a wall. The barrel leaked ale in a puddle as the man knelt and moaned.

On a street corner a Gray Friar in a soiled robe was praying loudly for Prince Hal, but the crowds paid him no more mind than if he were a yapping dog. They passed four men struggling to work a pushcart free, its wheels stuck in the muck. An acrobat in ragged motley tottered on stilts to the delighted shouts of a drunken throng.

Walking through the streets of the huge, strange city surrounded by armed guards, James gaped at everything, yet he hardly drew a glance. He was glad, but what kind of city was it where prisoners were so common? The Tower of London was out of sight now, and they were going in the wrong direction to go there. "Where do you think they're taking us?" he asked William in an undertone.

William shrugged, and from the glazed look he gave James, he was no less confused. The bells of the Angelus began to chime, and James looked up to see the gray stone of a minster rising before them. He nudged William with his elbow.

It wasn't a great castle. In fact, it was plain and unimpressive, though the entrance porch was polished stone with elaborately carved faces. Splendid flying buttresses on the sides supported the rather plain building. Men-at-arms threw open the carved, arched double doors.

As they were escorted through chamber after chamber, nobles in fine dress, servants in livery, and robed clerics turned to stare. The rooms were a jumble of multicolored carpets, statues, tapestries, carved benches, and burnished armorials beneath crossed swords. James had never seen rooms so awash in colors and furnishings. When he realized he was gawking, he snapped his mouth shut and stared straight ahead.

At last the doors to the audience chamber were thrown open. It was flooded with noonday sun through immense, arched windows. James blinked in the sudden light, trying to make sense of the sudden chaos in the vast chamber. Overhead, the beams soared to an unbelievable height, and around James and his little retinue, men bellowed laughter and shouted to be heard. They churned in a sea of colorful silks, and James could see no more than a few feet into the hall awash with courtiers. He chewed his lip as he slid his gaze to look from the corner of his eye at the earl. Orkney was white to the lips, his mouth pressed into a thin line.

James took a single step forward and squared his shoulders. One of the Englishmen, fine as a peacock in blue satin, nudged his neighbor with an elbow and sneered in their direction. James dug his nails into his palms as he forced himself to look through the beautifully dressed rabble as though they weren't there.

Trumpets blew at the far end of the hall, and the babble quieted to a murmur. "Our most dread lord, Henry, King of England," a strong voice shouted.

Orkney laid a hand on James's shoulder and squeezed so hard it hurt, but James gave a little nod. He kept his eyes straight ahead.

The men around them were bowing low, and at last James caught a glimpse of a throne on a far dais. The chamber was huge, he thought, bigger than any he'd ever seen. But then his breath caught. A burly man with a plain gold coronet encircling his dark hair and a neatly trimmed beard paused half way to the dais. He bent his head as a prelate in a crimson robe dusted with jewels put a hand on his shoulder and said something into his ear. In his rich black tunic and cloth of gold cloak, he threw his head back and hooted a laugh. James's stomach twisted in his gut.

Henry Bolingbroke, King of England, laughed hard for a

few more moments before he strode to the gilded throne and threw himself down in an inelegant sprawl. His squinting blue eyes fastened on James, and he called out, "Come. Bring my new guests before me."

An usher stepped forward. He motioned to the four of them. Orkney nodded, and side by side with him, James approached the throne. Sir Archibald and William followed on their heels.

A few strides from the throne, Orkney halted and his hand stopped James. They bowed deeply to their captor.

The king grinned as he looked James up and down, paying no heed to the others.

"A whelp of Scotland." He snorted. "James, they call you?"

"Aye, Your Grace. James, Earl of Carrick and Prince of Scotland, and this is my household." He motioned to the grim-faced Earl of Orkney. "Sir Henry Sinclair, Earl of Orkney, Sir Archibald, and my squire, William Giffart."

"You were fleeing to France, I am told, to be educated and properly schooled in French." King Henry leaned forward with his elbows on the arms of his throne, pondered James for a moment, and grinned. "Your father should have sent you to me straight away. I am, after all, the rightful King of France and speak excellent French, having spent much time there. There is none better to school you than I."

James gritted his teeth as his face flooded with heat. "Son Altesse Royale, vous me feriez trop d'honneur."

King Henry looked at him. There was silence, as though the men around them held their breaths. When the king snorted back laughter, chuckles rippled through the chamber. "C'est vrai, mon enfant. I have no time for schooling a child, but we shall see that you have a tutor who is suitable to your rank." His glance slid over William. "And you have a squire. That is seemly, but you have no need for a large household in the Tower."

"Your Grace!" Orkney's hand tightened on James's shoulder. "You can't mean to send the lad to such a terrible—"

"Silence," the king said, rising from his seat, his voice thick with annoyance. "I did not give you leave to speak. You will be allowed ransom, sir earl, you and the knight with you. Until then, I shall hear nothing further from you." A hush fell, and he glowered around the great chamber. "Now, where is Thomas Rempston?"

James glanced back and saw a slight, middle-aged man, dressed in rich blue, with a bald head and a beak of a nose threading his way through the press. When he reached the dais, he bowed deeply. "Your Grace?"

The king took his seat on the throne and nodded curtly. "Sir Thomas, as you see, we have more guests for you to lodge in the Tower. Young James here must have tutors and be kept in reasonable comfort." He eyed James and his companions with a smile on his lips. "Allow the earl messengers to arrange ransom for himself and the knight—as quickly as possible. I don't intend to support a large household for the boy."

James was sure Orkney's fingers would leave bruises, so hard did they dig into his shoulder. The man made a strangled noise in his throat, and words seemed to burst from him. "Your Grace! Surely a lad of such tender years—you cannot truly mean to send him to—"

"By the mass, I bade you be silent!" The king pointed a finger at Orkney. He turned to Thomas Rempston with a narrow-eyed look. "As my Constable of the Tower, you will see to them." He flourished a dismissive hand.

It was a stiff and shallow bow that Orkney offered the English king. James gave the earl a doubtful glance from the corner of his eye and followed suit. Sir Thomas Rempston motioned for them to follow him, and outside the chamber, they were once again surrounded by guards.

"It will take much time for arranging ransoms, lad," Orkney said through gritted teeth. "Much time…" Nothing else was said through the chaos of the London. At last they came to a long, open marketplace of tents and stalls of every color. On one side, cattle were lowing and bawling in an enclosure. Poultry honked and cackled within pens, adding to the cacophony of farmers shouting out their vegetables, women bargaining, and bakers' boys calling, "Bread. Fresh bread."

Their guards yelled, "Make way!"

People grumbled and cursed as they were shoved aside so the guards could march James and his household through to the other side. James sucked in a deep breath when he saw a moat. The bloated body of a dog and brown bits that James refused to consider floated in the stinking water. He reluctantly raised his eyes to the high, crenellated, gray wall, where armored guards paced. Their footsteps reverberated like drumbeats on the wooden drawbridge. The heavy gate screeched open, and James shuddered. Within the outer walls, on a rise, soared the stern, implacable face of the keep.

He went cold, and his vision swam. The next step was the hardest he had ever taken. James forced his legs to move. He walked through. The gates of the Tower of London crashed closed behind him.

CHAPTER 9

APRIL 1406

Through the high, arched window of James's Tower room, morning light spilled across the floor, bars laying dark stripes on the threadbare carpet. His straw-stuffed bed was hard and uncomfortable. James thrashed and kicked his light coverlet onto the floor. In his bare feet, he ran to the little garderobe and pissed into the hole as William, on his pallet on the floor, muttered complaints.

William filled a basin with water from a jug on the table. James washed his face and hands, donned clean hose, shirt and doublet from the chest that had been brought from the ship the week before and pulled on his boots. Then he climbed the two steps to stand in the window nook and look past its iron bars. He took a deep breath and leaned his forehead against the rough stone of the surround. Sunrise was a wash of red across a cloud of smoke that never seemed to clear from above London. He absently rubbed at the strange pressure in his chest as he wondered when he would ever see a blue sky again.

"That coverlet will nae be fit to use," William said. "With you tromping on it like that in your boots."

In the yard below, James spotted a man-at-arms following a dark-haired man, who sauntered across the patch of ground within view. It was certainly not Sir Thomas. Possibly another prisoner of this foul place? A lion's roar nearby made him flinch. It was answered with another. He turned to look around the bare chamber, with its narrow bed, small table and two stools, a thin carpet on the floor. But a fire burned on the hearth, they had been brought food by a gaoler every day, and the lions in the menagerie were only a sound in the distance. William said he had never heard of prisoners being given over to the beasts, but he looked nervous every time they split the air with their roars.

William looked up from pulling on his own clothes. "The English will allow you to buy more comforts when you receive moneys from Scotland. Your lands will…" William's comment died off at an echo of voices from down the hall. He kicked at the edge of the carpet with a sneer. "We will use it to send for thick carpet and hangings to stop the draft and decent plate for your table." Even in the summer's heat, behind thick stone walls, the air was chill.

James propped up the wall with his back. "I don't care anent that. I just want out of this room. I want to see the earl and to know if there is news."

"The king said you were to have tutors. I'm sure they don't mean to keep us locked up forever."

James strode a few steps and flopped down onto his bed. There was nothing to do here. He threw his arm over his eyes and bethought of sitting high on the tower of Rothesay Castle whilst his mother still lived, the land green all around until it slanted down to the rolling sea. Masts bobbed on the horizon, men in the fields scythed oats, a little goose-girl poured out grain for her flock. He tasted capercaillie stuffed with apple and pine nuts and thyme with sweetened caudle to wash it down. He could still hear the sound of the chapel bell, his brother's laughter as he rode out the gate, his mother's lilting voice. She wore the green that she loved, and it set off the red gleam of her hair and the gold of her coronet. He saw his sire's drawn, pallid face when they put her in her tomb. And he felt gooseflesh as the cold sea splashed over his feet as he waited that dark night for the ship Maryenknyght. The memories made his throat ache, so he sat up with a sigh.

"It's near time to break our fast," William said.

James didn't answer, but he supposed William was right, and the clatter of feet in the hall caused him to slide to the edge of the bed. His belly rumbled, ready for the bread that would break their fast. There was the noise of the bar being lifted, and the locks rattled, and the door creaked open.

James stood up in surprise when Sir Thomas Rempston stepped through the door. "Lord James," he said with a neutral sort of nod. "I have found a tutor for you, a monk from Eastminster Abbey well recommended by the abbot. He has both French and Latin, I am told. And the king has provided some coins for your upkeep, so if there is aught that you require for your wellbeing…"

"My freedom!" James exclaimed. At Sir Thomas's raised eyebrows, he lowered his voice. "Surely, Sir Thomas, I need nae be constantly confined so."

"It is not my intent. Once I am assured that you understand your position here, I will give you the freedom of the keep. But if you abuse that in any way, I will confine you." He crossed his arms and held James's gaze. "Do you understand?"

James felt his eyes widen at the threat, but he tried to keep his face blank. "Aye, sir, I do. I mean no abuse. I shan't challenge your authority."

"Good. There are others in the Tower who will be company for you." He snorted. "I have no doubt you'll soon

60

make the acquaintance of Gruffudd Glendwr. He's the nearest in the Tower to your age."

"Then I may leave? Go outwith this little room?" James couldn't help the eagerness of the questions. Why should he be grateful for being let out of a cage he shouldn't be locked into?

"Except for the walls, the deeper dungeon and chambers that are barred, I grant you and your squire freedom of the keep." Sir Thomas scowled at him. "In time long past, one of the Glendwrs tried to jump from the wall and fell to his death. Stupid! Since then, prisoners are forbidden there. You'll be escorted by a guard, but he'll not impede you unless you try to escape. But do not doubt, if you cause any problems, I shall be told."

James fiddled for a moment with a loose thread on his doublet, looked at the floor, and then nodded. "I understand you, Sir Thomas. I have no desire for durance more than I must suffer."

"Good."

"The Earl of Orkney? Will I be able to see him? I must need to speak wi' him."

Sir Thomas let out a breath. "He displeased the king with his impudence, but. . . I suppose there is no harm whilst he awaits his ransom." He gave James a somewhat kinder look than before. "The menagerie will entertain you, I suspect. We have five lions and a leopard for the nonce. Your confinement need not be so terrible."

James knew very well how terrible a confinement could be. He still dreamt of Robert in an oubliette, desperately gnawing his fingers as he starved to death in the dark. James tightened his mouth into a line, holding back a smile of relief to be outside if only for a few hours. "I ken it could be worse, Sir Thomas."

61

"Sensible boy." Sir Thomas nodded and turned on this heel to leave.

Behind him, a gaoler carried in a tray with a loaf of hot bread and a flagon of fresh water. James muttered a word of thanks as it suddenly occurred to him that it was a good idea to keep the gaolers sweet. He decided to mend his manners, though the gaolers were rough men and his inferiors. The man grunted and tromped out.

Grinning, James broke off half the loaf and tilted his head to William who grabbed up the rest. "Let's go!" He strode fast, not allowing himself to run, out the door and down the hall. Flickering torchlight touched the granite slabs underfoot, and shifting shadows danced across the rough walls. The winding steps were narrow and slick with wear and damp, but James barely slowed his tumultuous rush.

He pushed the heavy door open and stepped into the most precious sunlight he had ever seen. That it was dimmed by the ever-present London smoke mattered not. He was in the light and the air. He gaped at the high gray walls and the bailey yard. A guard in glittering steel paced atop, whilst another with halberd in hand stood at a corner.

The door crashed closed and he looked over his shoulder to see that they were indeed shadowed by one of the gaolers in the livery of the Tower rather than armor, but he had a sword at his waist. His heavy shoulders and thick neck below a blunt face made James assume he could use it. James decided that he should give him no reason.

A laugh came from around the bend of the tower, and a lithe figure wearing a battered helm and armor sauntered into view. When the man saw James, he pulled his helm off and held an arm wide in welcome. He examined James through large, dark eyes under arched brows.

"Well met, my lord," the man said in a strong singsong

accent. "I heard we had a new companion in this charming abode." His black curling hair was dripping with sweat.

James blinked at him and, after a moment, nodded in greeting. Obviously not a guard, the man was mayhap twenty with a sarcastic twist to his narrow lips.

"Forgive me. I am Gruffudd ab Owen Glendwr, eldest son of Prince Owen Glendwr." He snorted a wry laugh. "And fellow 'guest' in this fine English Tower."

James was reminded a bit of Robert Lauder. At least there might be fine company in this dour place. "I'm James." He shrugged. "Earl of Carrick and son of King Robert of Scotland, if any of that matters here."

Gruffudd threw a casual arm around James's shoulder. "Aye, it does, lad. You'd not want to be a villain in this place, stuck in the lower dungeons. Though my lack of coin makes my stay less pleasant than some." He looked past James to William and nodded a greeting.

"William Giffart, my lord," Will said. "Lord James's squire."

But James was moving back from Gruffudd. He reached for the blunted practice blade in his new friend's hand. Bouncing on his toes and turning the blade in his hand, he said, "They let us practice in the yard?"

"With blunted blades, certes, we may practice at sword and even tilt at the quintain when Sir Thomas feels kindly."

James's grinned, but then frowned. "My sword work isn't as good as I would like, Gruffudd."

"Then the three of us shall practice together." The Welshman winked. "They call me a fair hand with a blade, so I'll teach you what I know. It will keep us from dying of boredom."

CHAPTER 10

MAY 1406

*T*he courtyard rang with steel upon steel. Under his mail and helm, sweat trickled down James's face and his back as Gruffudd pressed his attack. Their blades met in a harsh clash and slid down until the guards locked. He looked up into Gruffudd's narrowed eyes. James heaved as hard as he could, throwing his opponent back.

His sword up, ready for the next swing, the tip of James's blade hovered a hand's breadth from Gruffudd's. Stronger and older, if James didn't defeat him quickly, he wouldn't. In a sudden fury of movement, he slammed an overhand blow that would have rung Gruffudd's helm like a bell—if it had landed. But it didn't. Gruffudd slipped to the left, out of danger, and brought his own sword across and into James's face. James yelped as he jumped back and spun to the side. He slashed up and around to hack at his opponent. Supple as a snake, Gruffudd dodged. Gruffudd slashed at James's stomach. James made a fierce downward blow to knock it away.

THEIR BLADES LOCKED AGAIN. James's breath was coming in

great heaves. He gulped desperately for air. Muscles straining, James leaning with all the strength he had left into the
blades. Gruffudd smiled and threw him back. James circled
him, panting, sword low and ready. Looking into Gruffudd's
eyes, he saw a flicker of amusement. James brought his sword
up. Gruffudd moved in, twisted behind him, and brought a
wide cut from behind to slap his blade on James's neck. A
bead of sweat dripped onto the sword.

"Yield you?"

"Aye," James said as Gruffudd pushed him away with a
slap to the shoulder. He rubbed a stinging welt across his
neck. "That hurt."

Gruffudd ripped his helm off and tossed his head to get
his dripping hair from his face. "Better, Lord James. You lack
strength yet, but for your years,"—Gruffudd nodded—"you
do not fight badly. You might stay alive against me when you
are fully a man."

James took off his helm and tipped his head back. The
May breeze felt good on his sweaty face. He leaned on his
sword, caught his breath with a shudder, and took a moment
to enjoy even faint praise from Gruffudd. Cheerful companion, he was also a skilled fighter, and the challenge was
exciting.

"Let me see your neck," Will said, glaring at Gruffudd.
"You shouldn't hit him so hard."

"Princes die in battle, like any man." Gruffudd looked
with an unfocused stare toward the top of the castle gate,
where his uncle's head rotted, and then jerked his gaze back.
"He'll only learn if he knows what hurt truly means."

Orkney, his face flushed red, came out the Tower door
and hurried across the yard. "Lord James!" he called. A gray-
haired priest in a soiled black robe and a gaoler in livery
trailed after him.

James tried to sheathe his blunted blade, but his hands

65

were bruised and clumsy. He got it in the battered scabbard on the second try. "My lord?"

Orkney paused a few steps away to tug at his doublet. He shook his head, not quite looking at James. He'd never seen Orkney look so—odd. James's guard nearby shifted, his armor creaking, and a raven croaked whilst Orkney looked everywhere except at James. He finally sank onto one knee and looked into James's face.

"Your Grace…" he said in a voice that shook.

James froze at the title.

"Your Grace, I am…" James could hear him swallow. "Dire news, sire. I must tell you… Your father… the king is dead."

James opened his mouth. Nothing came out.

William dropped to a knee.

"Your Grace," Orkney said. "You understand…"

James nodded wordlessly as the priest stepped forward.

The man bowed deeply and said, "At Bute Castle, sire. When… when word was brought to him of your capture, he turned his face to the wall. Would nae speak nor eat nor drink. And he died the third day."

"Dead…" Cold rushed through James and there was a sound in his ears like a rushing tide. "He… He didn't even try, then. To save me." James's voice was a whisper. He swallowed down a burn behind his eyes and looked up at the sky, where a muddy coin of the sun shone through the drifting layer of smoke.

His father. The king. Who had been no true king. His chest caught, and he could not breathe. He struggled—jerked in a gulp of air. The world spun. Closing his eyes, he just breathed until his head cleared. Then he opened them and looked at the men around him, who watched him, waiting.

He was the king. He must act a king. That is what they were waiting for, but he didn't know how. Again his mouth worked. "My lords..." he choked out. He unbuckled his sword belt and shoved it into William's hands. Slowly, he walked toward the White Tower. "Let me be. I—I must think."

CHAPTER 11

*T*he room was blessedly silent. James leaned his head against the cool, damp stone and hammered his fist into it as hard as he could. It hurt when the skin split and blood dripped down his wrist—a welcome pain. It made the pain in his chest seem less.

How could he? To give up. Their father had let Davey die. Now he had abandoned James—alone—imprisoned.

James turned and propped his back against the wall, cradling his bleeding hand against his chest and blinking back the burning in his eyes. He wouldn't weep. He wouldn't! Not for a father and king who cared so little for him.

The door creaked half-open, and Gruffudd stood in the opening, a flagon in his hand. "Sir Thomas sent this for you. He's not so bad, once you're in his good graces, and I think you need it." He closed the door behind him and poured some wine into a cup.

James nodded, but he looked away, swallowing. He felt as though his throat had closed up tight. Perhaps the wine would help, so he took it with his left hand, his right still dribbling blood.

"Have anything to wrap that?" Gruffudd asked.

James took a deep drink of the wine—sweet and not much watered. With a sigh, he hooked a stool with his foot and sank down on it. He turned his hand to examine the split. "It's nae so bad. It will stop soon."

When Gruffudd had helped himself to a cup of wine, he threw himself on James's bed, propping up a knee with an arm flung over it. "Your bed is softer than mine." He gave a wry twitch of his mouth.

"Is it?" James poked at the shallow split on the side of his palm for a minute, but the bleeding had already almost stopped. He looked up at Gruffudd, and the words tumbled out. "Your father. Do you... honor him?"

He gave James a rather apologetic look. "My father is a strong man, you see." He shrugged and took a sip of the wine. "Too strong, mayhap. He could not abide the English ruling over us. Grey de Ruthyn seized our lands, and because we are Welsh the English shrugged at it." He swirled the wine in his cup and looked pensive. "That doesn't matter. But... aye, I honor him—failed him though I did."

"I... I did nae... honor mine." James looked sadly at his cup of wine and swallowed down the rest in a gulp. "He was a bad king."

"I'm sorry."

He couldn't stand the hot anger burning through him, and he jumped to his feet. The stool toppled. He hurled the cup against the wall. "Hell take him!" It clattered onto the floor, a smear of wine marring the wall.

Gruffudd shook his head. "It may be that he could not help it. He was as he was."

James's shoulders slumped. He righted the stool, eyes burning with tears he would not let fall. He walked slowly back and forth across the room before he sat back down. Propping his elbows on his knees, he sank his hands into his hair and gripped. "He let them kill Davey. Did nothing. He never did anything. If he was so grieved at my capture, why did he nae do something? Only my mother did—when she lived. Wha' kind of king is that?"

"You will be different."

"Why do I feel so… so lost, though?" His voice choked. "I should nae care."

"He was your father. He would not have grieved so if he hadn't cared for you, lad."

James rocked where he sat, and tears began to run down his face. "That makes it worse. Don't you see?"

CHAPTER 12

JUNE 1407

*A*s he bent over the book on his table, James laid down his quill and ran a finger across a bright illustration that filled half the page. A wheel held a woman in finery at its height but had flung a king in ermine and a ragged peasant onto the ground. Kings, princes and beautiful ladies awaited their turn on the wheel. He was chewing his lip and frowning over it when a sharp thud on the table made him jump.

The black-robed monk, Brother Odo, rapped the thin birch cane on the table again, and James looked up into his piercing stare. The monk was a small man, no taller than James, slender and quick, with sharp features and threads of gray in his dark hair. The tonsure atop his head shone as though he polished it.

James bit the inside of his cheek to stop his grin, which hurt less than that rod would have, had it smacked on his hand.

"You were not given Boethius to daydream over."

"Aye, Brother. I only wondered wha' the wheel meant."

"The wheel means a wheel. *Consolatio Philosophiae* is but a story which Boethius wrote whilst imprisoned, as are you. You are to use your time more productively than staring at pretty pictures." He pointed a narrow finger at a word. "Tell me what those four lines mean—in English."

A word of his own Scots often earned James a stinging rap on the knuckles, or sometimes a caning, so he sighed and examined the line the brother was pointing to. His Latin was mainly that of the Church prayers, and Boethius's book made him struggle. He took a deep breath and licked his lips. He could grow to hate this foul tome, though the illustration made him think—perhaps too much.

"Who formed my studious numbers," he translated aloud from the Latin,

"Smoothly once in… happier days,

Now helpless in tears and sadness

Learn a mournful tune to… to…" He sighed, bracing himself. "…attollo… I don't remember."

"Raise!" The birch whistled when it slashed across James's shoulders. "Learn a mournful tune to raise."

It was only the sound that made James wince. The cane stung but was nothing to a blow from Gruffudd's practice blade. His knuckles were skinned from the day before, and his shoulders were bruised from being knocked from his horse riding at the quintain. Besides, even Bishop Wardlaw said that the sting of a cane was a fine aid to memory.

Brother Odo made a disgusted sound in his throat and motioned to the parchment, which was much marred where James had sanded out errors. "Write it out. Cleanly, boy." He thumped the can down on the table. "I expect the next ten lines written when I return in the morning."

"Aye, Brother Odo," James said, meekly keeping his eyes on the parchment until the door banged closed behind his tutor.

Smoothly once in happier days…

But there was no point in thinking of happier days. Those days were done, though later he would give more thought to that wheel. Brother Odo might be mistaken that it had no meaning when it cast men from the heights to the depths. The tutor never wanted to talk anent anything except the translation of the words, and James suspected the monk had no imagination at all. Shaking his head, he closed the book. He would write out all the lines, even if it meant burning down his last candle, but for now in the practice yard, he would find Gruffudd and William and perhaps some of the other prisoners and something fun to do.

He jumped up, checked both in the hallway to be sure Brother Odo was out of sight, and hurried down the narrow stairs, out into the sunlight. He gaped at a line of riders streaming through the open gates, two dozen in polished steel. And there rode the Earl of Orkney in the middle with on one side Master John Lyon, who had brought word of King Robert's death. James did not know the big man beside them, red-faced under his dark, wiry beard and belly straining against his embroidered doublet.

Orkney vaulted from his horse and tossed his reins to a sergeant, who was muttering a protest which the earl ignored as he strode toward James. "Your Grace, I have news I would give you privily."

The stranger was climbing heavily from the saddle. "He's no more 'grace' than I am. Less than my lord father," the man rumbled.

James looked past Orkney, who was slowly shaking his head, and took a slow, deep breath. "Murdoch?" James asked Orkney in a carefully controlled tone. If he had ever seen his cousin before, James didn't recall it.

Orkney jerked a nod.

Murdoch Stewart, Earl of Fife, eldest son of the Duke of

Albany, swaggered across the bailey yard. "If it isn't my little cousin, James."

Thrusting his trembling hands into his armpits, James narrowed his eyes at the man. "Aye. And my brother Davey was your cousin, too." His face felt scalded with heat. "Were you at Falkirk Castle when he was murdered? Cousin?"

Murdoch threw back his head and laughed, exposing trembling jowls under his beard. "Aye. And I was there when parliament voted that we had no fault in his death." His laugh broke off like a snapping branch, and he scowled. "Before the Battle of Homildon Hill, when I was taken prisoner."

James drew in a slow, steady breath and then another. He swallowed down the tears of fury at Murdoch's laughter. He had no doubt that his brother's murder was at least partially Murdoch's doing, but screaming at him or weeping like a lassie would gain nothing. "Och, my lord..." He forced the words out. "We are both prisoners, then, whether you think I am entitled to be 'graced' or nae. Our differences must wait until we regain our freedom." A pulsing pain began to throb behind one eye at having to speak to the man he was forced acknowledge as cousin.

"My father will ransom me. You may be sure." Murdoch glowered at James and then at Orkney and back to James from eyes that were bloodshot. "But do nae expect him to agree to any ransom for you to be freed, whelp."

"Your father is hardly the only noble in Scotland," Orkney said.

"But he is the regent." Murdoch shoved past Orkney. "Bring my supplies. I am thirsty," he called over his shoulder. A servant, who James realized had a badge of the Albany Stewarts on his shoulder, hefted a tun of wine onto his shoulder and plodded after Murdoch. Orkney squeezed the bridge of his nose and let out a long breath.

"His being moved here from Nottingham Castle was part

of my news for you. From wha' I have heard, he spends much of his time drinking, so I doubt his presence will be something you are forced ofttimes to suffer."

"I suppose I knew I would see him one day." James looked at Orkney's thin-lipped face. "Part, though? Wha' is the rest?"

The bailey yard was raucous with noise, men-at-arms talking and leading away their horses to the stables and a couple of sumpter horses being unloaded whilst William and Gruffudd stood near the armory watching. Orkney took James by the arm and led him into a corner where a wall met the tower.

"My ransom has arrived. I was allowed to return only to bid you farewell."

James felt his stomach lurch. Once Orkney left, he would be truly alone.

"Don't look so, lad. William will remain with you, and I convinced King Henry to allow you a chaplain, so Master Lyon will remain, also. He can arrange messages between us. Once in Scotland, I'll do wha' I can for your release. There is nothing I can accomplish here."

"But my ransom…?"

"Albany has…" Orkney took a pained sounding breath. "He has stolen your lands. A' your regality… You have nae funds for ransom or even for comforts, even if King Henry would agree to it."

"If?"

"Henry has sworn you'll be released if you swear fealty to him. Fealty as King of the Scots." Orkney scrubbed at his face with one hand. "If you agreed to it, I have no doubt he would give you an army to take Scotland. The damned English have done such before. The Balliols, Toom Tabard and his son, both of them, were put on the throne by English armies before we rid ourselves of them."

75

"But… wha' would that mean? If he put me on the throne? Would he throw down the Albanys?"

James's heart gave a lurch at the thought of destroying his enemies. If they would kill him, why should he not use the English against them?

"It would mean that you owed King Henry obedience, though how much power he would give you, I cannot say. A' Scotland would be under his heel. And never—never would our parliament accept such an agreement."

"So… I would be king at his pleasure and Scotland defeated." James tried to wrap his mind around the idea. "And if he didn't like wha' I did, wha' then? If I did the best for Scotland and nae for him?"

"If we already weren't under their heel, we soon would be, for there is no way we would win against him or even more so against Prince Hal of Monmouth. You would—" Orkney shrugged. "Probably, you would lose your throne, although he might let you keep it if you knelt at his feet."

"He has put no such proposal to me," James said. "Did he to you?"

Orkney nodded. "Though he says that you are yet too young to lead an army. But others might in your name in a year or two—especially once the English have put down the rebellion in Wales. I told him no. Eventually, the demand will be put to you directly." Orkney grabbed his shoulder and gave him a shake. "And you must tell him no."

James swallowed. "Though it will mean they keep me locked up."

"It will cost you dear, lad. But saying yes would cost us a' more—including you."

"But… How do I regain my freedom?" Too many thoughts were spinning through his head. "Albany seized my lands? Then I have no coin for my needs? For William's?"

"I will leave you coin from my ain purse. In Scotland, I

can work along with Bishop Wardlaw and the Lauders toward freeing you. But you must take my oath." Smiling a little, Orkney knelt on the ground and held up his clasped hands. "Take my hands between yours."

Blinking, James knew he should say something. He was sure he had seen his father do this, though it was long ago. He clasped his ink-stained hands around Orkney's larger ones.

"I do swear fealty and homage to you, my lord, James, King of Scots, and I will keep faith with you against all creatures, living or dead, and I will defend you and a' your successors against a' malefactors and invaders, as God and his saints help me."

James licked his lips and said, "I… I take you as my man and will keep faith with you and defend you and your heirs, as is my duty as… as your liege lord."

James raised his eyebrows for Orkney's approval, and the earl gave him a brisk nod of approval. For a moment, he grasped James's arm. "Do nae lose heart, Your Grace. However long it takes, we will free you."

CHAPTER 13

NOVEMBER 1412

"*B*eautifully written, Your Grace," Master Lyon said, leaning over two charters laid out on a long table.

The featherbed was plush with comfort, and James had piled pillows behind his back. He stretched his legs out, crossed his ankles, and strummed a note on the lute. It was a rare treat to be brought to Bishop Arundel's Croydon Palace with King Henry's court, dragged as a prize to increase the English king's fame and prestige. But James could almost forget for the moment that he was a prisoner, and he intended to take full advantage of it. "Nae badly done, though I say it myself. But you taught me, Lyon, so I suppose the credit is yours." James hummed a tune under his breath.

Lyon straightened and sat on the stool in front of the table. He studied James for a moment. "You were always a good pupil, though I am no tutor. You should have had better."

"Those provided me by King Henry were well enough, but none were Scots. And none as skilled wi' the lute and the harp as you. Forbye, you did nae cane me at every error. You were ever kind." James twitched a wry smile. "Except in your news from home."

"I wish I brought better. Albany has no intention of cooperating in your release—ever, even if it means they continue to hold his own son." He motioned to the charters that James had penned with his hand. "But these are a step you needed to take: the first documents sealed by you of your reign. And the Douglas of Drumlanrig will be much in your debt. He may even have influence wi' the Earl of Douglas."

James sat up, swung his legs over the edge of the bed, and laid the lute aside. "Thanks to you." He stood to smooth his doublet, worrying at a worn spot. "And you brought me funds from the bishop, for which I am much in your debt—and his. I hate when I my clothes are as ragged as a beggar's."

"They are nae that bad, Your Grace, though that you must plead for wha' is yours…" Lyon paused when the door opened and an usher in the king's red and gold livery bowed.

"My lord, I bring a summons from His Grace, the king."

The usher preceded James into the marble hall as Lyon gathered the documents and followed. Bishop Arundel must be immensely rich, James pondered, as they walked past walls hung with French tapestries and niches containing statues of Medea, Hyacinthus and other figures he couldn't identify. The usher opened a door flanked by statues of Cerberus, eyes of onyx gleaming in their snarling faces.

Prince Hal confronted James the moment he entered. Tall, lean, dark hair cropped in a ring above his ears, and hatchet-faced, a white scar on his left cheek from a Welsh arrow stood out livid against his tanned skin. "And here is Lord James fancying himself some sort of ruler in spite of our paying for his bread and wine." He had two or three inches on James, which grated almost as much as his sneers whenever they met.

James took a deep breath and looked past the prince to

King Henry, who sat beside the hearth speaking to two men: Sir William Douglas of Drumlanrig and his brother, both tall and wiry with red-blond hair, though Sir William's was thinning on top. Happiness was too thin a word to describe his leap of feeling to receive his own ambassadors, a blaze of delight.

Joy was a naked emotion. He couldn't hide it. Even King Henry smiled, as James strode to the king's side, ignoring the prince. It was the king, even though he was James's captor, who must be greeted first.

James said, "Your Grace, I am beyond pleased to see you looking so well."

That the king looked well was a vast exaggeration. His face was pallid and gaunt, and a livid boil was angry and weeping on his neck above the collar of his doublet. Yet the king's smile broadened, and he extended his hand. James took it and bowed over it—only courtesy.

Prince Hal swaggered to stand beside his father with a smile on his thin lips that was pure insolence. "Whilst you always look well, thanks to my royal father's care."

"His Grace has been generous," James said. It was less than true, but James had no intention of being provoked into an argument, however rude the prince was. "As is his receiving my ambassadors."

James turned with a smile to the two men who were waiting his attention so patiently. He held out his hand.

William Douglas of Drumlanrig dropped to a knee to grasp it. "Your Grace." His ruddy face was high with color, and a wide smile spread across it. "To see you... I cannot tell you my happiness."

James clasped the man's hands in both of his. He felt as though his grin might break his face, it was so huge. "And my joy as well. But I have more to share wi' you than joy, my friend." James looked past the Douglas to the other man, ruddy as well but several years younger than his brother. "And your brother—Sir Archibald." He held out his right hand. "Welcome."

Archibald Douglas knelt and kissed James's hand. "Your Grace."

When the men rose, James said, "Master Lyon brought me word of your efforts for my freedom, and I will nae have it go unrewarded. The charters are no less than your due."

Lyon carefully spread the two documents out upon a massive table against the far wall. "Writ wi' His Grace's own proper hand," he said with obvious pride.

James squeezed Douglas's hand before he strolled to stand beside the documents he had spent so much time penning and waited until the two men rose to join him. He pulled his signet ring from his finger, the one ring that he wore. "This is the seal I use for my letters, but they will be sealed with my great seal in time to come." He pretended not to hear the snort of derision from Prince Hal as he tipped wax onto the document and pressed his seal into it. "As I promised, this confirms to you the lands of Drumlanrig, Hawick and Selkirk." He did the same to the second parchment. "And restores the grant of Cavers to you, Sir Archibald."

Douglas of Drumlanrig took the long parchment from the table, examining it closely. "By your own hand, Your Grace?" He raised his gaze to look into James's face. There might even have been tears in his eyes. James lowered his gaze to the table for fear there were tears in his own. He briefly gripped Douglas's arm.

Douglas looked past him to the English king. "Your Grace, we would have your leave to discuss negotiations for the speedy release of King James."

King Henry leaned back in his chair, looking into the fire.

"Your Grace?" James said, but the king didn't reply or look his way.

"That will have to wait until arrival of news regarding ambassadors anent the Duke of Albany's interests," Prince Hal said smoothly. He could be smooth when he wanted, as James knew well. "His representatives left for France a few days past, we are told. Until I know that they do not conspire with our enemies, there will be no negotiations. Charles d'Orleans and the others of his Armagnac party are not likely to forgive the Duc de Bourgogne for his father's murder, which complicates the affair. Whether the Scots ally with one side or the other—" Hal seemed to decide against sharing his thoughts with James and broke off.

James opened his mouth, closed it. Then he opened it again to say, "The duke negotiating wi' the French has naught to do with my freedom, surely."

"His allying with the Duc de Bourgogne does, however. If you returned to Scotland, you would be no more than a tool to be used in his machinations with the French. I have no intention of letting that happen."

James's heart thumped against his ribs. "I thought that you were ready to negotiate." He heard how unsteady he sounded and closed his mouth. He looked at the king, who still refused to meet his gaze.

"When we are certain of the situation with France, mayhap," Prince Hal said. "Not before."

James felt his face flood with heat at the accusation that he would be his foul uncle's tool. He took a deep breath to stop the words that wanted to flood out. He would not give Prince Hal the satisfaction.

CHAPTER 14

MARCH 1413

*J*ames sat on the edge of his bed, listening to William snore softly. He walked to the narrow window and swung his leg out and sat straddling the stone. The March night sky was dusted with stars, and a sickle of the waning moon hung above the dark ragged pines that surrounded Nottingham Castle. Since Croydon, this had been James's most recent cage. But now King Henry ailed. They said that Henry of Monmouth had already seized power. James thought of Prince Hal's hungry eyes over the livid battle-scar on his cheek. Aye, he would believe it of the man.

Ducking his head, James pushed one shoulder out and squeezed through. The cold air nipped at his ears, and the night was quiet except for a dog barking in the bailey yard.

He bent his other knee and squeezed it outside so that his arse rested on the narrow outside ledge. Awkwardly, he shifted around, winding his arms back over the window opening. He dangled his foot down and felt for a space between the stones. The outer wall was all about strength, rough-cut and roughly laid. When he had a toehold, he lowered himself down. The irregular rocks gave him enough purchase for fingers and toes. Carefully, he lowered the other foot, inching his way down and touching the face of the rock beneath his fingertips, the grit of the mortar, the sharp edges of the stones. His hearing seemed sharpened by the darkness. An owl screeched, and the breeze rubbed together the branches of the oaks so they creaked.

His room was directly above the kitchen, and he was sure the cooks had already settled for the night beside the warmth of their hearth. Breathing deeply and sweat dripping down his face, he groped his way. When he was a man's height from the ground, he kicked away from the wall and dropped with a grunt. His bent knees took the force of his landing. He froze for a moment and listened. Something took flight overhead with a great flutter of wings.

He turned and darted across the grass to the narrow path that led down the hillside to the village. Keeping to the edge, he stayed in the shadow of the trees. He put each foot down carefully so as not to kick loose any pebbles or step on branches. A coughing sound came from beside the path, and a roe deer ran across, its light brown hide looking almost white in the pewter moonlight. In the darkened beech and oak woods, there were sounds that might or might not be owls and prowling foxes.

He pushed his hair, still wet with sweat, out of his face. The trees had begun to thin, and thickets of hazel and alder pressed close to the road.

At the foot of the slope, the path curved. Through the trees, he caught glimpses of lamplight from the inn. A nightingale trilled and swooped over his head to flutter into a tree, making the branches whisper. Then there was a burst of laughter, and someone began to sing in a squawking voice. Over the door, a painted sign with a crusader's cross swung in the breeze.

James stood beneath a spreading grandfather oak, watching. If there were guards at the inn, they would be sure to carry word to his current gaoler, Sir Richard Gray. And there were no horses outside the door. He snorted a wry laugh through his nose. Had he really been so daft as to wish for one? If he escaped so far from Scotland, they would recapture him within hours, and he would only look like a fool. Sometimes the days seemed like years and the years, centuries, and still no hope of freedom. But tonight… Perhaps for tonight, he would pretend to be free.

So he blew out a breath and strode toward the bars of light that shone through the shutters. Within was the common room, and James gawped at the benches half-filled with men at scarred tables bent over their drinks. The air smelt of ale and sweat and oak from the fire on the hearth. Torches cast a wavering light. He peered hopefully, for he had heard some inns allowed girls to serve, and some even took coin for a few minutes alone, but he saw only men. In the corner, a skinny youth of fifteen or sixteen, red-haired and freckled, plucked at a clàrsach, badly out of tune. How had a harp from Scotland come so far south?

An ugly man with a big belly straining at the laces of his stained jerkin and a shaggy beard covering his cheeks and chin stood with his arms crossed over his chest, glaring. "Are you coming in or no?" he snapped.

James closed the door behind him and felt his face flooding with red. "I was thinking I could buy a mug of ale." It wasn't his fault he'd never set foot in a hostelry before and that he had hoped for more.

"That's what I sell, but I'll have my coin before you taste a drop."

He hadn't a clue how much a mug of ale cost, but he had a few silver groats in his purse still from the last time Bishop Wardlaw had managed to send him coins, so he pulled two out and handed them over. The hostel-keeper turned the coins over in his hand and examined one suspiciously before he nodded. "Woman!" he yelled. "Bring a pitcher of ale and a tankard."

Through a doorway in the back came a woman in a faded dress, grumbling. She was thin with a pinched face, sharp nose and faded red hair. "Here I am. Quit your shouting."

"Sit you down, then." The man shook a finger at James. "Can't serve with you standing, can we?"

James took the table near the clàrsach player, and the woman banged the pitcher and tankard down in front of him. He nodded his thanks, keeping his tongue between his teeth. The man hadn't mentioned his Scottish speech, but there were not so many in these parts they might not guess who he was. He took the tankard in his hands and sipped, smiling. It tasted better than any he'd had in many a day—in the free air.

But when Red-hair plunked another note, James shuddered. "In summer, when the thicket shines," the boy sang with a sharp voice, picking out notes on the clàrsach that didn't quite go with the words, "and leaves be large and long."

"Wait." James shook his head to get the sound out of his ears. "Can you tune it before you torture us with that noise?"

The boy stared at James, letting his mouth drop open with a gormless look.

The hostel-keeper had been talking to one of the customers, but at the silence, he hurried over. "Why aren't you playing, you worthless git?"

The boy flinched away. "He said to wait."

"Never mind anent what some stranger said." He raised his hand to cuff the boy.

"Let me play instead," James said before the man's hand could fall. "And I'll tune it for him, so he'll sound better."

86

The woman came bustling over, frowning. "There's no music," she complained, as though no one had noticed.

James reached over and pulled the instrument out of Red-hair's arms. He rested the soundbox against his chest and turned the pins to tune the strings, plucking them one by one. "Wha' is your name?"

"Ralf." The boy had leaned close to watch, but James was sure he'd be no better the next day. It had taken years for Master Lyon to teach him the instrument, though music came easily to him.

The innkeeper clipped Ralf's ear. "Pay attention now. Mayhap you can learn something for once."

The boy was cringing, so James said, "I'll finish Robin Hood and the Monk, if you sing wi' me."

Ralf shifted in his seat as he rubbed his ear. "I will."

James ran his fingers down the strings. "Good." He bent over the instrument. "It is full merry in the fair forest, to hear the birdies' song."

Ralf joined in with James, slapping his thigh to keep time. "To see the deer draw to the dale, and leave the high hills free. . ."

The customers were beating on the tables along with the music. The singing and companions made the night seem brighter. It wasn't very long before the two finished the ballad. James leaned back, smiling, and the woman poured him another tankard of ale. He took a swallow of the smooth, tingly brew, and it left a bitter tang of hops in his mouth.

"Do you know any more songs?" Ralf asked. "I'd dearly like to learn some."

James nervously plucked a note. His was a song no one had ever heard, but it would do no harm to share it this once. He nodded. "High in the heaven's firmament, the heaven's stars were twinkling fire." He picked out a tune to go with the words. "And in Aquarius, Artemis the pure rinsed tresses like golden wire."

He sang what he had written, although he was sure there should be more to the poem that had yet to come to him. Ralf stared at him when he played the last note, his thin mouth spreading into a grin. Several men thumped their tankards on the table, but half a dozen others stood to toss silver groats that bounced on the table in front of him. The hostel-keeper applauded, and James smiled up at him.

Then James heard horses outside and the sound of men's voices. A moment later, the door burst open. A man-at-arms stepped in and stood aside for Sir Richard, Lord Gray of Codenore and presently James's head gaoler. He was a tall man, perhaps fifty, James thought, with thick lips, a bulbous nose, and thinning gray hair. His doublet was green velvet, and a fur cloak was tossed carelessly back from his shoulders. Through the doorway, James could make out the shape of a party of horsemen.

"Lord James!" Sir Richard exclaimed. "What mean you by this? I sought you and found you missing!"

James gave a long, low sigh and handed the harp to Ralf. He stood and gave the English lord a half bow. "I felt in the mood for drinking a tankard of ale and playing some music for these good folk."

"I gave you no leave to depart the castle. And certes not without guards."

James lifted his chin and looked Sir Richard in the eye. "I am King of the Scots." However much they denied him the title and respect due a king, he could not meekly accept such reproaches. "I ask no man's leave. Forbye, did you truly believe I was going to hie me home to Scotland—" He threw his arms wide. "—with neither gold nor mount nor men?"

"You are put in my charge by the king, sirrah. And whatever you think you may be in Scotland, here you are to do as you are bid."

James twitched a smile, which he knew was going to annoy the man. Sir Richard might be a noted campaigner and chancellor in the king's court, but he had no sense of humor. "Very well, Sir Richard, for I am indeed a prisoner here. Wha' is it you bid me to do?"

"Aldis, Lord James will take your horse." Stomping to thrust his face into James's, he said, "You will mount up and return to the castle to prepare for departure on the morrow. You are to be sent to the Tower of London at the bidding of Prince Hal."

James nodded farewell to Ralf. The boy pointed at the coins on the table.

"They're yours, lad," James said and patted his shoulder. Even though James could have used the coins, he wouldn't let the English see him scoop them up like a beggar. He sauntered to the door, Sir Richard's glare burning a hole in his back.

CHAPTER 15

*G*ruffudd pushed back from the table. His smile was a flash of white teeth as he jumped to his feet and tossed a half-eaten chicken leg into the trencher. James strode across the room and threw his arms around him. They pounded each other's backs, laughing. James thrust his old friend away to look him over. Gruffudd was less than welcome in the king's court, unlike James, for the title the English had stolen for Henry of Monmouth, Prince of Wales, rightfully belonged to Gruffudd's father.

"You look well," James said with a smile. In truth, Gruffudd was thinner and had a few threads of gray in his black hair, but James was too glad to see him to mention that.

Gruffudd snorted. "You've grown a bit—and put on weight. Did you spend all your time at Nottingham bent over a book?"

"Nae a bit of it. To Sir Richard's dismay, the king gave command that I was allowed to join them at the hunt, so I spent a deal of time riding." James tore the other leg off Gruffudd's roast chicken and stripped the meat with his teeth. After he swallowed it down, he grinned. "But they have better cooks than the Tower."

"Keep your hands off my dinner," the Welshman said, but he poured a cup of wine and handed it to James. "Where is William?"

"He said he would see to my things, but if that doesn't include gathering the gossip, I'm a Sassenach." James paused, eyeing Gruffudd, took a sip of the wine and then asked, "Do you ken why Prince Hal would have me brought here?"

Gruffudd put an arm around James's shoulder and drew him into the far corner away from the closed door. The walls were thick, but guards were always near, and voices carried strangely. He put his mouth near James's ear. "He is ailing again—the king. And already Henry of Monmouth has seized power."

"That I know. But why the sudden bustle?"

"The king was furious at his son overstepping his bounds, they say. I know that the king has been at parliament, where he forbad his son to attend, but I have not heard what he intends. And then they say he fell into a fit."

"A fit?" James asked in a low voice. "But he might still recover."

"Only God and the saints know. The guards gossip that he cannot rise from his bed, and that pustules cover his body."

"Is it truly leprosy, do you think?"

"Before I was captive, I'd seen lepers enough, ears, noses, and fingers rotted off. You have seen him. Does suffers so badly?"

James let out a breath he hadn't realized he was holding. When, for a short time, James had been sent to join King Henry's court at Croydon, he had knelt to take the king's hand numerous times. James shuddered and then felt ashamed. But leprosy was a fearful sickness. "His body seemed sound, except for the boils when I saw him last."

"That does not sound to me like true leprosy, and if he had it, surely the court would be kept away from him. But whatever it is that ails him, everyone says he will not live much longer."

James sipped his wine thoughtfully. "So, Monmouth will be king. The few times I've seen him, he struck me a hard man."

"Hard and one of the best commanders England has ever seen. The strategy he used to defeat my army at Pwll Melyn was a fine piece of work, curse him. Though if I had been wiser…" He shrugged. "The French will be hard put. Once his father no longer holds him back, he'll have his army at their door in a trice."

"But—" When the door opened, James broke off, but William motioned two other men inside, entered, and closed the door behind them. He was neatly kept as always, though the trip had been cold, his doublet brushed and his hair combed. The only mar was a purple bruise that covered one cheek.

A squire, slender with long arms and legs, his dark hair in wind-tossed curls and cheeks soft with fuzz, hurried to drop to a knee and grasp James's hand. "Your Grace, I am your servant." James smiled and raised him to his feet, nodding a greeting to the tall, blond-haired, burly priest who had approached more circumspectly, bowing low.

William was grinning at the squire's enthusiasm when he said, "Iain of Alway, sire, and Father Dougal Drummond. More prisoners have been brought to the Tower."

"Good God, man," Gruffudd said, staring at William. "Has James taken to beating you?"

James made a grimace. "No, I've started letting him take a

beating for me, and I am right sorry for it. Nae that Richard of Codenore asked my permission on the matter."

GRUFFUDD MOTIONED for William to help himself to the wine. "What happened?"

"His Grace left Nottingham Castle the night before last—through a window." William gave a wry laugh as he poured. "Sir Richard was most displeased when I could nae tell him where my liege lord was. Nae that I would have said, had I known."

"You escaped?" Gruffudd whispered to James.

"I could wish, my friend. It would take more resources than I have to make my way home, and I'm not such a fool as to give them reason to do me worse than they have, unless I feel the chance is one worth taking. No, the talk was that we were being moved back to the Tower, so I decided I would sample an evening of freedom." He tilted his head pensively. "I hoped there would be a lass there to…" He made a vague wave of his hand.

Gruffudd threw back his head and laughed. "And that kitchen maid I heard tell of?"

James gave him an aggrieved look. "You may laugh, but you've nae been locked up most of your life."

William rubbed his cheek with a thumb. "Allow me to go wi' you if you ever do that again. At least he didn't knock you about."

"I should think not." Gruffudd motioned William closer. "The tutors may have caned His Grace on occasion, but for one of the king's men to give him a blow... No, they would not."

"No. And were I about, he'd nae lay hands on my squire either," James said in a carefully controlled tone. He sighed and let his anger go for the moment. "Did you gather any gossip, Will? Why the new prisoners?"

"I took my time taking our goods to our room, chatted wi' the guards and shared some ale I had secreted."

"I have heard, Your Grace—" The priest paused until James nodded permission. He moved closer and lowered his voice. "I have heard rumors that Edmund Mortimer, the rightful king, plots to recover the throne; that his people may move against Prince Hal once his father is dead."

Iain of Alway gaped, but James merely raised his eyebrows.

"They say that the king will not last the night," William whispered, "and that he has told the prince that his soul is stained wi' holding you wrongfully a prisoner, Your Grace. Everyone is saying that he has told Prince Hal to release you wi' no ransom."

"That—can't be true." James shook his head. "The king has never once hinted that he would lessen his demands."

"It is what everyone is saying. And that he was furious when the prince removed the crown before times. The prince had to carry it back, and the king was in a rage, shouting at him from his bed."

"Could it be true, do you think? That the king has said I should be returned home? Released from this durance vile? I am afeart even to hope."

There came the sound of feet running in the hall. In the city, bells began to toll. "The king is dead," someone shouted. "Long live the king!"

CHAPTER 16

"You are to wait here, Lord James, until you are wanted." Sir Richard, Lord Gray, turned his back to stride out the door. It slammed shut and the lock clicked.

James stared after the man, grinding his teeth. At last, he ran a hand over the goatee he had grown since he returned to the Tower and paced across the room, spun on his heel, and retraced his steps, irritated that the scarlet carpets underfoot kept him even from the satisfaction of hearing his heels ring on the stone. A single large chair sat at one end of the long chamber, not grand enough for a throne. James continued his path back and forth. William stood at the narrow arched window, craning his neck to see into the bailey yard. No noise penetrated the walls, fifteen feet thick, atop the castle mound.

Since Prince Hal's coronation, there had been no word, no news, no sign of the new king. But both James and his cousin had been more closely guarded than ever before. The gaolers had been much excited about the latest news of some Lollard named Sir John Oldcastle. King Hal had quickly put down the man's rebellion. Oldcastle had been sent to the Tower, and a few nights later was slipped out of the prison. He was well known to be a friend of the new king. James snorted and made another pass across the room.

"Why were we brought but Gruffudd left behind?" William asked. "And why separated from your cousin Murdoch?"

After months of being closely confined within the Tower of London, James had been bustled to Windsor Castle at daybreak and hurried into the Round Tower. "Windsor. They have never before brought me here. Why is an excellent question. If it is true that there is pestilence in the city again…" James rubbed his forehead. "Gruffudd looked ill yesterday."

"I tried to see him to let him know where we were bound, and they had locked him in his cell." William turned from the window with a look of horror. "You don't think he has it?"

James paused in his pacing. "Holy Mary, I pray not. No one else in the Tower had been ill, and he is a braw, strong…" He shook his head. "No, it must merely be some ill humor that gripes his belly." James turned in a circle, scowling. "Devil take them, why do they have me waiting here?" James was grinding his teeth. "Do you have me presentable? Damn them." He held up his arm to show the frayed edge of his sleeve. "Look at that!"

"I'm sorry, Your Grace. It's mended the best that I could manage."

James sighed. He knew that. With as little money as he received from Scotland, William did as well as anyone could.

William returned to his vigil at the window, twisting his head to try to see what was happening outside. Where they were, in a side tower far from the main halls of Windsor, they could see only a bit of the yard.

James began pacing again.

"Horses are coming into the yard," William said hesitantly.

"I'm not fashed wi' you, Will."

William looked over his shoulder and twitched a smile. "You're impatient wi' being kept waiting."

"It is nae knowing, say. Why so close kept in the Tower? Why brought here? Wha' do they want of me?"

"Mayhap…" William turned and leaned back against the wall. "Mayhap Iain St. Clair and William Douglas of Drumlanrig have arrived, and the king has agreed to negotiate for your release, after a' the delays. That must be what has happened, and they need you for the negotiations."

James strode across the room again, clenching and unclenching his fists. "Delay. A nice word for it. Moneys for my ambassadors' expenses stolen. A feud between the Drummands and the Grahams, so that Lothian runs with blood. The Earl of Strathearn murdered. My own regalities stolen. I call it baudrie!" He gave a bark of bitter laughter. "My uncle does a braw job of ruling my realm."

William shook his head and turned back to the window. "More horses, dozens of them, but from here I cannot see who." He pressed his face as far through the window as he could. "Wait! I see the royal banner."

"It is Hal, then. Or should I now call him King Henry?" James said in an acid tone. "I suppose that I should. Though never once has he named me as a king." Coming to Windsor should have been a good change. He would have hoped it, but his reception had been harsh; he'd been bustled into a chamber and locked in to stew. "I'm sorry, Will. I do nae mean to inflict my ill-temper on you."

William smiled and shrugged. "You're my liege."

The long chamber was aglow with torches burning in gold sconces on the wall between the windows. A fire blazed in the hearth, filling the room with the snapping of pine knots. The heat was welcome. It was only October, yet the air was sharp with an early winter's chill.

James made another turn around the vaulted chamber. "Wha' do you suppose they use this room for? It isn't the audience chamber, is it? But Windsor is immense enough, they may have a dozen, for a' I could tell."

William's stomach rumbled and James had to laugh. It caught him by surprise.

"Mayhap it is a dungeon and they mean to starve us to death," James said. Normally that would not amuse him, but in this sumptuous chamber in one of the royal palaces, it seemed merely ridiculous that they'd not even been given food or drink in the hours that they'd waited. They listened as footfalls came and went in the hall outside and the stairway beyond. James made a few more passes around the chamber.

When the door was flung open, he spun.

"His Grace, Lord Henry, King of England and Prince of Wales," a page announced.

At the undeserved Welsh title, James blew out a quiet snort through his nose but kept his face a mask as the new king entered. He had obviously changed from stained traveling clothes into a red doublet with a gold chain draped around his shoulders and high polished boots. Sir Richard, Lord Gray of Codenore, entered with one of the royal family, who James liked the least, the old king's half-brother, Bishop Henry Beaufort. Oddly enough, everyone said that King Henry cared for his uncle more than he ever had his own father. There was something about Beaufort that made James's skin crawl, a hint of the foul under the sweet smell of perfume and his embroidered purple robe.

King Henry held out his hand for a greeting with a look from his large eyes that would have stripped the skin from

James. As James bowed over it, the king said, "I see you are well, Lord James."

James looked up in surprise. "I am, Your Grace. Was there a question of it?"

"Pestilence has broken out in the city," Bishop Beaufort said. "It has even spread to the Tower, so our more important prisoners have been moved. I commanded that all of the churches light candles and pray for the end of this new outbreak."

"The Tower?" James's stomach lurched. "I shall pray for everyone there, indeed." Beaufort hadn't mentioned praying for the victims. If Gruffudd did sicken, he would find no prayers here, considering King Henry's hatred of him.

King Henry waved a dismissive hand and strode to take the only chair. As the other two men took a place on each side of the king, it struck James that he was much like game being hunted.

"You will remain here until a return to the Tower is safe. But there are more important matters to discuss." King Henry nodded to Bishop Beaufort.

Beaufort favored James with his oily smile. "This morning His Grace commanded me to prepare a letter assuring you of his willingness to release you to return to Scotland." He withdrew a tightly rolled parchment from his sleeve and handed it to James. It bore the royal seal. James gave the king a doubtful glance and broke the seal with his thumb. He unrolled it and read it with growing disbelief.

Was there no end of what the English would demand of him? To bring him here with this demand and claim it meant they would free him was the twist of a knife. "You cannot think I would agree to this," he demanded indignantly.

"We kept you safe from your uncle. Fed and clothed you. The late king saw you were tutored as well as any man in

England." Sir Richard pushed his face toward James. "I hope we have not wasted our years of good care of you."

"Then it is wasted. I will nae."

"If you mean to return to Scotland, you will," King Henry said. "My father on his deathbed entreated me to release you without ransom. I agreed to do so—if, as King of the Scots, you swear fealty to me."

"The Scottish parliament would never agree to it," James said.

The king's mouth curved into a tight smile. "They will when faced with an army, which I am willing to give you. If you are my liegeman. An army you may use to defeat your uncle of Albany. Execute him, if you like."

"Why? Why would you give me an army?"

King Henry widened his large eyes and shook his head. "I would have thought that even you could see that. I mean to conquer France. Whilst I do that, I do not want the Scots at my back or aiding my enemies. You will accomplish that for me."

"And if I refuse?" James said with a chill in his voice. The condescension of the man stung.

"If you refuse, you will return to the Tower—when the pestilence has passed. And there you will remain, at my pleasure." King Henry watched him, like a lion with prey, judging and weighing every movement and word.

James tried to mutter a curse, but his throat was too dry. He stretched himself tall and lifted his chin. He had always told himself that, when it came to it, he would die well. Living well, doing what was honorable, that was harder, he suddenly realized. "If I must remain your prisoner, so be it. I will nae conquer Scotland for you."

King Henry studied James. "I suggest you consider your words carefully, Lord James. If you are to be freed, it is at my pleasure. And I assure you that your stay in the Tower can be less pleasant than it was under my father. For you will remain there unless you give me your fealty."

James felt cold to the soul. He turned his gaze out of one of the high arched windows to a bright autumn day: a day upon which he would give up his last hope of freedom. "There is nothing to consider," he said carefully, trying to keep the quaver from his voice. "I will never betray Scotland so." He turned his gaze to stare into Henry's face. "Never. That I do swear upon the Blessed Virgin and a' the Saints."

The king nodded to Bishop Beaufort. "If Lord James will not swear fealty to me, the Tower is the place for him. How comfortably kept he is there is not my concern." He inclined his head regally, dismissing James.

James turned and nodded to William to follow. He felt their eyes stabbing his back as he went. A snort of laughter went up behind him, but he didn't look back. Hell mend them, all of them. He'd not give them Scotland or his pride.

CHAPTER 17

*J*ames irritably told Iain and Dougal to return to their chamber in the White Tower. He'd had enough of sympathy since they'd returned to find that Gruffudd had died, alone and untended, locked in his cell. James knew that there was nothing that could have been done, but his friend shouldn't have died so. Had he cried out for water? Had he thought his few friends had abandoned him?

Yet if he let the English know that he grieved, they would count it as weakness. He could manage better alone. James plunged his hands into his armpits and, scowling, he paced the perimeter of the yard that was the limit of his world until he heard shouts and cheers past the bend of the Tower. Some contest of the men-at-arms, he decided and strode to watch. At least, they would not try to make him feel better.

As he came around the bend, a burly sergeant moved slowly forward, naked to the waist and his face blandly calm. A couple of the watching men-at-arms cheered when an older man, spare with hard, stringy muscles, his sparse black hair cropped short, stepped forward from the far side of the practice yard.

"You've gone old and bald, Berolt," the sergeant taunted.

"You didn't have to go stupid. Always were." Berolt pulled his shirt over his head and tossed it to a supporter.

The sergeant circled, arms spread wide and empty hands twitching slightly as he awaited an opening. "Not as stupid as you to challenge me."

Berolt rotated to keep the sergeant in front of him. They grabbed each other's arms, testing strength and balance.

The sergeant looked as though he might say something else but stepped forward instead, his shoulder driving into Berolt's chest, and his arm slipped around his waist for a throw.

"Watch out," James muttered under his breath. He had no fondness for the mean-tongued sergeant, who regularly screamed curses at everyone in the Tower.

Berolt dropped to one knee and grabbed the sergeant's leg, breaking his throwing hold, attempting to unbalance him. The sergeant leaned over onto Berolt's back, grabbed him in a bear-hug around the waist, and lifted him into the air, laughing. Berolt lost his grip on the sergeant's leg and hung, back pinned to the sergeant's chest, head down.

"No!" James shouted and jumped to his feet, sure Berolt would be dropped head first to the ground, but Berolt slammed his knees into the side of the sergeant's head, once, twice, thrice. The sergeant cursed in pain, and Berolt jerked loose, landing on hands and knees. The sergeant staggered backward to dodge Berolt's grab for his legs. He rubbed his ears and shook his head, face twisted in anger.

They glared at each other and then approached slowly, arms extended. The sergeant lunged into Berolt in another attempt at a throwing move, but Berolt sidestepped and tripped him. He went flying to the floor face first with Berolt on top of him. Berolt's arm slipped around his neck, and his bicep bugled as he strained to pull the struggling, heaving sergeant's head back in a death grip.

Finally, the sergeant pounded a palm on the dirt, yielding.

James was clapping and shouted, "Well fought!" What a fine skill and one James had not learned. If he were busy with a new skill, he wouldn't have time to think anent having lost his only friend or never returning home, so he strode to the man and said, "Can you teach me to do that?"

Berolt looked him up and down. "Who might you be?"

"That's Lord James, one of the king's prisoners," the sergeant spat out as he worked his shoulders.

Berolt tilted his head thoughtfully. "Can you pay?"

"A little." It would be well worth the few coins in his purse.

"Then meet me here this time tomorrow. But I won't make it easy on you just because you're some lordling."

James managed a smile. "Good. I shall be here."

It would take his mind off—everything. But that was tomorrow. Today he had to go back to his room and treat his people as he should. How unfair had he been to William all these years? James knew he owed his squire too much to let it continue, so he trudged through the yard and up the steep winding stairs, gaze fixed on his feet. Shadows flickered and writhed around him as he climbed. They seemed to fit what his life had become—for how long? Years perhaps. Forever perhaps. How could he know? Until he died here as Gruffudd had? Deus, misereátur… No, he would find some way to be free.

"Ha! There you are, you useless pig filth!"

Hell mend him! Murdoch Stewart, stinking of wine, was leaning on the wall. Big, red-faced under a wiry beard sprinkled with gray, his belly straining against a stained doublet. As James snorted, Murdoch straightened to block his path.

His cousin was there to make James's day more of a hell than it already was.

"Just let me be, Murdoch. You have nothing to say to me."

"This is your fault! If you'd only agree to what King Henry demands he would let us out of this cage."

James glowered at Murdoch. How could any branch of the Stewart line have come to this? "You're drunk."

Murdoch raised clenched fists, his face flushing scarlet. "You! Weakling son from a bastard line…"

James stepped forward, blood going through him in a hot rush.

"I'll make you agree," Murdoch said. "You're no king to have such power."

James spread his feet, wishing for a sword. But he wouldn't need one to handle a drunk. He gave Murdoch a thin smile and shoved him out of his way and stepped toward the door of his little room.

Murdoch grabbed his arm, twisting it behind him.

"You'll do wha' I tell you." Murdoch jerked upward hard on his arm.

Pain lanced through James's shoulder.

"You'll swear fealty to Henry."

"How dare you lay hands on me!" James smashed his heel down on Murdoch's instep. The man gave a cry of pain. James rammed his shoulder into the arm holding him, twisted free to face him. He knocked Murdoch against the wall, shoving his forearm into Murdoch's windpipe.

A booming voice cut through the murk of the tower. "What is this? Guard!" One of the liveried gaolers hauled on James's arm. James shook him off. A man-at-arm thundered up the steps. He grabbed James from behind. James let his muscles go slack, and the man shoved him across the hall.

"The Constable of the Tower will hear anent this! He'll deal with you lot." The gaoler strode away.

Murdoch rubbed at the red mark on his throat. "He tried to kill me."

The man-at-arms twisted his mouth into a sneer. "Return to your cell. Now."

James pushed his door open, his head woozy as the rush of fury drained away. His shoulder throbbed. Iain of Always, Dougal Drummand, and William turned to look at him.

"You'll hear from Lord Robert, you will," the man-at-arms shouted and stamped back down the stairway, cursing.

James closed the door behind him and leaned against it.

Iain looked at him with wide, alarmed eyes. "Wha' happened?"

A narrow shaft of light beamed through the window. James lifted his eyes to the sky, the color always dimmed and fouled by the smoke from thousands upon thousands of hearths. Even after all these years, the sight of it called to him to ride free, to see the true sky of home, feel the sea wind whipping in his face. Holy Mother of God, to be free... As he stood looking through the window, it overwhelmed him for a moment as it had that first day. But no, he would not meekly accept his fate like a milksop. He took another deep breath and said, "Some wine."

Iain poured a goblet, and when James took it, he saw that his hands shook. He gulped half of it down. "Murdoch threatened me, the drunken fool. We..." He shook his head. He still could hardly believe it himself. "We came to blows."

"Domine, miserere nobis," Lyon said, looking horrified. "It is lèse-majesté to raise your hand to the king!"

"Nae an offense I can presently punish. As if my imprisonment here weren't harsh enough, I expect he and I will both feel Robert de Morley's wrath over this." James swirled the wine in his goblet and swallowed the stone in his throat. There was something he must do, and it was hard. But he owed it to William.

"Wha' will Morley do?" William asked.

"Mayhap confine us to our cells for a time, nothing to worry over." James looked morosely at Master Lyon. "You still have King Henry's safe conduct to Scotland."

"Aye, Your Grace."

"I have letters you must carry to Bishop Wardlaw, the earl of Orkney, Sir John Sinclair, and Douglas of Drumlanrig. We are on a knife's edge. Henry has taken Harfleur. If he wins in France, Scotland will be next, so the French must be given every aid. And yet if I could promise that aid from Scotland would not reach them, it might be a price for my freedom that he would accept." James strode across the room and turned, his gaze fixed beyond the walls. "My allies at home must know my state here and give me their advice. You will leave forthwith. And take William wi' you. See him settled in a good place whilst you're there."

"Wha'?" William squawked. "You would have me leave?"

James ran two fingers over his moustache and goatee. He couldn't look at William, but this had to be done. He felt an odd pain in his chest. He must have pulled a muscle fighting with Murdoch, he thought, that was all. "You have been in this cage past long enough," he said hoarsely. "It is time you went home."

"My lord," William protested and took a quick step toward him.

Finally, James forced himself to look his squire in the face. William was no longer in his first youth, with no wife, no bairns, and had spent most of his life in a prison. James could no longer keep him here. "It is time, William. I owe you too much. Wha' kind of king will I be if I repay my friends with ill instead of good?" James forced himself to smile. "You will be there to welcome me when I return home."

"But... But your father commanded that I serve you."

"My father is long dead. I am the king now. I command you to go home."

"Then I must obey." William twisted his hands together, looking distressed. "I will be there to welcome you. As you say. And then you will be wearing your crown."

"Soon." James pulled William to him and embraced him. "God go wi' you."

William hugged him back. "Iain will serve you in my place."

"I shall," Iain said.

They broke apart, and James twitched an embarrassed smile. "Now you must go before there is time for more trouble to brew."

CHAPTER 18

NOVEMBER 1415

*A*cross London, bells tolled. The air had a stench to it of dead fish and wounds rotting and horse shit blown by a harsh wind that carried a hint of snow. James was chilled to the bone.

A maze stretched before him, close-packed with a cheering crowd. King Henry had returned from France in triumph. He would make a show of parading his prisoners, James amongst them, though James had been nowhere near the battle. James was clad in a doublet with the Lion Rampant of Scotland and shoved roughly into line with the French prisoners just brought off the boats. Hundreds of them were ragged and dirty although their wounds had been bandaged. But now they were tied by rope into three long lines. James clamped his jaw shut on the curses that boiled in his chest so they could not escape.

A yellow bitch with its teats drooping ran up and crouched to growl and bark at the countless French prisoners, until one of the men-at-arms rode his horse at her and she fled, yelping. A tall, dark-haired prisoner, the bandage around his head clotted with blood and his clothes covered in streaks of filth, collapsed face down in the mud and lay still, fingers twitching as he moaned. The rope looped around his waist jerked on a tight-faced Frenchman next in the long line of prisoners, who grunted as he stumbled and regained his balance.

Eyes wide, Iain of Alway looked James askance, and James nodded his permission. The lad scurried to kneel next to the man who had fallen. The tight-faced Frenchman turned the injured man onto his back and wrapped an arm around him, pulling him erect, saying, "Je vais prendre soin de lui."

Iain of Alway looked at James.

"Etes-vous sûr mon écuyer ne peut pas aider?" James asked.

"Un Anglais?" the man snarled.

James motioned to the device on his chest. "Un Ecossais." But the man gave a stubborn shake of his head, so James said, "He doesn't want our help."

A knight trotted up a Scottish Saltire tied to his horse's tail and dragging in the dirt. Rage shot through James like fire, but he kept his back stiff.

"The king is ready to proceed," the knight snapped at James. "You're to walk beside Charles, Duc d'Orléans and Jehan le Meingre, Maréchal de France." He pointed to the front of the lines of prisoners. They were to be herded like animals. Mounted men-at-arms were forming a column on each side of the prisoners. Rigid with outrage, James followed the horse that dragged the Scottish banner before him to the front of the horde of stinking, filthy, limping men. The knight pointed out a young, battered nobleman and the older Maréchal de France standing fix-faced beside him.

"Your Grace of Scotland, yes?" the young man said in a heavily accented voice as James stood beside him.

James nodded. "And you, Your Highness? Charles, Duc d'Orléans?"

The nobleman was a few inches taller than James, but many men were. A purple bruise covered half of his forehead. In spite of the soiled doublet and hose, the duke gave a scornful look at the crowd awaiting them. Then the wind gusted, and he shivered. "Yes, I am he." He grimaced, raising his arched nose to an imperious angle. "Do you know where they take us?"

The noise from the crowd rose to a roar when King Henry and his men clattered to the front of the procession, the king's banner as large as a ship's sail held high aloft. Shouts of, "Make way! Make way for the king!" echoed back to James.

The horse dragging the flag of Scotland in the dirt started forward at a slow walk, following the king's cortege. One of the sergeants yelled for James and the duke to move along.

"Windsor Castle, I suppose. Most of us, at any rate. The Tower of London is nae large enough to hold such a throng of prisoners."

The curious crowd gave way before the king, but the cheers turned to shouts of derision as the prisoners walked past. Servants, soldiers, merchants, and whores all gathered to howl insults. Bells tolled to celebrate. A gang of boys ran alongside him, stamping through puddles. James cursed under his breath when they splashed freezing water and mud. The rope around the Duc d'Orléan's waist jerked and made him stumble whenever one of the men behind him slowed or fell. James grasped his elbow to keep him upright, and the man gave him a haughty, reluctant nod of thanks.

James knew very well how much the humiliations stung. He trod carefully to avoid stepping on the captured flag they dragged before him and longed for some way to repay King Henry for the affront.

The gate of Windsor Castle was like a tunnel, but the thick walls made the crowd's shouts fade behind them. Yet the clatter of horses being unsaddled and led away, prisoners being untied, and the constant shout of commands was overwhelming. Before them, beyond the wide bailey yard, broad stone steps led up to Windsor's massive Round Tower. A man-at-arms swung from the saddle to untie the rope around Charles d'Orléans's waist and pointed in that direction.

Charles glanced at James and said, "I thank you, Your Grace, for your courtesy. If I did not seem grateful—I beg you put it down to grief."

As the horse dragging the shamefully abused flag was led away, James walked beside Charles toward the doors of the tower. Glancing around to be sure no guards were near, James lowered his voice and leaned close to ask, "Is it true wha' they say? King Henry executed prisoners who had surrendered?"

Charles's lips tightened to a line of white. He jerked a short nod. "Some of my own household," he said in a voice like gravel. "They gave up their arms. Were surrounded by guards, no threat to the English. He ordered them slaughtered."

"I knew he was a hard man, but—" The dark, iron-banded doors were thrown open with a crash. A shove from behind in the small of his back caught James by surprise and made him stumble to one knee.

"See that the prisoners are taken within and those who are injured given aid," Bishop Beaufort said to a dour sergeant, who had removed his helm and waited to the side. "Lord James and Monsieur le Duc will remain."

Beaufort's calm gaze was a thousand times more threatening than a man-at-arms' casual shove. Within folds of fat in his doughy face, it concealed more than it told. He continued in his oily voice, "No need to kneel. Save it for declaring King Henry your liege lord."

James ground his teeth and surged to his feet.

Charles gave James a wary glance from the corner of his eye and stepped forward. "When will your king seek ransom for me and my people?"

"It is being arranged as we speak—for most. Some... are more valuable in our possession." Beaufort's pause said that Charles would be part of that number. "You will share a suitable quarters with Lord James. With so many to house, we do not yet have room to give you separate chambers. Once we are able, you will be more suitably housed." He motioned to a sergeant who had been shouting orders as the hundreds of prisoners were hurried indoors. "See to our two guests at once." He turned and walked away, his rich robes flapping in the sharp wind.

James only had time to mutter, "Sleekit creature makes my skin prickle," to the white-faced duke before they were marched through the doors and up the winding stairs.

At the highest part of the tower, the guard opened a door for them. Iain followed them in, and Charles collapsed onto the chair. He plunged his hands into his hair. "I almost died on the field, buried under the bodies of the fallen—my own knights who died protecting me. Now I wish that I had."

Iain knelt to light a fire. At least there were faggots in the hearth. When James spotted a flagon and cups, he poured the wine and handed one to the duke, who straightened to take it. James took a stroll around the room. Being jerked hither and yon, never knowing how long he would be imprisoned in the Tower of London or another castle at the whim of the English played with his patience. There had been days when James had felt exactly as the young duke did, but something he had heard anent Charles made him turn and look him over more closely. "They say you're a poet."

Charles was staring into his cup, swirling the malmsey pensively. "I attempt it."

"You will have a new theme to write, then." James jerked a corner of his mouth up into what he hoped was a smile.

Charles breathed a laugh through his nose. "That I shall."

"And I'll ask you to read my own poems. I am never sure if wha' I write is worth the scraps of parchment I use."

"It will serve to pass the time. And I fear we may have much time to pass." Charles tipped up the goblet and drained it. After a moment, James did the same. He feared the duke was correct.

CHAPTER 19

AUGUST 1416

All the gaolers had been whispering that Henry would soon leave England for Calais to plot with Emperor Sigismund and John, Duc de Bourgogne, to finish the defeat of the French king. Charles could not hear the Bourgogne's name without cursing him for his murderous treachery. The talk of it only frustrated James, locked as they were in the Tower, although James had come to prefer it to Windsor. The men-at-arms were always glad to give him a round with the sword. Wrestling was now his favorite, though. And when Charles wasn't cursing the treachery of the Burgundians, he was good company. James had promised him a new verse, since it occupied the time read each other's work. He frowned over what he had written:

THEN WOULD I SAY, "If God had me devised
  To live my life in prison thus and pain,
  Wha' was the cause that He me more adjudged
  Than other folk to live in such a ruin?
  I suffer alone as though I am nothing,

A woeful wretch that no one may aid,
But every man in life of help has need."

JAMES TOSSED DOWN HIS QUILL, and ink splattered across the page. Where could he go with the verse except more bewailing of his estate? He had had enough of it. Perhaps in the bailey yard he could find someone who would work him until he was too tired to think, too tired to moan that he was a prisoner still—after ten years that had stretched out like a long black tunnel—dark days without end.

He jumped to his feet, took a deep breath and released it. Very well. To the bailey yard. The man-at-arms flinched when James banged open the door. James gave him a curt nod, knowing he would follow. Taking the steps two at a time, James plunged down the winding stairs and out into the smoky sunshine, through the bailey, and into the practice yard. He slapped his hands on his hips. "I can defeat any man here in a wrestling match," he shouted. "Will any of you try to prove me wrong?"

"I can prove you wrong any day, Lord James." The sergeant James had seen wrestling Berolt some time back sneered. He worked his heavy shoulders as he strode toward James.

James unfastened his doublet and tossed it aside. A murmur of anticipation was spreading through the grounds.

James swung his arms to get the blood flowing.

The man stopped in the center of the practice yard in a half-crouch, arms cocked, a grin lifting a corner of his mouth.

Moving around him in a slow circle, careful to stay beyond his reach, James said, "You ken my name. Wha' is yours?"

"Adam." He wheeled to keep James in sight. "Not that it

matters when I have you pinned. I plan on making you eat dirt, Scot."

Dashing forward, James grabbed for an armlock. Adam slapped his hands away and went for James's shoulders. James let him close, and Adam had him by the arm, using his hip to throw him to the ground. As he went down, James grabbed Adam around the chest, taking him down with him. As they rolled, James used his powerful shoulders to throw him off. They both jumped to their feet and backed away.

"Make me eat dirt?" James jeered. "I'll feed you horse shite first."

Adam rushed in and seized James in a bear hug, lifting him off his feet. He squeezed, and James thought his ribs would shatter. The man had more strength than anyone James had ever fought before. Desperately, he put both his hands to the man's chin and pushed, forcing his head back. Adam grunted, squeezing harder. James straightened his arms, locked his elbows, and broke the hold.

James landed with his knees bent, took a step back. Adam was burly and fiercely strong, but he wasn't fast. They circled each other, and James considered how to take advantage of the man's slowness.

James feinted. Adam answered by trying to encircle him with his arms, but James ducked under and grabbed him around the waist as he wheeled behind him. He locked Adam's arms in a tight bear hug. Then, stepping his right leg over, he twisted Adam over his hip and slammed him face down to the ground. Whilst Adam lay stunned, James grabbed his legs, crossed them over his thigh, locked them in place with one arm, and sat back onto Adam's spine.

James grinned. "Shall I make you eat shite, Sassenach?"

The man was growling and heaving his body, but James had him pinned.

The ring of guards who had gathered to watch were

whistling and calling out for Adam to get up. "Throw him off, Adam. Have at him," one shouted.

The man was in pain, but James had him firmly secured. Each thrust to break free only increased the strain on his legs.

James, sweat dripping off his head and shoulders, laughed as he pushed, twisting Adam's legs further back. Adam screamed. James rocked back again and again until Adam slapped a hand on the ground in surrender.

"What is to do here?" a voice bellowed.

James looked up to find King Henry glaring at them, his mouth in a hard line. "Up from there, both of you. Now!"

The watching guards had scattered like a flock of geese. James cuffed Adam's shoulder and rose to his feet. He looked around and found his doublet. As he donned it, the king barked, "You. If you have nothing better to do than fighting our prisoners, I'll see that your commander mends matters."

At King Henry's elbow, Beaufort looked on silently, dressed in flowing red robes of silk and reeking of some flowery perfume, whilst the king's guards looked on open-mouthed.

Adam was backing away, stuttering apologies and excuses as he went. Henry's scowl at James would have flayed the hide from a boar, had one been there. As it was, James laced his doublet and then bowed with a half-smile.

"Were you seeking me, Your Grace?"

"God damn you, James. Playing at fighting with guards? You have more important things to think on." King Henry looked around the practice yard as though expecting some help to appear. "After all these years, have you gained no sense? You force me to hold you under harsh durance from your obstinacy, and you learn nothing."

Beaufort gave the king an unctuous smile and laid a pudgy hand on his sleeve. "I understand your disappointment in Lord James. It gives me no joy to see a nobleman play the ruffian. Yet you must remember your own dignity, and the matter you came to discuss with him is serious. It is best discussed privily, do you not think, Your Grace?"

King Henry's face flooded with color, and he shook off his uncle's hand. He turned on a heel and stormed into the White Tower, down the narrow hall, and into the chapel, never once bothering to glance to see if the others followed. He stood for a few minutes, seeming to stare at the watery light which filtered through the stained glass windows. When he turned, his expression was mild. "When my father allowed you at his court, I always said you were a fine hand with a harp."

"His Grace does me too much honor. I dally with both harp and sword." James crossed his arms and grinned. "I am trying to convince your Constable of the Tower that we need a tennis court. I believe I would enjoy that as well as I do wrestling."

"So, you are happy enough to remain my prisoner? You will not seek your freedom? Are you truly so craven?"

"No, Your Grace." James fought to keep the anger out of his voice and failed. "It is you who denies me freedom, whether I would seek it or nae. Have you forgotten?"

"Denied it?" Henry had the gall to look incensed. He pointed at James. "I deny you nothing. You deny it to yourself. Swear your fealty to me, and you have your freedom. I require nothing more. And count yourself blessed, for I am defeating the French even with the Earl of Buchan and his followers from Scotland taking their side. Albany is too craven to do so himself, but thousands of Buchan's followers are in France." Henry stepped closer to glower into James's face. "I shall defeat them with or without your fealty."

"The king is all kindness," Beaufort said. "I have advised

His Grace against freeing you, but his conscience pricks him that he promised the late king."

James slowly shook his head. "I cannot. You ken that I cannot."

"I do not know that." King Henry stepped even closer to him and spoke slowly, softly, as though to a child. "Think, James. Soon I shall have France in my hands; after, I shall not long leave an enemy at my northern border. But I would not lead my armies against a sworn liegeman. It is the only way you can save Scotland. The only way you will free yourself. I weary of waiting for you to see sense."

To his amazement, James was sure Henry believed what he was saying. "You truly believe that my people would accept an English overlord? That they would nae throw me off if I did such a thing? Because I assure you, they would."

"The French are coming to accept me, however much they have fought the idea of being ruled by an English king."

"Have you terrorized them enough that they will in truth? Burning a' the way to Agincourt… The slaughter of prisoners…"

A deep red climbed up from Henry's velvet collar until the deep scar on his cheek stood out bone white against his flaming face. "There was no slaughter!" When James just raised an eyebrow, Henry visibly took a deep breath. "You know naught of battle. I could not risk the prisoners rising in the midst of my men."

James opened his mouth to ask if Henry had forgotten to have his prisoners disarmed that they could be such a danger, for James knew they had been disarmed, but from the look on the king's face, decided that there was wisdom in silence. He snapped his mouth closed.

After a pregnant pause, James motioned around them. "Aye, it is true I know more of imprisonment than of battle.

But I will never give away my kingdom. Nae to any man on this earth."

"God damn you!" King Henry shouted, the words roaring out of him as though he could no longer contain his ire. "I am out of patience. Enjoy your imprisonment, if you can."

"So be it, if I must, but I will nae kneel to you to give you my fealty."

Henry's eyes narrowed, and he jabbed a finger at James. "Get out of my sight. Out! Run back to your cell like a craven."

James turned on his heel. As he marched from the chapel, he could feel Henry's stare stab his back. As he reached the doors, he heard Beaufort say in his sleekit tone, "The Scots will be nothing for you to defeat, Your Grace. Now we must prepare for your departure for Calais."

CHAPTER 20

MARCH 1420

*J*ames rubbed his eyes. He didn't know how long he had read, but the fat tallow candle had burned down to a stub, and the light of morning lit the room. His copy of Chaucer's *Troilus and Criseyde* he had received just before he was brought to Windsor Castle lay on the table. He had much to learn from Chaucer's work for his own poetry. Forbye, it was all that kept him sane some long days. With a sigh, he turned to read:

Tisiphone, help me to compose these woeful verses that weep as I write, that flow like tears from my pen.

He closed his eyes and groaned. The sound felt as though it must have come from his very bowels. He could not read that now. Miserere mei, Deus! He had enough to lament in his life without their misery as well!

He should have slept, but last night he'd not even touched his bed. The words in his books called out to him—he read until he fell into the stories, as though his cage did not exist. Iain would scold, but he had been too angry and restless for sleep. The longing for freedom he kept within tore at him until sleep was a long-lost memory. It ripped at his heart, and death seemed preferable to life.

It was wrong that the knife in his belt meant for cutting his meat at table should call to him with its siren's song. The only thing that kept him from a plunging it into his chest was that men would call him a coward.

A nightingale twittered outside. He pushed back from the long table, stiff as a board and his legs half-asleep. He shook out the stiffness, went to the window, and looked out. The little brown bird trilled as it fluttered into the leafy branches of a tree by a pond. Months ago he was allowed for a time the freedom of the gardens. He was still a prisoner, yet the ability to come and go into the courtyard had given him an illusion of liberty that had eased the darkness for a few days.

He leaned his forehead against the cool stone of the window, wishing it would cool his fevered thoughts. King Henry… war… freedom… home… They circled in his mind, day after day which turned into year after year, until he felt he might go mad. But the breeze carried a scent of green and spring rain. The hawthorn hedge around the garden below was studded purple with berries. He wondered if there was pestilence in the city that had him moved once more from the Tower to Windsor Castle. He had more freedom of movement within the Tower, for they feared less that he could escape.

At least the view from his window, even in this corner tower where he was stuck away, eased his melancholy. The pond shimmered in the morning sunlight, and a willow hung over it casting shadows that ruffled when a fish darted to the top. Sun sparkled on a little marble bench. The nightingale trilled again, clear, first soft and growing louder.

It burst with a rustle of the leaves to a higher branch when a small, white dog rushed up to the tree, yipping fiercely. The dog jumped, bounced in a circle, and propped its feet as high as it could reach, panting. James couldn't help but smile. What a silly useless creature, yet it brought a spark of joy into his dark thoughts.

A golden-haired girl hurried up, her skirts swishing about her feet. She knelt, scolding the dog as she fastened a gold leash to its collar. He was entranced by the vision. If it was a happiness he could not share, it was one he could watch. It was like soft rain on a parched soul. She looked up at the sky, and even from his window, James could make out her inscrutable smile. When she stood and tugged on the leash, he decided she was older than he had first thought: a young woman rather than a girl, her long neck white as cream and her shape softly curved. He strained to make out more of her face, but she bent, speaking to the dog that first pranced about her feet and then darted to nose in the grass next to the pool. When a frog leapt and it growled, she threw back her head and laughed. Something in James's chest burst free.

Unmarried, she must be, her hair a loose tumble of curls down to her waist under a sheer chaplet. Her green gown shimmered like silk in the sunlight as she sank down upon the bench. She took a small ball out from a purse at her belt and tossed it across the grass for the dog to run after. When she bent back her head, eyes closed, as though she drank in the sunlight, he saw a gold chain about her neck hung with a heart-shaped pendant, ruby red against the white of her throat.

James realized he was open-mouthed, watching, and snorted a small laugh. But she had brought him more joy in these minutes than he had felt in years. She took the ball from the dog's mouth, bent to kiss its nose, then rose and strolled past the pond, its leash in her hand. James cursed under his breath as he thrust his head further into the window and craned to watch her slender back as she walked through the gate.

He turned and threw himself down at the table to pull a parchment close. He dipped his quill in the inkwell. His hand was shaking as he wrote as fast as he could to keep up with the sprawling words that rushed through his mind:

AH, sweet, are you a worldly creature
  Or heavenly thing in likeness of nature?

OR ARE you god Cupid's own princess
  And are come to free me of my bonds?
  Or are you very Nature, the goddess
  That has painted with your heavenly hand
  This garden full of flowers, as they stand?
  Wha' shall I think? Alas, wha' reverence
  Shall I devote to your excellence?

IF YOU A GODDESS BE, and that you like
  To give me pain, I may it nae escape.
  If an earthly being is that does me such,
  Why does God make you so, my dearest heart,
  To do a wretched prisoner hurt.

HE PROBABLY WOULD NEVER SEE her again, whoever she was. But she was fixed in his mind forever, of that he was sure.

CHAPTER 21

*B*ishop Beaufort's apartments were every bit as lavish as James had expected, although Windsor was, of course, not the Bishop's own dwelling. Half a dozen thick carpets covered the stone floor, and every inch of the walls was draped with embroidered tapestries of men at the hunt, ladies sending knights off to war, and nobles feasting. A fire crackled in the marble hearth. There wasn't a cross or religious item anywhere in sight. James snorted a soft laugh.

Beaufort was humming to himself when he strode in the door, dressed in his flowing red robe and reeking as he always did of a flowery perfume. When he saw James, he nodded with an unctuous smile. "Lord James."

James gave a half-bow. "At your command, Excellency."

"It is good to see that you have been well cared and provided for. It has been some time since I have had cause to see you. How long has it been?"

"Three years, I believe."

"I hope they have not been excessively tedious."

James managed a thin smile. "I have kept myself occupied. And Charles d'Orleans is good company. I confess, however,

126

that I am curious why you summoned me to Windsor." He motioned. "And to your own apartments."

Beaufort closed and barred the door. "It is a good place to talk privily."

"We have reason to talk so? Odd. I thought the last time I spoke with King Henry that he gave me his final word."

"Few things in life are final, my lord, you may find as you grow older." The bishop crossed to a table and picked up a gold-chased flagon. "Will you join me?" he asked as he poured a cup.

James shrugged. If the bishop wanted him poisoned, surely he would not do it in his own apartments when it could be done any day in James's cell, so he nodded and poured himself a cup.

"You are aware that Murdoch of Fife was ransomed by his father? The ransom was considerable."

James jerked his head back and felt the warmth drain from his face. "I knew he was no longer at the Tower of London, but…" James felt as though he had been slapped. Money had been received from the Pope in return for letters and support James had given that some thought might tempt Henry into changing his mind, for he needed funds for his endless war. Had Albany managed to lay hands on that? Where else would he find so large a sum? "No. I did nae know."

The bishop smiled. "The king has decided to give you another chance at freedom as well, Lord James. He is most fond of you, though I have never understood why."

Nae this again, James thought. "A puzzling way to show his fondness, keeping me close confined."

A wicked snicker burst out from the bishop. "He can be puzzling, Lord James. Even strange at times, though if you repeat that I said so, I shall deny it."

"So strange that he has forgotten wha' I said the last time

he demanded it? I will gladly repeat it for you, Excellence. I shall never swear fealty to him."

"Fortunately for you, he does not ask it. He will take your parole and allow you a year's freedom in return for hostages. Many hostages, of course. After all, you are, you claim, a king."

James's breath hitched. "Hostages? Has this been negotiated with ambassadors from Scotland? Who is he demanding? How many?"

"No, this is a proposal for you alone. Agree to it, and we will send the demand to Scotland for you."

"How can I agree when I don't know who you are demanding?"

"Why, they are right in front of you." The bishop pointed to a parchment weighted down by a marble statuette of a woman in remarkably few clothes.

James raised an eyebrow as he moved the statuette and picked up the parchment. He scanned the long list of names in three columns. James opened his mouth, and then he laughed. "You jest. This is a list of near every noble in Scotland. It is impossible." James was not nearly such a fool as they seemed to think him. "They will never agree to it."

"You cannot be sure of that. Mayhap they will, and you would return home. Nothing would please my nephew more. He has agreed that you may go to Raby Castle to await word. Under close guard, of course."

What a strange offer. Raby Castle was far north, nearer Scotland and home than James had been since that day he had climbed aboard the Maryenknyght. But King Henry had to know that his demand for this many hostages, the highest nobles in Scotland, was insufferable. He had some other plot in mind.

James chewed his lower lip. Would he be best served by agreeing? Holy Mary, Mother of God, but he wanted to accept. To be so far from London and so near home… There had to be some trick, a hook in the bait. Yet he could not see it.

Perhaps it was merely that they thought a taste of freedom after being close kept would soften him to their demands. Or it might be some deeper plot.

He would take the bait and see what they would want of him. "Very well, Excellency." James gulped down his wine and gave the bishop a grin that felt more like a grimace. "I will put my seal to it and wait at Raby Castle. But they will nae agree."

Beaufort bowed. "Then, if it please you, my lord." He motioned to the table and waited with a smile that made James shudder as he tipped wax onto the document and used his ring for a seal.

"You and your people will leave in a few days' time. I shall need so long for the messages to reach Scotland, as well as arranging for suitable guards. I've summoned Sir John Water and a dozen men-at-arms to oversee you. Tomorrow, you'll be sent back to the Tower, but you may join the court tonight for supper, such as it is with the king absent.

James left the document, which he was sure was useless, lying upon the table and considered the bishop, wishing with all his might he knew what was passing through his mind. Whatever it was, James's benefit was not the goal. Still, it had been a long time since he had dined with the court, and he would not pass the chance to see a certain gold-haired lass. She had been bejeweled and finely dressed as only a lady of the court would be. If he were blessed indeed, he would see her one last time.

The rest of the day crept by as slow as a flow of honey on a cold winter's day. James climbed to his tower room and tried to distract himself yet again with Chaucer's Troilus and Criseyde, but he could hardly see the battles of Troy for imagining sunshine gleaming on a head of golden hair. In the afternoon, he called for hot water and scrubbed himself until his skin was red. He sat still, although his fingers twitched with restlessness, while John shaved his cheeks and trimmed his goatee.

Once he was trimmed and smelled sweet rather than of sweat, he had John pull all of his clothing out of the chest it was carried in and lay the dozen pieces across the bed. He scratched at the hair on his chest as he looked them over. There was no way he would compare to the peacocks who would strut at the court.

At last he settled on what passed for his best doublet, white, embroidered with the red Lion Rampant, the one he had worn the day the French prisoners arrived. Now it had places worn almost through the fabric. He had no jewels except the signet ring on his hand. It was when he was dressed and looked down at his threadbare court clothes that he realized the extent of his madness. Did he truly think she would look his way? A foreign king, imprisoned and impoverished... As he waited for the page to summon him, he thought, but whatever you wear, however poor, you are a king.

The sun was setting behind the castle wall when the page opened the door and had James follow him past the yard to the great hall in the royal apartments.

"I shall ready your belongings to leave tomorrow," Iain said as James left.

With the court in residence, although the king was in France with his army, even the sprawling Windsor Castle was crowded. The guards at the door of the Round Tower ignored him, accompanied as he was by his own guard and the page. Near the doors to the main residence, a group of men-at-arms were crouched, tossing a die. One shouted a curse when he lost. James earned a bay of laughter when he observed that the loser next time should wager that he would still be King Henry's prisoner next year. He then followed the page up the short flight of stairs to the main doors, which were flung open.

The hall was an eddy of satins, silks and velvets with jewels glittering amidst the waves. Some of the guests were finding their places on the long benches. Others were milling about, chattering like magpies and enjoying music from the lutists in the gallery. The page led James around the edge of the room as everyone they passed gave him sideways looks and edged away.

He was always an embarrassment at the court. As a member of a royal family, they couldn't sit him low at the tables, but he was a prisoner, so couldn't be set high. At last, the page bowed and motioned toward a place at the distant end of the high table on the dais. For once, James thought he was glad for it as he sat between two knights, no doubt members of some great lord's tail. He smiled as he scanned the throng. This would be a perfect place to watch the pageant of finery and spy one nightingale in particular. He frowned and shook his head. That was bad poetry. As beautiful as a nightingale's song was, it was a plain bird, brown and ordinary. No, that would never do, not for his beautiful lass.

The smell of roasted meats and fruits baked into sweets carried in from the kitchens. The heavy hangings in dizzying colors on the stone walls kept out the chill of the early spring night. A singer joined the lutists, but James could not make out the words over the clatter of servants filling cups and the mutter of a hundred guests finding their places.

A herald called out the names of the Constable of England, John de Beaufort, Earl of Somerset and of Lady Joan de Beaufort. From his place in the side, James had a good look at them. The earl was tall and dark, but then James saw Joan and nothing else.

She was even more beautiful than he had thought when he saw her in the garden. Her creamy gown was worked with pearls that could not match the luster of her skin. Her movements were graceful and studied, her skirts swirling around her feet as . Her stepfather, Thomas, Duke of Clarence, kept her arm on his as he helped her up the steps of the dais and to her seat, his head bent as he spoke close to her ear. She kept her eyes modestly down, but her straight spine and the firm line of her mouth hinted at a strength within her softness.

Others had followed whilst James stared at the lady, and he realized the chairs and benches had filled. Bishop Beaufort rose and gave thanks, mercifully brief, since when he stood he blocked James's view of Lady Joan. A servant filled his goblet, and James took a sip of the purplish wine. When the rich taste with a hint of plums and currents filled his mouth, he leaned back, smiling. He could be quiet and simply look his fill.

Perhaps she felt his stare, because she looked in his direction and cocked her head. Her eyes met his. She seemed to study him, but her stepfather spoke to her and she turned away. His stomach grumbled again at the scent of a capon redolent with hyssop, rosemary, and sage, so he cut off the leg. He stripped the meat with his teeth, tossed the bone in his trencher and went back to watching.

"James Stewart? Is that truly you?" a familiar voice asked close at hand.

James looked up and gaped at a face he barely recognized after so many years. "Henry Percy."

One of the knights interrupted regaling them with his story of a glorious fight at Agincourt to make room for the man who was now Earl of Northampton. Percy sat with his back to the table and stretched out his long legs. James signaled for more wine, and they saluted before they both drank. "It has been many a year, my friend," Percy said thoughtfully.

"It has." James smiled. "I'm glad you finally reached home, Henry."

Percy leaned an elbow on the table to be closer to James. "Albany traded me and a room full of gold for his heir. He was desperate to have Murdoch back."

James glanced at Joan de Beaufort, who was laughing at some quip, before he turned back to Percy. "Was he? Why do you suppose now, since he took his time about it before?"

"You know Albany opposed Pope Martin?" When James nodded, Percy lowered his voice even more. "The new Pope may see that he pays for that. He is at odds with all the bishops. Of a certainty, he cannot live much longer, as ancient as he is, so he needs his heir. And his others in his family do whatever the devil they please. The monasteries are a scandal all over Scotland. Forbye, he's near at war with Douglas over sending troops to the French." He grinned. "A few months back, the Earl of Douglas attacked Berwick and Roxburgh, but I saw them off, so the king named me Warden of the East March."

James drained his cup. "You cannae expect me to congratulate you for defeating them, though."

"Why not? It's not as though they are your friends."

James realized that knights around them had fallen silent, and this was not a conversation to be noised about. Nor would he mention the letters he had managed secretly to send to the Douglas. "Mayhap not." He drained his cup, and a page refilled it, doing the same for Percy. The tables in the middle of the room were being cleared. James stood and nodded toward Joan de Beaufort. "Is she betrothed?"

Percy stood too, and they moved around the table as the

musicians played the chords of a quadrille. "The Beaufort girl? She's past an age when you'd think it, but her stepfather seems none too eager to marry her off. Odd too, since she would be quite a prize, so I am sure they have a good reason for waiting."

Across the dance floor, Joan put her hand on her stepfather's arm as the music began. Five other couples joined them, and she floated through the figures, smiling up at each man whose hand she took as she gracefully circled.

"You have an interest in her?" James's heart thudded.

Percy laughed, slapping his thigh. "I forgot to tell you. I married this year. If not as beautiful as that lady..." He nodded toward Joan, who was curtsying deeply to a man dressed so brightly in blues and greens that he outshone peacocks. "...he is a Neville, and has connections I needed."

James clouted Percy on the shoulder, beaming with relief. "Well done."

The quadrille ceased and dancers scattered, but Lady Joan accepted the hand of the peacock, so she was taking the floor once more. James spun in a circle, desperately looking for a possible partner. When he spotted a restless looking matron, her tapping foot peeking out from beneath her skirts, he bowed and held out his hand. She looked at him with narrowed eyes, but then she curtsied, and he led her out on his arm as another quadrille began.

He bowed and held the lady's hand as he circled, allowing her to dance around him. The dance turned. The ladies skipped to a new partner, curtseying when they reached him. Another spin and James had to admit he enjoyed dancing even when Joan had not reached his place. Then she held out her hand. He bowed over it and turned, his face burning with fever as she smiled up at him, her eyelids crinkling. She had eyebrows like wings over blue, glittering eyes and a long slender neck, smooth shoulders sloping down to hidden breasts. He stumbled a bit in the turn. By the Holy Rood, James, he thought. Remember the steps or she'll think you a fool.

Her hand slipped from his when she skipped to a new partner, and then the dance ended. He backed slowly off the floor as she walked to her waiting father. When he took her hand to lead her to their places, just once she peeked over her shoulder in James's direction, and his heart tried to beat its way out of his chest.

Percy put a hand on his shoulder and laughed. "Don't think it, my friend. She's for some deeper plot than any to do with you. You may be sure of it."

CHAPTER 22

APRIL 1420

*S*ir Richard de Neville swayed in the saddle but managed to right himself, as he tossed down his shattered lance. He yanked the reins and turned his horse to ride back for a second pass. James handed John his broken lance and took a new one. "I hope this holds up better," James jested, and John grinned up at him.

Neville spurred his horse to a hard gallop. James couched his lance and galloped to meet him, leaning forward as he rode and holding his lance as steady as steel. As they met, he saw Neville shift in his saddle. James tried to jerk the same direction, but it was too late. A force like thunder exploded into his chest, and he was flying. He crashed down on his back, the wind forced out of his lungs. His head whanged on the ground. He saw stars. Or maybe it was bits of dirt dancing in the sunlight. He blinked, trying to clear them away, coughed, and gulped for air that wasn't there.

Iain was shouting, "Your Grace!" and hauling him to sit up.

James coughed again and gasped, "I'm a' right, Iain." His riderless bay was trotting to the stable. James pulled at his borrowed helm, already dented when he had put it on, but it wouldn't budge. The handful of men-at-arms who had gathered to watch were hooting and calling out taunts. At the entrance to the practice yard, the gray-haired Sir Ralph de Neville, lord of Raby, was laughing loudest of all. Dougal Drummand came to help, and between the three of them they wrested the helm from his head.

A wave of nausea hit James. He bent, swallowing bile and breathing deeply. *By'r Lady, I'll not humiliate myself by spewing after a joust.* Sir Richard swung from the saddle and strode over. "Do you need our physician, Lord James?" he asked.

James gingerly shook his head and then regretted it, but he felt sure now that his belly would not shame him.

"Good." Sir Richard turned to walk away but then turned back and nodded to James. "It was a decent match."

In truth, James knew he needed more practice at the tilt to judge his opponent better. His skill with the horse and lance he had no doubt of. But judging men…

John was tugging at him, and James let his squire put his arm around his waist and help him limp to the armory, Drummand carrying the dented helm. James sank onto a bench so John could strip off his borrowed harness and sweat-soaked, padded arming doublet.

Shadows danced around the armory from the brazier that burned at each end. The only sound was their breathing and the clank as John dropped the gauntlets onto a table with other pieces of armor.

Dougal said, "John, I need to check His Grace to be sure he is nae injured. Put off doing that for a bit." He gave a significant nod toward the door as he passed by John and came to kneel next to James.

James crooked an eyebrow at him. Putting a hand to his head, Drummand tilted it back, coming close to stare into his eye whilst lifting an eyelid. "Thomas Payn has contacted me

137

with a plan. Whilst you jousted, I met with him," he whispered. "He has a list of inns where there are Lollard confederates between here and Edinburgh."

Dougal Drummond released James's head, and James closed his eyes, taking a deep breath. He could feel his body quiver. He gripped his hands into fists and forced himself still.

Dougal looked to be sure John was still guarding the door as he moved to the other side and checking James's eyes again. "He will have horses for us at midnight outwith the postern gate."

"You are sure we can trust him?"

"Since Oldcastle's execution, he has been on the run. He has as much reason to reach Scotland as you do."

James rubbed his forehead. The situation was nearing desperation. If Henry married the French princess, as they said was agreed in the Treaty of Troyes, it would truly be disaster for Scotland. "And wha' is the price?"

"Merciful treatment for Lollards who flee England to Scotland."

"Their argument is with the Church, not with me," James whispered. "I will not pursue them if they aid me. I can make no promises for the Church. But escaping the castle will be no mean feat. There's a guard on the postern gate."

Dougal just raised his eyebrows, with a grim tightness in his face. When James nodded, his mouth hard with the knowledge of what he was called upon to do, Dougal stood and called to John, "His Grace suffered no injury, but he should rest."

James put an arm around Dougal's shoulder, as though for support, and said in his ear, "They're watching the roads to Berwick. Supposedly for the expected hostages." His voice dripped with scorn. "Does he ken?"

Dougal jerked a nod as he put an arm around James's

138

waist. John was hurriedly tossing the pieces of harness into bins, whilst with Dougal's aid James limped out into the sunshine. James entered the east tower and climbed the winding stairs, the back of his neck prickling for someone to seize them.

In his room, he was grateful to stretch out on the bed. His head still pounded from his fall, though for a time excitement had made him forget it. John roused him when a page came to the door announcing supper. He was tempted to plead injuries, but the last thing they needed was attention, so the three of them dined quietly at the far end of the dais before returning. James took out the knife he used at table and sharpened it. The snick, snick, snick on the whetstone seemed like the beat of a dance he had yet to learn.

John knelt before their chest and said in an undertone, "You must have a change of clothes."

"One only. We must not weigh ourselves down." James stripped and donned his darkest blue doublet and hose and picked up his riding boots. He threw a dark cloak over his shoulders and waved away the gold pin John would have used to fasten it. Then he looked the two of them over. He would have wished for black or gray, but only Dougal's priestly gown was of black. It would have to do. A look and nod passed between the three of them.

Silently, he slipped down the stairs, the only sound their fast breaths in the quiet of the night. At the doorway he paused to listen before he eased it open and scanned the empty bailey yard. Stealing across the castle yard made his nerves jump under his skin. He slid his back along the rough stone of the wall in deep shadow, the others copying his movements. He could hear the thud of the guards' feet on the parapet walk above, but they would have had to look straight down to see him. His heart was pounding so loud he was surprised the guard couldn't hear it. But the footfalls faded around a corner, and James let out a breath.

"Stay. I'll give an owl's hoot twice when it is done," James whispered. He slipped through the shadows around the corner tower. His fear was a tangible thing; it writhed within his belly. The only weapon he had was the knife he used for meat, and he had never shed blood. But the knife was sharp. It would do the job. The postern was a narrow oaken door with bands of iron set in a corner of the wall where it met a tower. One man stood guard before it, but there were guards nearby on the parapet. Whatever happened, the guard must be silenced.

James chewed his lip for a moment as he considered. There was no way he could sneak up on the man, so he straightened his shoulders and strode boldly toward the shadowy shape in the darkness. He made no attempt to hide. The guard didn't move, but James knew he'd been seen, so he nodded. When he got close, he saw that it was a tall, wide-shouldered youth, his eyes big in the faint moonlight. A lock of brown hair stuck out from under his mail cowl to fall across his forehead. Is there some way I could let him go? The idea of killing the lad made his stomach clench. But no… He didn't dare chance it.

James took another step and said, "A braw night for taking some air."

The lad snorted. "I'd be in a warm bed if I had my choice."

James could see the gleam of the young man's mail armor, but only the sides of his throat were covered by the cowl. James wasn't sure his knife would have penetrated the mail, but it wouldn't have to. For a moment, he felt cold to the core. He could return to a warm bed and prison. Instead, he said, "Mayhap an ale will make up for your pain. You've been courteous, so let me reward you with a few groats to buy a treat."

"A reward?" He sounded doubtful but stepped closer anyway.

James reached into his purse with his left hand, fumbling around in it to give himself time, and the guard's gaze followed the movement, his mouth dropping open. James slipped the knife from his sleeve and plunged it hard into his throat, grabbing him with the other arm to haul him close. The struggling guard opened his mouth and made a gurgling sound. Warm blood gushed over James's hand and down the front of his doublet. He held a dead body in his arms.

James gasped in a breath that felt like a sob and whispered, "Réquiem ætérnam dona ei."

Outside the walls, a dog barked. James heard a footfall on the parapet. His breath came so fast he might have been racing across the moorlands. When the body stopped twitching, he lowered it to the ground, lifted the bar, and softly eased the heavy door open.

Outside, James pressed his back against the rough stone of the wall. Despite the cool night wind, he could feel sweat drip down his face. Twice James's hoo-hoo-hoo-hoo broke the still of the night. When Iain and Dougal hurried through to join him, he was wiping his sticky hands on his tights, his stomach roiling at the coppery smell.

"Wha' if they find his body?" John panted.

"We'd best be awa' before they do," Dougal said and pointed toward a copse of beeches that formed a distant black hump some hundred yards away. "Hurry!"

James gripped the knife in his hand as they ran, wishing beyond words for a good sword. Perhaps Payn would have one, he hoped. In a few steps, James was in the lead. John and Dougal followed. Dougal stumbled when he stepped on his robe. A dog was howling near, and James could hear John panting. No one spoke as James pressed to run faster, cold fear crawling up the back of his neck.

He was only a few yards from the trees looming in front of him. A silhouette of a man showed in the shifting patterns of moonlight and shadow. There was a shout.

"Who goes?" Horsemen rode out of the darkness, harnesses ringing and swords thudding against their saddles.

The shadowy figure in the trees turned, cloak whirling about him, and ran. A horseman pulled up his shorting horse in front of James. There were shouts and curses. "Don't let him escape!" A horse whinnied.

Breathing hard, James ran his palm down his face and winced at the tacky feel of it. He leaned forward and rested his hands on his knees, panting for breath. A' for naught! He wanted to rage and to weep at once. Instead, he gritted his jaws and kept silent.

"Got him!" a rough voice growled, sounding triumphant.

A man, short and sturdy, from what James could make out in the moonlight, stumbled out of the trees, prodded along with a sword at his back by a horseman. Now men with weapons gleaming in the moonlight streamed out the postern gate, and an alarm was being shouted on the parapet.

His doublet only half-laced and hair a gray nest sticking every which way, Sir Ralph de Neville pointed to the new prisoner and said in an icy voice, "Get that miscreant to the dungeon." He stood for a moment, his gaze fastened on James. "Where is Sir John Water?"

Sir John was panting and fumbling to fasten his sword belt as he replied, "I am here, my lord."

"Then escort Lord James to his chamber. And put a strong guard on the door."

CHAPTER 23

MAY 1420

*J*ames paced back and forth across his chamber like one of the caged lions in the Tower menagerie. In the weeks since the failed escape, Dougal had apologized at least a dozen times and could hardly look James in the face. John was silent and downcast.

John Water had said no more than was required whilst they waited another two days at Raby, not even mentioning the dead guard. When it became clear that no hostages would appear crossing the Scottish border, he grunted that his commands were to proceed to Southampton. Southampton Castle was a square, gray, gloomy place, but the parapet had cannons. James itched to examine them, and planned to harass Sir John until it was permitted. Though the man had been oddly absent in the week since they had arrived, except when he appeared for meals. However, there were ever two guards on James's door with orders that he was not allowed to wander, although the command still did not apply to his household.

They had never dragged James to Southampton before, and it nagged at him. "Wha' are they planning?" he asked

Dougal, who stood staring morosely into the hearth where a small fire sputtered. "Obviously, Henry has changed his mind anent wha' use he has for me, but why? How? I thought of a certainty after… after…" He sputtered to a stop to spare Dougal mention of their failed escape that he blamed himself for.

"After my failed plan for your escape." Dougal turned and gave his king a wan smile. "I feared harsh confinement in the Tower as well."

"I have told you times enough that it was not your fault that Payn was being watched. You could not have known. So let it be. I am much more interested in why I've been brought here."

"With Beaufort's resolve to wipe out the Lollards, I should have guessed they might have spies on his heels." Dougal rubbed the back of his neck. "But I have managed to sniff around Southampton. Discreetly, mind. And it seems that Sir John is ordering goods: tents, armor, even banners and horses. Seemingly, he plans to join King Henry in France, or I can think of no other reason."

James tugged at his lip and made another of his circuits around the chamber. "If he is merely preparing for joining his king, why bring me along? I have never known Henry to do anything without good cause. Much as I dislike him, he is far from a fool. And John Water would not act without Henry's orders. Not when it comes to my confinement."

Dougal nodded, staring pensively at his feet.

John's stomach grumbled loudly enough to make James chuckle. "I'll go to the kitchens and bring up our lunch, Your Grace," he said.

There were voices outside the door, and James stilled John with a raised hand. When the door opened, Sir John Water, his weathered face crinkled into a scowl, stepped through and made a sweeping motion with his arm. "I need to speak privily with your lord." He waved a dismissive hand at the others. "You might find lunch in the great hall, I suppose."

Dougal's look at the knight was icy, and Iain gave a questioning look, but James said, "Aye. As you please. Leave us."

Sir John stood in the door watching until the two men were out of sight. "See that we are not disturbed," he said to the guards and closed the door. He stared at James and shook his head. "I have not conveyed the events at Raby Castle to the king. It may be I will not."

That left James speechless for a moment. "Why not?"

"Neville agreed to keep the matter quiet—for our own good. If the king knew how close we had come to letting you escape, how far we had failed in our duties, he would be furious. Of that, you may be sure."

"I failed in my attempt. That is a' that matters."

"The king would not see it so. He tasked me with seeing to your safety and that you do not escape. My failure is what he would see, and I cannot afford to lose his trust." Sir John had a scar across his forehead that twisted when he scowled and a habit of looking down his crooked nose, which surely had been broken at least twice. "In France, my duty will be even harder, but I shall not fail in it. At no time will you be without guards within at your side, unless you and I can come to some agreement. If you give me your parole… Swear that you will make no further attempt, and I will at least somewhat loosen your leash."

James knew he was gaping, but the astonishment felt like a rush of heat through his entire body. "France? How in France?"

"The king is in Troyes and is to wed Catherine of France."

Everyone knew that. "Wha' has that to do with me?"

"Beaufort did not tell you, then?"

When James wordlessly shook his head, Water shrugged.

145

"The king has commanded that if hostages did not reach Raby within a week's time, you are to be brought to France. And I believe we will proceed with him to take part in the war."

France… The Douglases were said to have a huge army there helping the Dauphin Charles, who now was King Henry's only barrier to conquest. But Henry held Normandy, Anjou and all the northern provinces and might well take Paris. He held the mad king, who had promised to name Henry as his heir. Or perhaps that was the work of the Queen Isabeau and Philip of Bourgogne, who control the poor madman. James slowly paced around the edge of the room, running his fingers across the smooth wood of the table, pursing his lips.

"I want your word, sir. Swear to me that you will not make another such escape, or I will keep you under such guard as you have never before seen."

James was sure the man was speaking exactly the truth of his intent. In France, if he escaped, he might have a chance to reach the Douglas, but whether that would be for good or for ill, he could not know. It could be a leap from one evil to a worse one. Yet, if there were such a chance, could he swear he would not take it? For now, such an oath would serve him, though. And if he did not escape, he would still have a chance of learning war from Henry of Monmouth, whom, God wot, was as good at that art as any man alive.

"So, you believe we will join the king's army? To take part in the fighting?"

"I know of no other reason for the king's commands: to acquire a courser for your use, palfreys for your household, armor, tents, banners bearing your lion rampant. They would be of no use unless you join the king with his army, and they are at the king's own very particular command."

James nodded as his mind flicked through thoughts like

flipping the pages of a book. "My household has not been given their stipends in many months. They must be paid. And my own purse is empty, as it is a year or more since I've received funds from Scotland. I have debts which must be paid."

"I have the funds to resolve those concerns. Do I have your oath? Will you give it? You will still be under guard, but I will loosen it as much as I am allowed."

James ceased his pacing and turned to look Sir John in the face. "Aye. I will give you my oath." A corner of his mouth twitched in a wry smile. "If you would have me swear on a holy relic, I shall do so for you. No more escape attempts." Excepting if a very good one appeared—one that would succeed. Then he had no doubt that Bishop Wardlaw would give him absolution for breaking an oath.

Sir John looked at James with his dark eyes narrowed to slips. "I shall inquire for the location of a suitable relic for your oath, Lord James." The man gave a brisk nod and left James pondering France and war.

CHAPTER 24

*J*ames noticed a grave the first hour of their ride out of Dieppe, a small raw mound with a tilted cross made from sticks. A few hours later, Iain pointed to a row of them. After that, hardly an hour passed that they didn't see a few, some freshly dug and others beginning to sink into the ground.

Sir John Water rode beside James with Iain of Alway, Dougal Drummond, and John Lyon trailing on adequate palfreys. A dozen sumpter horses carried their tents and harness. James had turned up his lip at the courser he had been provided with, of inferior quality to what a king should ride. But above their heads flew the royal banner of Scotland. If it was limp in the heat of day in late May, for the first time in his life it was there. Though riding through a land that reminded him of a priest's sermon on hell destroyed his pleasure.

As far as James could see on either side of the road were great swaths of devastation. They rode through miles of ruined fields with no sign of plowmen, and past orchards where trees grasped toward the sky with branches like blackened fingers. The farmhouses were burnt-out shells. At a crossroads, they came to a gibbet that dangled with what was left of dead men, empty eye sockets staring, tattered rags flapping on the rotting bodies. James choked on the stench and used his cloak to cover his mouth and nose. At the clatter of their passing, ravens flapped into the air.

They traveled sunrise to nightfall, with Sir John Water anxious to have James in Troyes in time for the wedding. The few travelers they passed were armed, some just with a hefty staff, others with falchions or axes—farm implements but they could kill, and here and there James spotted a rusty sword. They scattered off the road like quail from a hawk at the sight of their party, but James noted that they fingered their weapons and gave lingering, hungry looks as the troop passed.

In camp, James lay awake in the dark, looking up at a sky scattered with a thousand stars. Sir John had claimed there was no time to set up the tents, but James welcomed sleeping in the open air. The night smelled of freedom, even if it was false. He could hear Dougal's grunting snores, the fire's crackle as it sent sparks heavenward, one of the horses whickering softly, and the sentry's footfalls as he paced around their little camp. James was obviously not the only one who had noticed the avid looks of the passing travelers. He rolled himself in his blanket and watched the flames dance, as the night wore on.

They circled the towns, too many of which were controlled by the Dauphin's army, and made a wide swing south around Paris, but when they neared Troyes, Sir John finally let them stop to wash and don fresh clothing. The hostelry was barely worthy of the name—a stable for six horses, and two guest rooms upstairs. James thought the wine good, better than they ever had in England, where it spoiled so fast. "King Henry will be regent once he marries

Princess Catherine," a solid merchant in a good wool gown said. "Not that the Dauphin Charles will give up easily, but clearly King Henry can beat him."

James wondered if the man were really so eager for an English king or if it was the company of English knights that made him say so. But maybe peace and no more war would be enough for the man. Did he care who ruled if they left him alone? That made James think—ideas that he had never before considered. What king was worth the devastation they had ridden through?

"Queen Isabella had to sign the treaty for the king," the hostel-keeper said to Sir John, whom they had quickly identified as the one with coins in his purse. "He's in one of his drooling, mad periods, may God show the poor man mercy."

"It is we who need the mercy, us with such a king," the merchant said with a snap. "King Henry is ready with a hanging, but he doesn't drool into his soup."

James sat silent, sipping the rich wine, listening to all the words and wondering how similar his people of Scotland would sound in their inns. Would they curse him if he gave way and swore fealty to the English king? Would he be cast out as King John Toom Tabard and his son had been? Or was he wrong? Had he wasted so many years fighting the wrong war?

Sir John insisted they ride hard the next day. His king would be furious if James weren't in Troyes in time for the wedding. When he saw the spires of the city dark against the soft afternoon sky, James cantered to ride beside him, behind a man-at-arms carrying the Scottish banner. "It doesn't stink as badly as London, at least."

Sir John snorted. "Comparing a minnow to a whale. I'm glad it doesn't reek of ash, though."

It was true that most of France had a stench of death. At least the English hadn't put Troyes to the torch, since it had opened itself to the English king like a whore spreading her legs.

They rode past wagons loaded with casks of wine, stacked with bales of hay, and piled with vegetables, so James knew somewhere there must be parts of France that Henry hadn't ravaged. But every wagon had a guard or two walking beside it with a sword or war axe at his hip.

If the people of the city of Troyes were sorry at having been conquered, James couldn't tell it. The brick and half-timbered houses stood whole and untouched, and the spire of the cathedral towered whitely over all. Sir John led the way through the crowds. A dozen soldiers staggered, drunk, one lolling against a wall to stay upright. Servants scurried to carry baskets of goods from the markets. Whores with white breasts half bared in unlaced bodices leaned above window boxes flowing with flowers and called invitations to passing customers. The bells of the Angelus began to toll. Black-robed friars in a long line threaded their way as they chanted, Ave Maria, gratia plena; Dominus tecum. Someone shouted, Au voleur! as a lithe figure darted and dashed to escape into the crowd. A peddler pushed a cart yelling, "Moules! Moules fraîches!"

Riding through the crooked streets with French spoken on every side in the bright June sunshine, for the first time James felt some pleasure in being dragged into Henry's war. They had to themselves the top floor of the little house that had been reserved for his use, a surprise and a welcome change from the castles where James was usually confined. Iain was settling them into their quarters, whilst Sir John hurried off to receive his orders concerning James. In the meantime, James stood at the window, looking out at the pleasant bustling street. "Mayhap if Sir John is indeed willing to loosen my leash, we can enjoy some of the pleasures of the city."

Iain's face lit up. "Aye, I've heard so much of French-women. And the food!"

Dougal managed one of his more priestly looks. "I hope you are nae thinking of wenching, Your Grace. That would be below your dignity. Better that you keep yourself chaste for a lady such as that sweet Lady Joan you saw at Windsor Castle."

James felt himself coloring and was sure he had said nothing to Dougal anent the lady. "I may never see her again, so if I find myself with a something sweet to hand I'll enjoy that instead of dignity." James laughed. "But there are churches you might visit, so you don't see my violation of my royal dignity."

Lyon shook his head, although the severe look he gave James seemed a bit false. "Even if Sir John will agree to such feats of Venus, you must remember who you are. Forbye, I am happy to rest from our dash across France. Churches will wait until another day, however handsome they may be."

Iain was nearly dancing as he made the bed with James's linens and shook out the clothes, well wrinkled from travel. "Do you really think he will agree to it?"

"I'll see wha' I can do," James said.

A servant fetched them hot water, and James nearly scrubbed his skin off to rid himself of the stink he felt had soaked into it. His chaplains had already laid out their pallets, and Dougal was snoring softly in his sleep when Sir John came banging in the door.

"We made it barely in time. The wedding is tomorrow." He tossed Iain a bundle. "Clothes for his lordship."

As Iain shook out the blue silk doublet and smoothed the tights, James wandered over to sprawl in the only chair, his legs stretched out and booted feet crossed at the ankle. "My chaplains are fair weary, but it seems to me that the rest of us could find some food and mayhap…" He shrugged. "… some company or even a hostelry with a player would not be so ill."

"And I suppose the cost would come from my purse."

"Or King Henry's." James grinned insolently. "He is paying for this wee jaunt, is he not? And I have seen nothing of that 'loosened leash' you promised me if I gave you my word."

An hour later, James sauntered out of the door of the half-timbered house accompanied by Iain, Sir John and only one squire as guard. The streets were still busy as the sky grayed toward dusk, and for a city surrounded by war, they were peaceful. Shutters banged closed, and bars thudded into place. A man stood in the door of his shop scolding an apprentice for his tardiness.

A few women bargained for the last vegetables in the stalls in the market. A baker was shouting that he had a loaf of bread left in his basket. "Have you heard how much food is reaching the city?" James asked.

Sir John shrugged. Food for a foreign population wasn't his business. "I've been told the king says that we have to keep the people sweet so we can trust our backs. But the important thing is for the army to be fed, and that you may be sure of. You won't go hungry with King Henry."

James hadn't supposed it, but he let the subject drop when the knight pointed to a hostelry with a hanging rooster painted on a sign over the door. When they rode into the little enclosed courtyard, two boys ran out to take their reins.

A burst of laughter met James when he strolled into the long common room. A fat, gray-haired man greeted them at the door, bowing. "There's no rooms, my lords," he said in accented but understandable English. "We're full up. All the English army has been at my door looking for shelter better than their tents, and they've taken every bed."

"Some supper and a good flagon of wine will suit us, if

you can manage that," Sir John answered with a look down his crooked nose.

"And company, if any such is to be found," James put in, smiling broadly.

The hostel-keeper gave a hrmmph. "I don't run a whore-house, my lord. But I suppose if one of the girls takes a liking to you, that's not my affair."

James raised his eyebrow at that, suspecting the man would take his share of any 'gift' the girl required. Even he was not so green. The hostel-keeper sat them by the window, and James could make out through the oiled linen the fading light of the summer evening. As the darkness ate the world outside, James wished he had someone to advise him. If only the Earl of Orkney were here. He trusted his household with his life, but they could not advise anent the quandary that clattered in his mind.

There was a row of wine kegs at one end of the room and an empty hearth at the other. A woman was drawing wine from the kegs, and three serving girls were running back and forth with flagons and cups and trenchers stacked with sausage scented with thyme and sage that made James's mouth water. The tables were crowded with townsfolk and soldiers mingling happily enough, or so it seemed. Five men-at-arms by the hearth wore the blue and red badge of the king's brother, John, Duke of Bedford. One slapped at a server's arse, but she danced away as she flashed him a smile. There was also a large party of Welsh archers in simple chain mail. At another table, a tonsured priest in a brown robe and a man with the shoulders of a smith sat with a hard-eyed merchant.

Sir John ordered the four of them sausages and wine in an arrogant tone, and the girl scurried to bring it. "Don't scare her awa'." James held out his hand. "I'll pay. Your voice would flay a mule, much less a lass."

With a sour look, Sir John dropped a few coins into James's hand. Once James had handed them over, the girls laid thick trenchers of bread filled with browned, steaming sausages dripping with juices in front of them.

One of them filled his wine cup and looked at him from under her lashes. There was a gap between her front teeth when she smiled, and her smock was stained, but she had a sweet smile. Besides, she was plump, and her cheeks were round and rosy. "It's lonely for poor soldiers a long way from home," James said in French. "Would you be kind enough to keep me company for a while?"

"My master might be angry if I don't serve the tables," she said, looking modestly down.

"Wha' if I gave him a coin or two? Mayhap he could spare your time to sit with me."

She gave a glance toward the hostel-keeper, who was watching them with a bland look on his round face. "There is no chair for me, my lord."

James pushed his chair back to make room and said, "I have a lap that will serve nicely. But if you sit in my lap, you must tell me your name."

"Béatriz," she said as she settled herself on his thighs and slipped an arm around his neck in a much less modest move than he'd expected, but he decided he had no complaint. He could feel the softness of her breast against his chest.

James drained his wine cup. "Do you have a room here, Béatriz?"

"I do, my lord, but it is small, with only a bed and a hook for my Sunday kirtle."

James gave her his best winning smile. "There would be more room than on my lap there. And if I gave you a little gift out of his sight, you master would not have to know."

"But you promised coins for him so he wouldn't be

155

angry," she said, pushing out her lower lip. But her lips were pink and inviting, and James shrugged.

"Of course. But you must have one for yourself." He lifted her off his lap with both hands on her waist, and she held out her hand. The back stairs to the third floor were narrow and dark, with only a single torch to light them. Her garret room at the end of the hall had no lamp or candle. But the sun had set, and it was bathed in pewter moonlight. She wriggled her kirtle and under dress over her head and tossed them aside. James gaped her soft skin and soft breast, and no underclothing. His hands were shaking. She was deft and sure unfastening his clothes. It had been far long too long since he'd had a woman. Many months ago, once in a kitchen garden, there had been a servant who had been glad of him—or of his few coins. But a prisoner… Then he thought of it no more as she murmured soft words and pulled him with her onto her bed.

CHAPTER 25

From his place at the side of Saint-Jean Church, James leaned a shoulder against the thick marble column and squinted. Flashes of red and gold light from the stained glass bounced off gold candlesticks and the white marble. They were like splinters driven through his eyes. Gusts of incense that boiled out of the censer a priest was waving about made him gag, and James swallowed down bile that tasted of last night's wine. The church was already full to overflowing with guests, except for two chairs at the very front.

A blare of trumpets made James flinch. A small, dark woman in a red silk gown cut so low that James felt his eyes widen and a high headdress flowing with veils, entered with a lady-in-waiting on each side. James had heard so many stories of Queen Isabeau of France, but somehow she looked nothing like the stories had led him to expect. She turned when a wavering voice made some indecipherable noise of protest, and then a thin man, pale as whey, and supported under each arm by a page, was helped through the door. His black, embroidered, velvet doublet hung on his thin frame, and his trembling hands fumbled at the rings on his fingers. The pages lowered the poor mad king of France into a throne-like chair at the front of the church, and the queen took a seat in the one beside him.

Another flourish, and a choir sang in the gallery as the bride walked from the main doors on the arm of a reedy, grim-faced nobleman, the Duke of Bourgogne, James supposed. She was slender and graceful in her silk gown, with a skirt covered in fleurs-de-lis picked out in pearls and wide sleeves that brushed the floor. He could understand the rumors that Henry was much taken with her. Her gold hair was bound in a bejeweled roll under a sheer veil. Her face still had a bit of childlike roundness, but over her blue eyes, her eyebrows were fashionably shaved, and she smiled confidently up at the awaiting Cardinal of Troyes when he took his place in front of the altar.

There was a crashing fanfare of bells and cymbals, sackbuts, and trumpets. James put a trembling hand to his pounding forehead, and his stomach lurched. But like the rest of the hundreds of nobles packed into the church, he turned to see King Henry striding up the center aisle with his brothers, Thomas, Duke of Clarence, and John, Duke of Bedford, behind him.

The axe-faced king was dressed with his usual severity in a black doublet, the sleeves slashed in crimson, and a chain of gold thickly set with rubies and pearls. He wore only a simple coronet on his dark head.

James shifted restlessly as his stomach roiled. Perhaps he should have been more moderate, but his rare chance to carouse had been too good to give up, although Dougal had snorted when he staggered in at midnight, and this morning Iain had complained that he looked like something a castle cat had thrown up on the bed.

The nuptial mass droned on, and James dozed on his feet

in the shadow of the column. Another violent fanfare jerked
him awake. He breathed a soft chuckle when he realized he
had missed the blessing of the couple. A rainbow of light
from the stained glass windows danced around the two as
King Henry offered Catherine his arm and walked her
toward the door. The church bells tolled. The cathedral—and
James kept wondering why the wedding had not been there
as had been the signing of the treaty—joined the clamor.
Soon the tintinnabulation spread across the city.

He hoped he would be able to slip away from the feast
early and either return to his own rooms—or mayhap find
more congenial company, although he had few coins without
Sir John to pay the cost. He smiled at the thought as he
followed the procession from the church. The cheering
outside blended with the clanging bells. People were
throwing flowers and shouting the princess's name. Perhaps
they saw her as a path to peace with the warlike English and
an end to the destruction and death as Henry clawed his way
to the French throne.

He stepped out into the dazzling June sunlight. Sir John
shouldered his way through the press, and James had to grin.
At least the wedding had separated him from his watchdog.
"I was afeart you wouldn't find me," he quipped.

James thought the man snorted but couldn't hear him for
the cacophony.

A line of men-at-arms surrounded the broad marble steps
of the church, where King Henry and Catherine stood with
King Henry's brothers, as well as the Duke of Bourgogne and
Queen Isabeau. He saw no sign of the king, who must have
been shambled off out of sight.

Sir John grunted an agreement when James nodded
toward the king, so they shuffled their way with the queue to
offer their congratulations. James bowed over Catherine's
hand and was happy to be shoved ahead by those behind him

waiting their turn. The crowds were shouting King Henry's name along with Catherine's, to James's surprise, the shouts growing even louder. He had to escape the press of the crowd making his head throb, and the questions that buzzed in his head like flies.

Even through the pounding in his head, James was tempted to laugh as Sir John stuck to him like a burr in a horse's tail. Did the man think he was going to try to flee from the middle of the English army? But he could pay for their food. Something greasy and a flagon of wine would surely cure the hangover that made the bright sunlight stab his head like a dagger. The nearest hostelry, with some sort of fish over the door on its sign, tempted him within, and he found a quiet corner to collapse into.

A boy brought them trenchers and dipped cassoulet, redolent with onions and duck amidst the beans, and a golden wine the hostel-keeper said was the best in the region. James downed the wine and bent over the table to spoon up the food.

Sir John paused with a spoon halfway to his mouth. "I'm to escort you to the bishop's mansion for the feast. The king's own command. He expects you there especial."

"I am one of his prize trophies. Why wouldn't he want me there?"

James sighed gratefully as the pain in his head eased and the wine and good food relaxed the muscles in his neck that had felt as hard as a rock. He wished he could ease the doubt anent what he should do as pleasantly. He brushed a hand over the doublet that had been provided—blue silk with red slashing in the sleeves. "These are my best clothes. There is no need to return to our rooms." James motioned the boy over. "And this is indeed the best wine I have ever had, so I'll have some more."

James drank it looking out the open window as the

shadows crept across the cobblestones, brooding over why
Henry had brought him to France after so long and what he
wanted of him. And if James should agree. Fourteen years he
had been a prisoner, and he was—weary. Besides, was it truly
worth the fight? Would anyone truly care? Many kings had
an overlord. If Henry was his, what might he demand? If it
were something that James could not give, the cost would be
terrifying.

"Lord James." Sir John was standing already. "It is time for
us to leave for the feast."

James decided he might get drunk again tonight. "Very
well. Let us go make merry." He drained the dregs of his cup
and slammed it down on the table.

They walked briskly through the crooked streets to join
the river of peacock colors streaming into the bishop's
mansion. As usual, James was an outcast to the English, but
they didn't quite dare ignore him since obviously the king
had desired him here, so he received nods and even half-
bows as he wended his way through the crowd.

When he reached the door, Sir John grinned. "I only have
to see you here, not put up with the crush."

James laughed silently. "Och. I would it were me. But
mayhap they have more of that wine I liked."

Although dusk was an hour away, the great hall was
ablaze with torches burning in bronze sconces.

"Lord James, son of the late King of Scots," the herald
called out as he entered.

He pressed his lips into a thin line. It wouldn't cause them
harm to give him his title. It was just another prick Henry
used against him, but one that hurt every time. He could feel
their eyes on his back. I'm naught but a showpiece for Henry
to parade his power.

The guests wandered amongst the tables, talking and
laughing, as heralds called out the names and ranks of the

new arrivals. Above in the gallery, fiddlers, harpists, horns, and drummers were trying to compete with the noise.

When he turned, James saw that Queen Isabeau's dark eyes were fixed on him, and she motioned him to come to her.

"Your Majesty," he said, bowing over her hand.

"These geese are as skittish of you as they are of me. The fools actually believe the lies my enemies put about." She smiled and the wrinkles around her eyes deepened into creases. "And you would think from their faces that being a Scot was catching."

He supposed it was true. Everyone had heard stories that she was a witch and an adulteress, though considering how mad her husband was, it was perhaps no more than human failing. They all gave her deep bows and curtsies but edged away as though she rang a leper's bell. Him they merely gave uneasy looks, not sure how to treat a king who was not truly a king.

She put her arm through his. "I do like the company of a handsome young man, and since they say terrible things about me anyway, you may keep me company and let them say what pleases them. Come, and you can sit beside me when my daughter and King Henry grace us with their presence."

James let her guide him toward the dais and even politely helped her up the steps, trying to decide how to handle this rather terrifying woman. "I am sure, Your Majesty, that my place is further—"

"Pfffttt... I am still Queen of France, even if your King Henry now rules it. At least, the servants won't argue with who sits beside me."

He bristled. "Not my king, Your Majesty."

She patted his arm and ignored his irritation. When they had arrived at places just left of the seats of honor, Queen

Isabeau leaned close to say softly, "You have fine eyes, Lord James, and I enjoy the pleasant company of a young man, but do not worry yourself. I have no designs on your honor." She lifted her nose toward the crowd and managed to sneer without changing her expression at all. "I merely amuse myself with them."

James could feel color creeping up his face from his collar and wondered if every eye in the huge hall was upon them. Did they think he was dallying with the Queen of France? She had been beautiful once, he supposed, but the thought made him queasy.

Trumpeters blew a flourish, and a herald proclaimed, "Our most puissant and dread lord, Henry, by the grace of God, King of England, Prince of Wales, Duke of Normandy, Lord of Aquitaine, Brittany, Maine, Anjou, and Guyenne; Regent and Heir of France, and his lady wife, the Princess Catherine, Daughter of France."

King Henry and Catherine walked into the hall as pages strewed rose petals before them. The king still wore the same clothing for the feast as for the wedding. Catherine had changed her gown for one as low cut as her mother's in light rose with a tight bodice and sleeves that swept to the ground. Yet her smile was sweet and modest. The king took her elbow to help her onto the dais and to the seats beneath the banners of the King of England and France. There were no English ladies with the army, so the tables were filled with a very male company. The king's brothers sat on the other side and gave James frowning looks, but the king nodded pleasantly enough.

Queen Isabeau took her daughter's hands and kissed her on both cheeks. The Duke of Bourgogne kissed her fingers and then her cheek, and then the king's brothers kissed her as well. The queen pulled on James by the arm, almost shoving him forward, and he took Princess Catherine's hand

and bowed over it whilst the king looked blandly on. The Cardinal led a long prayer before at last King Henry and his bride took their seats. James had not expected to be seated so near Henry. He supposed he should take it as a rise in his status in the court, but his doubts anent Henry's intentions made him wish he was as far from the royal couple as could be.

Queen Isabeau patted his hand and looked like a cat that had got into the bothy. "They make a beautiful couple, do they not, Your Grace?"

The cupbearers were filling the wine cups, and James watched eagerly. "Certes, Your Majesty. Your daughter is a bonny lass."

The king rose and lifted his cup, and a hush fell over the hall. "To my bride, Princess Catherine, soon to be crowned Queen of England." He turned to one side and the other with his cup high as shouts of "Princess Catherine! Princess Catherine!" resounded back at him.

James lifted his cup to the two of them and drained it. He held it up to be refilled as soon as he sat back down beside Queen Isabeau. The Duc de Bourgogne was giving him grim looks on his other side, and James was sure the man thought he had been displaced below his rank, but could not say anything to the Queen of France.

The first course was a dish of oysters steamed in almond milk served in gold chased bowls. James had filled himself at the hostelry, and it would be a long feast, so he picked at the dish, although it had a luscious smell. Half of France is burnt to a cinder, the people starving, but Henry's army will not go hungry. He twisted a wry smile. Looking around the crowded hall, most of what was here was indeed an English army. The mayor of Troyes had his lady wife with him, looking satisfied where they sat at the end of the high table, but they were among the very few.

The realization made James frown as he looked at the war-hardened men around him. He felt possessed by the question of why Henry had brought him here amongst them. Not that James had failed to train for war in the bailey yard. But he had never once set foot on a battlefield. So green a fighter was of no use to Henry who did nothing without reason. He started to take another drink before he realized he had drained his cup once more.

James held up his cup for more of the golden wine of Champagne. As the server poured it, the next course was being placed before them: a golden plate of goose in a sauce of grapes and garlic. A herald announced the first of the minstrels waiting to perform, and a lutist and harpist began to play. They filled the room with sweet notes. Queen Isabeau picked at the dish, looking bored, and asked him about his stay in England, which was nothing James wanted to talk about, but when he told her he was well acquainted with Charles of Orleans, he managed to turn the topic.

Soon darkness had fallen. Another minstrel entered and began playing I want to stay faithful, and James was sure King Henry hid a yawn behind his wine cup. This one bowed his way out of the hall as James toyed with a serving of fruited custard in a crust.

Abruptly, Henry stood and held up his hand for silence. Everyone jumped to their feet, though James rose more slowly.

"I command all my servants that, on the morrow, we all be ready to go besiege Sens. There we may prove our daring and courage, for there is no finer way to do so than at war. So I bid you retire and prepare to depart."

James gaped as the English king held out his arm for his bride, who stood, blinking up at him in obvious astonishment. Henry turned his gaze on James and said, "That includes you, my lord. You are to be ready to ride with my army at sunrise—without fail."

"But—" Queen Isabeau protested. However, the king was already striding from the hall with the young, wide-eyed soon-to-be-queen on his arm. Isabeau looked at James in consternation. "On the morrow? How can he leave so soon after the wedding?"

James raised his eyebrows. "He always has his reasons, madame, and I suspect his reason is that he wants the rest of France under his power."

"But could that not wait even one day?"

Philip, Duke of Bourgogne, offered the queen his arm, although his thin face was so tight his expression was almost a snarl. "King Henry's side was chosen for us by your murderous son, and there is fighting to be done. It must be so."

The queen paled, but she nodded. She gave James a faint smile. "We so rarely have true choices in this life. Is that not true, Your Grace?"

James had to agree, but he merely kissed her fingers and bowed to the duke as they took their farewell.

$\mathcal{T}$he people of Troyes had gathered in crowds to see the English army march away. There were no cheers, though a few whores had called out for them to hurry back. Behind, the morning Angelus had tolled from the church bells as the army spread out of sight, the knights and mounted men-at-arms in the fan, followed by their thousands of archers, and the baggage train trailed for miles behind it all. The king had not called James to attend him at the head of the army, where he rode under his huge banner, and James was glad to avoid him. With his little party guarded by Sir John, two other knights, and ten squires, James rode in the middle of the host, choking on dust and seemingly ignored in the crush.

Unhelmed, he threw his head back to let the hot summer sun bathe his face. The wind ruffled his hair and dried the sweat on his forehead. Steel armor was hellishly hot in the summer sun. He felt as though he were baking, but he stroked the hilt of his sword. Though many had grander, never before had he been allowed to go armed.

King Henry gave stern commands that no one was to

leave the columns of the march without permission. Still the squires sneaked away to hunt. When Iain came galloping up with his helm filled with wild strawberries he had found, James took a handful. It was like eating a velvet cloud made of honey. He licked the juice from his lips and told Iain to share them with Dougal and Lyon.

Now that they were at last on the move, Sir John was cheerful as a jester, grinning and telling James that he was like a maiden before her wedding night, but his first battle would cure that. James just laughed and said at least he was not too old to wield his sword like some he could name. The other knights roared with laughter at the thrust.

That night they made camp in the open fields beneath stars scattered like diamonds across black velvet. Another sunny day followed and then another, when they made camp outside the town of Sens. A thousand tents sprang up, and squires scurried about building campfires. Five heralds rode to the town gate to proclaim that it must surrender or its defenders would be hanged.

James didn't expect a fight, but he still paced nervously in front of his tent.

Sir John chuckled at him. "They don't have the men or the steel in their backbones to stand against King Henry."

He was right, and a short time later a messenger came to tell them the town surrendered. King Henry, the Duke of Bourgogne, the king's brothers and a score of guards rode to the castle to accept the surrender. James chewed his lip as he watched them ride out, asking himself once more why he was here. Something Henry was keeping back, some scheme. The longer it was secret, the more James was convinced it was dire.

The world grew hotter and brighter as they rode toward Montereau. There, Philip, Duke of Bourgogne's father had been murdered by followers of Dauphin Charles, and everyone said that the duke would have his revenge. They rode along the bank of the River Seine that flowed in gray-green ripples. James's saddle creaked softly in time with hoof beats in the dirt, the sound almost hypnotic. The world was empty, save for the moving army. It felt as though all of France had fled before them.

Across the waters of the wide moat, the towers of Montereau Castle appeared at last, its square gray towers squat and solid. Horns blew at the head of the march, and a squire came at a trot, having to wend his way through the press of mounted men, shouting, "Lord James, you are to join the king!"

Anxious to see what was happening, and if the castle would surrender, James spurred his horse and let the others follow as they would. By the time he rode through the half mile of close packed men, the king's pavilion had been pitched on a small rise within sight of the walls. At the base of the rise, there was a clamor of hammering and sawing as a gibbet quickly went up, and a cluster of prisoners were tied together like animals at its base. Some were kneeling, others standing and motioning toward the castle. James had no doubt the English had much practice at buildings such structures.

A table covered in red velvet had been set up under a spreading oak, where King Henry sat. Behind him were ranged the dukes and earls of the army in their polished steel as the king looked down on a man in simple mail kneeling beside the table.

"Please, Your Grace," the man begged, his hands tied together before him. "I did not intend to kill him. It was an accident. Truly. Mercy, I beg you."

Henry looked up at James as he swung from the saddle and tossed his reins to one of the footmen. The king's face was taut. He looked back down at the prisoner. "You raised you hand to a knight in a quarrel. Is that not so?"

The man's whole body was shaking. "I—I have served you well."

Henry nodded, and there was a flinch in his face. "You have. But I have learned to my sorrow that mercy has no place in justice. You will hang with the others."

A guard grabbed the prisoner by the arm and dragged him, gabbling and crying, down the slope. James gave the king a courteous bow. *Now we shall see what he truly wants of me.*

"Come, stand by me, Lord James," Henry said. He folded his hands on the table before him like a steeple. "I was fond of him. He often led my horse, but I cannot temper justice. Not for anyone."

James walked slowly to stand beside his nemesis, chewing the inside of his cheek. He looked toward the grim spectacle he had been brought to watch. "I understand, Your Grace. But the others. There are…" He counted. None seemed to be wounded or even in armor. "…eleven men. Why are they to be hanged as well? Did they each kill a knight?"

Henry tilted his head toward the roofs of the city barely visible in the distance. "I had them taken as hostages in Montereau. My van has captured the city. The governor and a handful of knights fled to the castle. If the castle surrenders, these will not hang. But the governor has refused."

"Mayhap he will change his mind when he sees that it is no mere threat," John of Bedford, a vacillating stork of a man, put in. "They cannot hold out against us. Refusing is madness."

"What do you think, James?" the English king asked.

James thought it was cruel and bloody business to kill men for revenge because someone else did not surrender, but it was useless to voice his true opinion. "Lord John has a point that they should surrender." He fought to keep his face blank.

The workmen were throwing ropes over the top rail of the skeletal gibbet. James gripped the hilt of his sword until it bruised his palm, his jaws tightening, as he forced himself to watch as the first of the men, thrashing, and his screams drifting up to the onlookers, was forced beneath a dangling rope and the loop slipped over his head. Three men pulled on the end, and the hostage kicked and twisted as he was hauled into the air.

Cold washed through him. James desperately swallowed down a gush of sour bile filling his mouth. He had killed a man himself. Thousands and thousands had already died in this war. What difference did eleven more make? Carefully, he took a deep breath, knowing Henry's eyes were upon him. He would know if James looked away, would judge it weakness. Another was hauled to the waiting rope, and James shook his head, scanning the walls of the castle. He could make out shapes of men upon the parapets. Why don't they surrender?

But they didn't, and a few minutes later twelve bodies dangled, casting long, writhing shadows in the bright June sun. James wondered if he was as pale as he felt.

"We will camp here," Henry said. "They don't have enough food to last a week, so I won't waste my men in an assault."

Duke Philip's pinched face was coldly fixed. "And when they surrender, any within who helped in the murder of my father must join those on the gibbet!"

James turned his head and examined Henry. He had known the man was hard, but he had never quite appreciated the depth of that hardness, not even after hearing of the executions of prisoners at Agincourt. Perhaps that was the lesson Henry brought him here to learn. He had a dire feeling it wasn't the last lesson Henry had for him.

"Was there aught you wished of me, Your Grace?" he asked in a carefully even tone. When Henry waved him away in casual dismissal, James climbed into the saddle and turned his horse's head with much to consider.

Within an hour, a blast of a trumpet sounded from the walls. A herald from the king rode to accept their surrender, and James heard the groan of iron chains. The portcullis slowly rose, and the bridge thudded down with a crash. A shout went up across the English camp.

CHAPTER 27

JULY 1420

*T*he last day of their journey to Melun was hot and dusty. The scent of thyme trampled under the horses' hooves mixed with the acrid dust of the road and the sharp smell of horse sweat. They rode through a stand of chestnut trees with leaves that drooped sadly in the heat, and James drained the flask of water that hung from his saddle-bow. Sweat dripped down his face and ran into his beard, itching like fleas. It was late morning when they sighted the high, white walls of the city rising above the Seine, drenched in golden light and seemed higher than any James had ever seen. The towers with their cone shaped roofs seemed impenetrable to attack. This will not be an easy fight, he pondered, wondering how King Henry planned to hammer the place open. It would not be starved into submission in a week. It was rumored the Sire Arnault de Barbazan had sworn it would not fall.

By midafternoon, before the walls, tents and cook fires spread out in their own city in orderly array. Squires ran to tie the horses at the picket lines on the east side of the camp. Workmen were digging latrines well downwind of the king's pavilion, and the other lords' were being raised around his. James shrugged and pointed to a spot on the edge of the camp well away from the king. "Raise our tents and plant my banner," he told Iain.

James could see crossbowmen moving on the parapet behind the crenellations. Above them fluttered the banner of the Sire de Barbazan, the sheaths of wheat quartered with rampant silver lions. But the highest tower flew a different banner, one that James was sure would drive King Henry to a fury: the blue royal banner of France.

"I think this will be my first real siege," James told Sir John.

The man barked a laugh. "If it isn't your first real battle, I'll buy you a flagon the best wine in the city. Once we take it. They are going to put up a fight."

"You think so?" James grinned with a rush of excitement. "You think it will come to a hand-to-hand fight?"

"King Henry is not content to sit on his arse and wait for a city to fall. Nor will Sire de Barbazan wait for us to take it from him, if what I hear is true."

Soon the camp rang with hammers as three trebuchets were being erected. Between them, workmen were building the frame of a turtle to protect sappers, who would try to undermine the walls, and a wagon piled with rawhide for a cover was being unloaded. Sergeants were assigning guardsmen around the perimeter. King Henry said he didn't expect an attack, but he also did not take chances.

A footman trotted up to James. "The king has summoned a war council for in the morning, my lord. You are to join it at first light."

They gathered as dawn stretched pewter fingers above the eastern horizon. A squire was fastening the clasps on King Henry's greaves. Standing around a table spread with papers, maps, ink, and quills were the king's brothers,

Thomas, Duke of Clarence, Humphrey, Duke of Suffolk, and John, Duke of Bedford. Behind James as he entered the pavilion came the Earl of Warwick, the Earl of Salisbury, and the young Earl of Suffolk, and the Earl of Richmond.

Philip, Duc de Bourgogne, a pallid, thin man with a high arched nose stood, arms crossed representing the French allies. The duke wore armor with gilding in elaborate scrolls worked into the steel, but his visage was grim. "I shall have the men who murdered my father," he announced.

"That is agreed upon, my lord," Henry said as he impatiently dismissed the squire. "The men responsible for the murder are yours."

John of Bedford gave a snort. "First we have to take the place, and the walls of Melun aren't going to fall at your whim."

Philip of Bourgogne's thin lips drew into a hard line. "Justice for my father is no whim. I will lead an assault and give the miscreants a taste of my blade."

"The walls of Melun will not be easily breached. Sire de Barbazan might be willing to give you a taste of his own blade in return," said Earl John, and Thomas of Clarence laughed.

"Enough," King Henry said. "This is a war council, not a gathering of fishwives. The sooner we are done with Melun, the sooner I can return to my bride." He glared at James. "And many of those men defending the city are your Scots."

James nodded, his mind grappling with the sudden attack as every man in the tent turned to stare at him. "Aye. There are many Scots brought over by the Earl of Douglas," he said in a careful, neutral tone.

"Douglas—with whom you are in contact, my lord—has his men defending the Dauphin. Did you think I did not know?"

"On the contrary, Your Grace. I assumed that you did."

175

"They fight wrongfully for the man who was once the Dauphin. Wrongfully! For I am the regent of France and heir to the throne. Douglas has no right to take up arms against me. Nor against his own king."

"King? When you have time after time denied me my rightful title. To this very day! You would nae have me king. You command me as a captive."

"So, you do not claim the title of King of Scots?"

James felt the color rising from his collar and stubbornly stared into Henry's eyes, keeping silent. Someone shuffled his feet. John of Bedford cleared his throat, the only sound in the profound silence.

"Do you?"

"I do."

King Henry's look was glacial. "Then they are your subjects. You will issue a proclamation commanding they lay down their arms on pain of treason against your royal self. You will sign and put your seal to it today."

Henry's blazing gaze bored into James's eyes.

"You are, Lord James, my prisoner and here under my command. And you will do as I bid. You saw at Montereau that I mean what I say."

He relishes this, James realized. It pleases him to demean me. "Any proclamation I sign has no authority. It is extracted by force and a' ken that is so. No Scot will obey it—nor should they."

"Obey it they will." King Henry snatched up a parchment and threw it against James's chest. "Now sign."

James automatically grabbed the document, and after a moment he held the thing out to scan what it said. The pounding in his ears was like the surf at Bass Rock, and it deafened him. Whether anyone spoke as he read, he couldn't say. The entire world narrowed down to the lying document

King Henry would force him to sign and the thundering in his head.

He dropped the parchment onto the table and grabbed up a quill to scrawl his signature. "You may observe, sire, if any of my subjects obey a command that was forced from me." He pressed his seal into the wax so hard it went through to the parchment, turned on his heel, and marched out, flinging over his shoulder, "I tell you they will not."

As he left the king's pavilion, a summer storm was blowing in, and the wind was gusting through a stand of chestnut trees, making the branches whip and sigh. He marched toward his campfire across a field of raw earth torn up by hoof and by boot.

At the cook fire, one of the squires offered James a slice off a rabbit he had caught. Sir John told him the best way to defend against a pike in an assault. Two of the squires practiced their sword work with blunted blades, and Dougal laughed at them. But James squatted by the fire, staring up at the walls. No Scot would obey a command torn from him by force. And what would Henry do when he realized it—if he didn't already?

CHAPTER 28

AUGUST 1420

*J*ames found a whetstone in the chest and sat upon his narrow camp bed. Iain held out his hand to do the chore as a squire should, but James shook his head. Keep your sword sharp, Gruffudd had often told him long ago whilst they trained together in the Tower. He would never forget all the Welshman had taught him.

As the stone made a snick-snick-snick sound on the blade, James thought of sitting high on the tower of Rothesay Castle, the land green all around the wide moat that sparkled in the midday sun. A peregrine circling lazily in the distance against smoky-blue mountains… His brother whooping and shouting as he rode out of the gate. James shook off the thoughts. Better to concentrate on the morrow. He tested the edge of his blade and smiled. Sharp as death on a dark night.

"Battle is not like a tourney, you know," Dougal said.

"I never thought that it was." The air was warm, and the tent smelled of sweat and oil from the polishing of weapons and armor. There was something comforting in it that made James feel at home.

Iain looked up from bending over James's cuirass. "Where do you think he will place us?"

James twitched a wry smile. "Where Sir John can keep close watch on me." Henry would take no chances on James escaping, not that his guard was ever far enough to make that a possibility. "Duke Philip is leading the attack, and we are in his forces. He wants to be first over the wall."

"The walls are high and strong," Iain said, rubbing hard to try to put a shine on James's dull plate armor. He complained that it was plain with no gilding or embossment, as the English lords had on theirs, but tried hard to give it a shine. "And so many defenders. Can it really be easy?"

"I suppose it may work, but I suspect King Henry is giving Philip his head to stop his complaining. I think he doesn't expect it to work." When Iain looked horrified, James laughed. "Henry is playing a game to keep Philip sweet until he has the rest of France well under his heel. It's worth a failed attack on the wall. For the nonce, give over with the armor. You won't polish it to be better than it is."

It was inferior but at least not the tourney harness that James had worn in England. Iain set the cuirass aside and put away the cloth. "Duke Philip must ken that an assault probably won't work."

"It's hard to tell. He has a face with the expression of a stone saint. Now the tunneling under the walls—that I think Henry has hopes for. But whatever the chances may be, tomorrow we'll fecht the French."

"But not the Scots?"

"Sancta Maria, Mater Dei! I pray not."

"Aye. As do we all," Dougal said.

James sheathed his sword and hung the belt on the tent pole. Yawning, he let Iain help him out of his soiled clothes and stretched out on his bed. He pulled his coverlet up to his chest and lazily scratched himself as he closed his eyes. I should feel more anxious, he thought, and went to sleep dreaming of steel singing on steel.

He awoke sure that he should already be dressed for battle. Woozy, he pushed himself off his bed and ran his hand through his tangled hair. He looked around the tent in the dim light from a single brazier that burned in a corner, and there was no sign of Iain. Dougal was still snoring softy on his pallet.

When he pushed open the flap of the tent, streaks of silver spread across the azure sky, and mist floated in streaks around the tents and over the trench around the city. The dirt was gritty beneath his bare feet. Men were blundering through dawn's murk. Iain hurried up with a pitcher of water. By the time he had splashed his face, the squire stood holding out his padded doublet for James to wear under his plate cuirass. As he pulled it over his head, Sir John came trotting out of the haze, already armored, his bowl helm under his arm.

"How long until we form for the attack?" James asked him.

"Duke Philip is already calling for you," Sir John said. "So you'd best be fast into that armor."

"See that your own men are ready." James went back within the tent. Iain's hands were shaking with excitement as he latched James into this cuirass and put his gorget around his neck. "Hurry," James said. "You'll have to ready yourself as soon as I leave. Why didn't you rouse me sooner?"

"I'm sorry. I thought you needed to rest."

James snorted a soft laugh as he pulled the gauntlets on and Iain knelt to fasten the greaves. "Henry will have my hide if I delay the attack." James shoved his feet into the pointed metal boots, and Iain handed him his close helm. James tucked it under his arm since it narrowed his world to a slit straight ahead. He fastened his sword belt, heavy with his

longsword and dirk, around his waist and gave it a tug.
"Don't dawdle."

It was strange to think of fighting afoot, but horses would
only be in the way as they clambered through the dry moat
with its sharp slant down ten feet and up the other side to
climb ladders that the footmen would carry. He ducked out
of the tent. Sir John saluted him with his sword. James cuffed
his shoulder and trotted toward the knot of men where Duke
Philip gathered his forces. James's stomach made a hard knot
in his belly, and his heart pounded like a racing steed. Behind
him, Sir John and his guards thudded in their armor to keep
up. Pale gold spread across the sky as the edge of the sun
peeped above the horizon. James wondered how much a
wound would hurt. He wondered if any of them would die—
if he would die this morning. In the warm summer air, a chill
ran down his back. Was he a coward because his belly
cramped at the thought?

James gathered his wits as he saw the array of men gathered around Duke Philip's banner. He shoved his way
through, and when the duke saw him, he sharply motioned
him over. The rising sun was burning off the wisps of mist as
the duke nodded to him. "You are to guard my back in this
fight," he said, and James nodded.

The duke's chaplain mumbled a quick blessing, and then
the duke cleared his throat and raised his voice to be heard
by all the hundreds of men gathered. "You will all be
rewarded. That goes without saying. But all the gold in
France will not bring back my father's life. I will have
revenge for the treachery that he suffered." He paused, but
there was only a ripple of murmurs at his words. "We will go
in and take this city. You know what you must do. Now we
will deal out blood and death to our enemies. Anyone within
the reach of your blade should die!"

That won the duke a cheer as the he drew his sword and

pointed it toward the wall. James lowered the helm and fastened it into place on the gorget. His stomach eased as they surged toward the dry moat. On each side, a dozen footmen carried long ladders. His feet slipped in the dirt as he went down the edge of the trench. Behind them were rank on rank of knights and men-at-arms with swords and war axes. James watched the longbowmen checking the arrow bags at their belts and their bow strings. They would be of little use until they were over the wall, though.

The thud of their feet was a rumble, and there were soft curses as men slipped. Someone laughed. But there were no trumpets to allow the city time to muster their defense.

Panting, Iain caught up to James and coughed out, "Here I am, Your Grace." James gave him a cuff on the shoulder as they scrambled into the bottom of the deep trench. A wind tunneled by the shape carried the smell of sweat and metal.

On the city wall, a horn cried out: Harooooo, harooooo…

James dismissed every thought from his mind but the task ahead. Climb the ladder and take the wall. He slid his foot up the first part of the incline, careful of his balance in the treacherous dirt.

The horn blew again: Harrroooooooo…

Figures were silhouetted between the merlons of the battlement, one in each opening. James realized they were out of time and began to run up the slope. "Up!" he shouted. "Up with the ladders!"

A deadly rain whistled down on them. The first footman carrying the ladder next to James died before he hit the ground, a bolt through his neck. Their longbowmen began to fire, but there was no way at that angle their arrows would arch over the wall. The crossbowmen dodged, jumped back out, and a second volley fired down. Men collapsed with shrieks of pain, cursing as they clutched arms and legs ripped through by the razor-sharp bolts. James stepped over a man-at-arms writhing with a bolt through his belly.

Two of the ladders were raised on the wall, and men began to scramble up.

The duke spun and shouted, "Raise the rest of the ladders!"

James looked up to see a cauldron tipping and jumped forward to grab the duke's arm and sent him sprawling into the trench. The man shouted a curse as he tumbled to his knees. Oil splattered, sizzling, as James leapt to join him, and he fumbled his sword free from its scabbard.

There was a voice bellowing, "Attack!" One of the ladders crashed to the ground; defenders shouted cries of triumph, drowning out the cries and screams all around.

"Look!" James shouted a desperate warning, pointing with his blade at a postern door and the enemy that were boiling through it. They broke into a run. "Iain, back to the camp!" he yelled, though he couldn't see the squire. He had no more time to speak or to think. They were upon him, their swords silver flashes in the morning sun.

The duke had already jumped to his feet and was sweeping his sword at an attacker.

"To me!" James shouted. An attacker let his sword drop as he came, and James ran him through. Another charged, his blade glinting as he swung. James barely dodged the blow, jumping to the side, and smashed a blow into the man's face hard enough to cave in his visor. He dropped, screaming and clawing at the blood that welled through the slits. James finished him with a thrust through the eye and planted a foot on the corpse's chest to jerk his sword free.

The duke backed up as a second enemy went down to his blade. James dodged and attacked. Sir John stabbed the man in the back.

James shouted, "Call retiral! This is lost!" As he did, they got a little luck as a longbowman managed to get two shots off and took out two knights to give the duke a breath.

"Retire!" the duke screamed. "Back to the camp!"

Another knight came at James as he backed up the side of the trench. James swept a cut at him. He recoiled, so James smashed the flat of his sword two-handed at his throat. He dodged again, and James backed up another step. He rushed. James blocked hard enough to send the sword flying from his hand. But a knife in his off-hand punched into a gap above James's gauntlet. Pain shuddered through his hand and arm, so desperately, James slammed his hilt into the knight's face. The man staggered and went down, skidding to the bottom of the trench.

James hurriedly backed the rest of the way up in a crouch, sword low and ready. Blood dripped from his injured off-hand. Sir John grabbed his shoulder and dragged him backwards. "Run for camp, you fool!" he shouted at James.

James bellowed, "Retire!" at the men still straggling up from the trench. A deadly hail clattered down, and a few more dropped.

James turned and ran for the camp. Dazed and panting, when he reached the first tent, he cradled his arm to his chest, pain hammering through it. He looked back. The fight was over. The city's defenders shouted taunts, and one turned to drop his drawers and showed his arse.

The sound of hoof beats coming from behind him made him turn. King Henry reined up and looked down at him.

"They were waiting for us," James said. "They couldn't have gathered defenders so fast."

Henry nodded. "I spoke to the duke. He has praise for your skill in the fighting."

James managed on the second try to sheathe his sword. His whole arm was throbbing, but at last he had a hand free to strip off his gauntlet and let it drop to the ground. His arm was coated in drying blood, but he thought, though it pounded with pain, that it wasn't too bad, a long gash across his arm to the bone. He wiggled his fingers to be sure they worked. "He is too kind."

The king bent to look at the injury. "Your first battle wound." He smiled amiably. "Have it tended. Wound fever kills as many men as the injury itself."

"I will. First I must find my squire."

James trudged wearily toward his tent, hoping that Iain had headed there, but before he had gone more than two steps he saw Iain standing with a group of the men-at-arms, waving his arms as he talked anent the fight, and James breathed more easily. "Wha' are you doing there?"

Iain colored bright red. "Waiting for Your Grace. To tend you."

James snorted, but even that hurt. "Find me some wine, and let us shed this armor," he said through clenched teeth.

CHAPTER 29

SEPTEMBER 1420

King Henry was sitting, legs sprawled, on his camp chair, wine cup in his hand and more relaxed and smiling than James had ever seen him. Thunder rumbled like rocks down a cliff, and the canvas rattled overhead. After two days of dreary, late-summer rains, the ground outside was sodden, but that hadn't prevented the miners from almost completing the tunnel under the walls. Henry said he and Philip would lead the way through on the morrow. But tonight, he gave a feast for his seconds in command. Being included did not mean James had a command, but he had only shrugged when ordered to attend.

Henry waved a careless hand at his minstrel on the last note of his song anent a knight pursuing a shy lady love. "Your song bores me. Give over." He looked around and grinned at James. "Lord James would do better. Will you not, cousin?"

Duke Philip, as tightly strung as a bowstring, stood to the side silently watching while the king's brothers, Thomas, Duke of Clarence, John, Duke of Bedford, and Humphrey, Duke of Gloucester sat crouched over a table throwing dice.

The earls of Warwick, Salisbury, and Suffolk were talking in an undertone in a corner. Richard Beauchamp, Earl of Richmond, a tough and grizzled old man, had his mouth full of roasted swan, and a servant was refilling the wine cups, although the wine was well-watered. Henry tolerated no drunkenness before battle, but they would take their ease.

"If it pleases you, I'll play." James held out his hand for the instrument and plucked a few notes to test the tuning. James frowned and bit his lip as he tried to think of the right song for the night. "Not one of my own, my lords. Something more martial, I think."

He played a few notes of a well-known song by Bertran de Born.

"I DO LOVE the cheerful spring
    When the flowers are blooming;
    I also love the trilling peal
    Of birds in the woods echoing;
    I love to see tents and banners
    Spread out upon the meadow;
    And my spirit soars when I see
    Knights charging into battle.
    Maces, swords, and plumed helms,
    And shields split and broken,
    Amid the midst of bloody battle;
    Vassals struck down are there,
    And steeds of the dead do flee;
    When mingled strife is spread,
    The noblest warriors join in
    To cleave both limbs and head—
    Better than captive is an enemy dead.
    Nothing more my soul can cheer,
    Not banquet nor soundly sleeping,

Than the shout of "Lay on!" rung
From each side in battle closing
And on both sides, I hear the noise
Of riderless horses neighing,
Screams of "Help me! Help me!"
When both small and great do fall
All alike into the grassy trenches
And yonder lie in a mangled pile
Splintered lance bedecked with pennon.

PASSION MUST TAKE a valiant lover
Skilled both in arms and service;
Who speaks well and greatly gives;
Who knows what he should do and say
As becomes a knight's great power—
One full courteous and lively.
A lady who lies with such a knight
May say she has chosen wisely."

KING HENRY SLAPPED his hand on the table and exclaimed, "Well done, James. Just the song. De Born knew battle—a great troubadour."

James strummed a final chord before he handed the lute to the waiting minstrel. "I suppose he did, Your Grace."

"It is a shame our age has none such as he." The king unwound from the chair like one of the Tower's lions rousing from rest. "You're learning war as well. It's all that makes life worth living. De Born was right anent that."

James rose, as did the king's brothers. John of Bedford, a pale imitation of his brother, gave James a look down his high-arched nose. "You're sure Lord James is up to the fight? To have him at your back?"

For the first time, Duke Philip spoke up. "He did well when we fought together. I am pleased to have him at our side. If his subjects learn to be sensible enough to join us as well, all the better."

King Henry laughed. "I may have to give him a knight's buffet one day. He fights and takes his wounds like a man." He gave James a speculative, considering look that sent a prickle up the back of his neck. "I brought him to teach him war, not wrestle in the mud with all my men. He can help me close the curst Armagnac's counter-tunnel like any of my men might."

James bit his lip hard to keep a response behind his teeth.

John of Lancaster shrugged and went on speaking to his brother. "This rain is miserable for fighting. Mayhap we should wait one more day to see if it is more fit for battle. Simply withdraw the miners until then. The tunnels are knee-deep in mud and water at best. They must be even worse with the rain."

The king gave his brother a scorching look. "We have fought before in the rain. It does not serve to let de Barbazan think he can drive us off. It gives them heart for holding out. I will have that barrier down and collapse their counter-tunnel. Too many of our miners are dying to their attacks."

"And I will have the murderers who escaped to reach Melun," Duke Philip said in an acid tone. "This siege has already taken longer than I would have expected from the great English king."

The king's face twitched at the remark, but he nodded a pleasant enough farewell. "Gentlemen, I expect you to be ready at daybreak. We will hold the way. A man's glory is in battle. Remember it."

A noise like a mountain coming down shook the night as James slogged through the muck. He turned toward the wall, frowning. When had they begun using the cannon at night?

The monstrous thing was dangerous enough during the day. The huge one called London had blown up the first time it was used and killed the four men who were firing it. But the stone it fired had arched over the wall and the noise when it hit had rocked even the walls of the city.

The rain had begun to turn cold as the siege crept into September. He absently rubbed at the tender scar on his arm. Certes, de Barbazan would be desperate to defend the tunnel he was using for their attacks. Dozens of King Henry's miners had been killed. It could be a dire fight.

Yawning, he let Iain strip him out of his sopping clothes and towel his hair. As James stretched out in his bed, he said, "You will wait here for me to return tomorrow."

"What? But—"

"The king is not taking squires with us into the mine. There isn't room for enough fighters." James sighed and rolled over onto his side, pulling his cover up to his chin. "'God's truth, I'm glad of a little fighting. I've wrestled and jousted with every man who doesn't run at the sight of me. This siege has lasted too long."

From his pallet, Dougal huffed out a laugh that James was sure he was not intended to hear.

When James ducked out of the tent in the morning, Sir John saluted him with his sword and fell into step beside him. The rain had stopped, but the world was sodden. Mud coated his boots and sucked at every step. He saw dark shapes of men dart between the merlons. A single crossbow bolt thudded into the cover of the turtle. This would be no surprise attack. Sire de Barbazan would be waiting for them.

In the silver light of dawn, the opening of the mine was a black, gaping maw beneath the shelter of the turtle. Duke Philip hunched on one knee on a pile of oak beams, peering within. King Henry crossed his arms as James pushed his way through the miners carrying huge coils of rope and pick axes to bring down the barrier and the walls of the tunnels de Barbazan had dug and past scores of knights.

A footman trotted out of the dark opening, holding a torch aloft. "The barrier is in place, Your Grace," he reported. "We killed their guards, but the fight had to have been heard. It was not silent."

"Form up!" King Henry drew his sword. "We mean to take this city, and the evil men who stand in our way will not stop us."

James almost snorted but held his reaction in as he picked up one of the torches piled by the opening and stuck it to the footman's. Several knights did the same, and the footman led the way.

The top of the tunnel was bathed in soft morning light, but it grew smaller behind them as they went into the pitch black. Their footsteps echoed off the dirt walls, and light from their torches flickered into weird shapes. A drop of water seeped through James's helm to run down his face, and they breathed in the smell of wet earth. His first step into the water was like ice. He could feel the cold creep up his legs as they splashed further, and the light of their torches glistened on the ripples.

Almost laughing in relief, he saw a pool of light ahead, torches stuck into rough sconces in the wall and heavy beams hammered together to make a chest-high barrier Water flowed around the feet of a dozen footmen, who held pikes and stared ahead as they kept guard for an attack.

Water lapped at his legs as he sloshed his way to the barrier. His foot slipped in the sludge, but he caught himself with a hand on the wall. A shouted echoed from around a dark corner. The torchlight danced and shone against wet cuirasses and helms.

"Bring it down," King Henry shouted to the miners.

A dozen men rushed up to it and started to swing their

axes. Two of them ripped into the same beam and jerked it free. When it smacked into the water, water washed up as high as their hips.

Another shout from the darkness sounded nearer: "Sus! Sus, mes amis!"

Now four miners worked on the same place and jerked another beam loose. The rampart was now no higher than a man's knee.

James could hear the slapping of men's feet in the water; he knew it must be dozens of them to be so loud. Harnesses and weapons rattled. James pulled his sword and held it low and ready. One of the miners, frantically fleeing back the way they had come, knocked into him, but James gave him a shove the way he was going.

His hand twitched around his hilt.

King Henry and Duke Philip both had their blades free. The torchlight wavered on the swords like golden flames as they crouched near the opening in the barrier. James eased closer, and his breath hitched. Then there was no more time to think. The enemy advanced at a run and boiled through the narrow opening. "Fida muris usque ad mures!" they screamed as they came. "Sus! Sus!"

James felt a queasy fluttering in his stomach as he evaded a blade and then plunged his sword with all his force into the man's belly. It went through steel and muscle and bone. King Henry was laying about him with his sword, a look of battle madness on his face. James backed up a step. If he died, he didn't want it to be to Henry's sword.

"St. George! St. George and King Henry!" men all around him were shouting, and their cries mixed with the shouts of their enemies.

James saw the duke catch a man-at-arms full in the neck with his sword, nearly taking off his head as the fool ran by him. A halberd whooshed at James from the right, and he barely had time to drop to his knees as it hissed over his head. He jumped to his feet and slammed the pike aside. The Armagnac raised the halberd high for another swing, lost his footing in the slippery mud and fell flat on his back. James made a sweeping side cut and blood gushed from his enemy's throat.

James looked around for a moment, gasping for breath and dizzy from the excitement. King Henry was surrounded by three enemies, but he lopped the hand off the first man who swung at him and raked his sword across the belly of the next on a back slash. An English knight lay slumped on his stomach across the barrier, a pike buried in his back. When James saw one of the Armagnac run up and grab at the haft of the weapon, he charged.

His prey met him, sword raised, flickering light catching on the metal. He had immense shoulders and was wearing a polished cuirass that was splattered with blood. James stepped forward, his sword coming in hard at the Armagnac's belly, but the knight angled his blade in a block and then swept his sword up and around. James met it with a blow that jarred up to his shoulders. Their swords slid and locked, James helm to helm with his opponent.

They broke apart, and James gulped for air as they circled. The Armagnac's blade whipped toward James's shoulder, but he blocked. When the knight tried a cut from the other side, James swept his sword, and it squealed as it scraped across the knight's steel-encased arm.

Then the two traded blows, one after another, faster and faster. James wasn't sure he could defeat the man. He was strong—and fast. James moved, flinching at a hard strike, and turned to the side. The man gave a grunt of triumph as he followed James forward, but James was already moving. He rammed his shoulder into the man's chest. The man stumbled, off balance, and James looped his leg behind the man's knee to dump him on his arse in the water. He aimed his sword down through the narrow opening in the knight's helm and pushed it home with all his weight.

Afterwards, it seemed to James as though he dreamt that long fight. Side by side with King Henry and Duke Philip and the score of men-at-arms still standing, he swung and dodged and parried and stabbed. James gritted his jaws shut on his own war cry as men around him shouted, "St. George and King Henry!" They trampled on bodies that had fallen. The Armagnacs' own barrier worked against them, but they kept coming. One hacked with a halberd so hard he lifted an English knight off his feet. James scythed him down from behind. Then there was another. And another.

Duke Philip chopped at a shield until it flew to pieces and then hewed the man in the face. One of the Armagnacs fled from the duke's blade, tossing away his sword as he ran. The charge broke as another followed. Suddenly, they were throwing down their weapons and running from the barricade. At the turn in the tunnel, one of the men grabbed two of his fellows and tried to form a line. A few more turned to stand with them, but the duke leapt through the gap. James and King Henry followed with their men streaming behind, shouting, "King Henry!" Then those few were fleeing too.

"Halt!" King Henry called to his men who ran in pursuit. "Find the miners! I want that counter-tunnel closed."

James sheathed his sword. His arms were numb from weariness, and he bent to rest his hands on his knees as Henry strode past him back to the barrier. In a minute, the miners were running up, talking and laughing in triumph as they fastened ropes around beams and loosened them with their pick axes. "Back, my lord," one said to him, so he straightened and walked dazedly toward the others. Henry and Philip were squatting as they waited, surrounded by their men.

Behind him, James heard a groan like the earth was in pain and a tremendous craaaack. A gust of dirt billowed. When the miners dashed out, covered in grime as though they had wallowed in it, Henry said, "Finish pulling down the barrier and return to your digging."

CHAPTER 30

NOVEMBER 1420

*T*he sky was gray and thick with roiling clouds. Blowing sleet stung James's face as he walked across the camp. Beside him, Sir John jerked at his cloak and cursed at the cold. A gust of wind sent dead leaves pinwheeling around them. After five months of siege, even the Tower of London sounded like less of a punishment, dry and with a fire on the hearth and wine in a flagon, whilst he wrote one of his poems, and his household was around him. His shoulders and back ached from the constant weight of his plate armor, the tent was never truly warm, and he was sick of watered wine and boiled beef. And he was sick of war councils, where they did nothing but quarrel, whilst King Henry glowered and fumed at the city's refusal to submit. That all the work to undermine the walls had been for naught put the English king into a rage. Stubbornly, the walls stood, and the city resisted.

Sir John bowed, remaining outside the doorway, as James entered. The others were gathering quickly. The earls of Warwick, Salisbury, and young Suffolk joined them, standing beside the long trestle table waiting for their king to take his seat. Richard Beauchamp, Earl of Richmond entered with Duke Philip. All of them were clad in their armor, though they'd eschewed helms and gauntlets.

Humphrey of Gloucester, the handsomest of the royal brothers, accosted him as he entered. "What are you going to do to bring those Scots out of the city? Six months we have held here and not one has submitted to your command."

"I told your royal brother they wouldn't," James said coolly, but politely. "As long as I am a prisoner, my commands have no weight."

Humphrey bristled. "If you mean to imply, Lord James, that you were forced—"

"I say wha' I mean. A king held prisoner cannot give commands."

King Henry turned from speaking to John of Bedford and said, "Enough. Both of you."

Humphrey made a particularly obsequious bow to his brother. "Thomas sent his squire to tell me that he is indisposed and cannot attend today."

John snorted. "Is he drunk again? Or so hungover he cannot stand?"

Humphrey pressed his lips together and eyed his brother. "And you are never in your cups? A siege is deadly dull. I cannot blame him for seeking to break the ennui."

"Our brother has an enormous amount of ennui to break it would seem."

The Earl of Warwick grinned, and Suffolk laughed aloud.

"I said enough. My council is no place for wrangling like fishwives. We have a city to take." King Henry took his place in the high-backed chair at the head of the table. "Now tell me if any of you has something to say to the purpose."

James sat near the foot of the table, more than willing to let the English lords wrangle amongst themselves.

The Earl of Suffolk shook his head. "The miners should

197

be put back to work undermining the walls. That it is near winter should not make a difference. If a few lose fingers or toes, what matter?"

"It is too late in the year for that to work," said Duke Philip. "The tunnels are waist-deep in water from the rains. Soon we would have collapses, and they'd lose not merely fingers and toes, and for what gain?"

"We won't need to tunnel under the walls soon. They were eating rats for their only food a week ago." King Henry lifted his lip in a sneer, and the scar on his cheek twisted. "Their motto is 'Faithful to the walls if we have to eat rats' but what when they no longer have even those? How long before they starve?"

"I have known Sire de Barbazan for many years, sire" said Richard Beauchamp. "He will not let his men starve if matters in the city are truly so sore. Let me go and negotiate with him rather than sending heralds. I believe he will listen to me if I offer him honorable terms."

"They have been offered terms. And de Barbazan spat on the terms," said Suffolk. He was a willowy man with a mass of brown curls and sharp blue eyes. He'd only inherited his title when his elder brother died at Agincourt. "The man is too God damn stubborn to even save his own people." He jerked a rude gesture toward the walls of the city.

Beauchamp slammed his hand down on the table and growled, "Don't tell me about a man I knew when you were in swaddling clothes, Jack a' Naples!"

Suffolk jumped to his feet. "Call me that with a sword in your hand, old man."

James almost laughed as the veins on Beauchamp's face popped out with his rage. Beauchamp rose. "Come outside and challenge me, if you dare!"

"I'll not have a sword touched in my presence!" King

Henry said, and his eyes blazed. "Sit down." When the two men continued to glare at each other, he thundered, "Now!"

Suffolk seated himself, but Beauchamp glowered at him. Finally, he turned to the king. "Let me prove the whelp wrong, Your Grace. I know de Barbazan. Allow me to go to him."

Henry gave an angry look around the pavilion. "I shall not turn away even a slight chance to end this siege." He stood, and James, along with the others, rose to his feet. "We are done. If you do not bring me a capitulation, tomorrow I have built siege towers and will assault the walls. Whatever the cost, I will have Melun. If he yields, I will take them captive and offer them treatment as befits their rank, even accept ransom." His eyes scorched them as he spoke. "But if I must command an attack, I will give the city over to my men. Make sure that de Barbazan knows that. His knights will fight whilst so weak with hunger that they can barely raise their swords, and when the battle is done, every one of his men still alive will hang."

The icy wind was blowing from the north as James stepped from the pavilion, and he could smell the stink of thousands of men and horses and a foul stench from the bloody flux that had plagued the camp for a month. Atop the city walls, the banners of Melun and the Dauphin hung sodden and limp.

Richard Beauchamp followed, shouting for heralds, his squire and his courser. James saw a man-at-arms carry a white flag on a tall pole and the earl swing heavily into his saddle. Everywhere men stopped what they were doing to watch as the party rode toward the city gate. Lyon walked slowly to stand beside James, ashen and thin from a bout with the flux that had nearly sent him to his maker.

"Wha' do you think, Your Grace?" he asked in a weak voice.

"I think I pray to the Holy Virgin that he succeeds."

CHAPTER 31

*S*ir John shoved the prisoner, his hands bound behind his back, and the man stumbled into the cobblestone square. He was a dark, slender man with a thin nose and lank hair. Under a thick, dark cloak, he wore sturdy clothes, as though he had been prepared for flight. Certes, he had left that until too late. James stubbornly crossed his arms. He refused to lay a hand on the Gascon they had hunted down, Bertrand de Chaumont. He was no gaoler. If he had to take a part in this, it would not be an active one.

The King of England, in the center of the square, didn't so much as look their way. So angry that his face was scarlet and the white scar on his cheek stood out like a blaze, he jabbed a finger at the knight standing proudly before him. "Who led the Armagnacs out of the city? Where are the men who murdered Jean the Fearless? Either you tell me, or you will suffer for your evil."

Duke Philip looked on, his face icy but his eyes dark holes of fury. But he always burned like the fires of hell when his father's murder was mentioned.

"My evil?" As skeletal as he was, Sire Arnault de Barbazan

was lordly. Though unarmed, he wore polished armor and a surcoat of red with his coat of arms on the chest. His gray head was bare and his beard thin with age. "I defended my city as I was sworn to do."

James wondered if the man had any idea how dangerous it was to enrage the English king. Since the city gates had opened and Henry led them through, King Henry's men had gathered together the soldiers who had defended the city. They were being herded like cattle outside the gates and some into boats to be taken by river to imprisonment. But James had no part in that, though he had watched for Scots and seen none of them. He had led his guards and a score of men as they searched for all the supporters of Dauphin Charles. He and his men had searched the city twice over. The Dauphin's friends who had aided in the murder of Jean the Fearless were nowhere to be found.

"I agreed to surrender the city, not keep count of every man in it. It is not my fault if some have escaped." De Barbazan made a sweeping gesture. "The city is yours. I have kept my word, and I am sure, my lord, that you will keep yours. Where are my men, and how are they to be treated?"

"The friends of the Dau—the former Dauphin did not escape on their own. Who aided them?" Henry pulled back his lips, baring his teeth in a snarl. "Or mayhap it is your will to take their punishment for the miscreant?"

De Barbazan's face stiffened. "Richard Beauchamp gave us your word that we would be treated with honor. Did he lie?"

"You would not be the first man of your rank I have imprisoned. Or higher rank than you."

James felt his face flame as the King Henry's gaze flicked toward him.

Henry continued, "I am the regent of the king of France. Had you submitted to me as you were obliged to months ago, we would not have come to this." Henry called for a guard. "Find me carpenters. I need a narrow cage built on one of the wagons. Sire de Barbazan needs lodging." He turned a cold smile on the aged knight. "And long may you enjoy it as our guest."

De Barbazan's thin face paled, but he gave King Henry a straight look. "I have never in my life been called a coward. If this I must suffer, I shall do it."

"Then so you shall." The king turned his back and walked a few paces to look toward the ruffled blue-green of the River Seine, where a barge was being loaded with prisoners.

I just want this to be finished, James thought as he stepped forward. "We found the man Chaumont, but the men the duke named as murderers were nowhere to be found."

"If not in Melun, they will be in Paris," Henry said in a calmer, determined voice. "They were helped to escape. Sire de Barbazan has chosen his cage over speaking, but others have said they saw the miscreants with Chaumont." He shook his head. "My vassal, who fought at my side at Agincourt. And he has betrayed me."

Sir John gave Chaumont a hard shove in the middle of his back with both hands, hard enough that he stumbled almost into the king. A guardsman grabbed each arm and forced him to his knees. James pressed his lips into a tight line. He had no hope for mercy for the man. Perhaps he didn't deserve it.

"I thought you honorable, Chaumont," Henry said. "Now I give you a chance to salvage that honor. Confess, or I will find more of de Barbazan's men to share your punishment with you, and you can watch them die before you do. Mayhap they will curse you as they hang."

"Your Grace—" Barbazan shouted in protest, but Henry cut him off.

"Gag him if he opens his mouth again." Henry looked down at the prisoner. "Well?"

Chaumont was shaking and his voice broke when he confessed. "I led them out of Melun. I knew the way through one of the contre-tunnels out of sight of your camp." He looked up at Henry with an expression that begged for mercy but showed no flicker of hope. His Adam's apple bobbed up and down when he swallowed.

"And where did they flee?"

Even with his hands tied behind his back, the man managed a shrug. "I do not know, Your Grace. Away… Where Bourgogne could not find them."

"Traitor." Henry looked around and pointed to a burly, bristling man-at-arms armed with a heavy war axe. "You. How many blows will you need to take his head off?"

Chaumont was struggling to climb to his feet, but the guardsmen grabbed him again and held the thrashing man in place. After a moment, he slumped, head hanging down, hair covering his face.

The guardsman was staring at his king, open-mouthed. "I don't rightly know, Your Grace. I never tried."

"Make a good job of it and you shall be my headsman when we're on campaign."

The guardsman hefted his axe and walked warily to stand beside Chaumont, eyeing him much as though he were a log to be chopped. The two guardsmen forced Chaumont forward so his shoulders touched the ground. He made a single sound that James thought might have been a moan or perhaps a prayer. The man-at-arms raised his weapon high over his head and brought it down with all his might. Blood sprayed across the cobblestones and seeped into the cracks.

"I'm sorry, sire." Chaumont's head lolled, still attached by skin and gristle, his eyes wide and blank.

"Again."

He raised the axe high once more, and when he brought it down, the head rolled free.

"Not ill-done for your first time," Henry said. "James…" He motioned James over with a friendly gesture and put an arm around his shoulder. "I shall follow the prisoners to Paris. It is opening its gates to me. I have already received word. But after we celebrate Christmas there, we are for England and you by our side to crown my queen. But for the nonce, you'll go to Rouen. Some of the prisoners will be sent there, and you are to be in charge of the arrangements of their ransoms."

James wasn't sure why his stomach felt like it was twisting its way up his chest, standing next to the crimson puddle. He had seen blood enough before. He cleared his throat and said, "Wha' of the Scots, Your Grace? Have nae seen them. Will they be sent to Rouen as well?"

"They are outside the walls awaiting you. But they will not go to Rouen, I fear." He patted James on the shoulder and turned to Duke Philip. "We shall find those who escaped. Of that you may be sure."

James stared at Henry's back, feeling as though every bit of blood had drained from his face.

Sir John strolled to join him, smiling. "The guardsmen are bringing our horses, Lord James. It will not take long for our men to pack the tents and gear, so we can leave at first light."

James nodded dully. He looked once more toward Henry, considering with horror why the English king had him sign that proclamation. James had never considered that Henry might use it himself.

Beyond the square, the streets were narrow and crooked, and the red-roofed houses blocked off much of the sun. But they were of solid gray stone and might have been pleasant had they not been so silent. Nothing moved. The towns-people were in hiding. Even the rats were gone, eaten no doubt. No pigeons fluttered. Eaten as well, he supposed. The silence was eerie and made his skin crawl, but better to think about that than what awaited beyond the gate.

The walls of Melun were so thick that it was like riding once more into the depths of one of the mines before emerging again into the watery autumn light. The sky churned with dark clouds. The earth was icy muck. A horse snorted behind him from amidst his guards. A flock of ravens, blue-black wings shining, flapped overhead, gruffly laughing. His horse's hooves kicked up clods of mud from the broken ground.

He rode, keeping his back straight as he stared. Two long gibbets of raw wood stood, and two rows of bodies dangled there. Twenty bodies. He counted them one by one. Koww-koww-koww echoed back and forth as ravens ripped at their flesh and hopped from corpse to corpse, quarreling over their dinner.

James turned his horse's head and nudged it closer to the first body. A crow screeched and flapped away. The man twisted on his rope, mouth agape, purple tongue protruding. His red hair lifted in the wind.

Sweat broke out on James's forehead and dribbled down his face. The crow had eaten out the man's eyes, leaving gaping, red hollows. Black swarms of flies rose and sank like storm clouds. The air reeked of shit and piss.

His head swam from the smell, but James forced himself to ride to the next man, neck twisted by the tight rope and a livid scar up his bare chest.

A gaunt dog, ribs like ladders in its sides, crouched below the body, snarling. James rode to the next body and the one beyond that and the one beyond that, Scots all. Dead because they obeyed their own liege lord and ignored the command James had given. The wind caught the next, and the body turned slowly, as though protesting.

This was not my doing. I refuse to claim it. Scottish corpses, stripped of their armor and dignity after making an honorable surrender. Not my fault. This cannot be my fault.

With a lurch of his stomach, he knew the lie he told himself. He signed that proclamation, never thinking that Henry would use it so. He should have died before he signed it. To truly live, with honor, was to have something worth dying for. He should have died before he allowed them to force him to put his name to this deed. It was a stain that nothing would erase from his name or his soul. He had learned a harsh lesson—and others had paid the cost.

He had actually considered swearing fealty to Henry. He had thought perhaps it would save suffering. His stomach heaved, and his mouth filled with bile. He forced it back down with a swallow, though it burned like a heretic's fire. But the English would not see him spew. And they would not receive his fealty. Never. Let Henry think wha' he will. This was a lesson that would stay buried until he used it. And use it he would.

CHAPTER 32

"Iain," James called. "We both need practice."

His squire was wiry and fast, too light to be a great swordsman, but James never forgot his duty to see that he had enough skill to stay alive when Iain followed him into battle. Not that they would see battle today, or any day soon, beneath Rouen's chill gray sky.

The city was long since repaired from the siege when Henry had taken it. Its spires rose high to pierce the clouds, its brick walls solid and slate roofs whole, protecting from the Christmas cold people who now served the English. Rouen was little more than a way station for Henry's war. James had but little to do in Rouen, though it had women and wine enough when the lonely winter sent him out to seek company. He was tossing aside a blade that didn't match his requirements, the blunted practice sword rusted and notched, when Iain came in and tugged on his arm. James raised his eyebrows at being handled.

"Your Grace, come look. Sir John is riding in with riders under a flag of truce. And they fly the Douglas banner." A banner one couldn't miss with its large red heart for the

Douglas ancestor who had carried the heart of Robert the Bruce on crusade.

"Which Douglas?" James strode out into the wintery light.

William Douglas of Drumlanrig swung from his bay and hurried to drop on a knee before James.

"Your Grace."

Sir John dismounted. "He bears a safe conduct from the king and news for you, he says."

"Sir William." James gripped the man's arm as he rose, gladder than he could begin to say at a friendly Scottish face besides that of his own folk.

The Douglas gave James a somber look. "I have much news, Your Grace. But nae news I would give you here."

"We'll go in out of the cold. I have comfortable enough rooms." He nodded to Sir John. "Iain, see that we have wine and food for my guest."

Flecks of snow swirled on the wind as they walked together through the narrow street. A dark-haired whore in a wisp of a nightdress pushed open the shutters and called down that she could service the both of them. James shook his head at her and said, "Not today." They went into the narrow brick house and up a winding stair to the rooms James shared with his household. Sir John and his guards took the level below. Since his chaplain and secretary were away on their own errands, they had the place to themselves.

James sat, propping his elbows on his knees, and gave Douglas a serious look as he waved him to a chair. "It must be serious news to go to Henry."

"First—" Douglas took a seat and let out a long breath. "Albany is dead."

James felt as though he had had a great fall and the air knocked completely out of him. For a moment, he couldn't breathe, and then he sucked in a great breath. "Dead." He stared blankly into the distance. "I spent my whole life knowing he wanted me dead. And he is the one who is gone. Strange to have an enemy who shaped my whole life—dead."

"He was ancient. Though strong of body and mind, even in his age. Not that I ever understood his mind. He was regent, yet used his power little, except to increase his own lands and keep you in chains."

James laughed. "You exaggerate, my lord. I, at least, have never been in chains. But I ken your meaning. He did everything to see I wasn't ransomed. But now?" James got up and strode to the door, calling for Iain and wine, and Douglas rose. "How stands Scotland? Who rules as regent?"

"Murdoch."

James turned, his mouth opened to protest, and burst out, "Who agreed to such a thing? That wine pot? Regent? That idle weathercock? Did Orkney agree to it? He could not."

Iain stood in the doorway, a wine flagon in one hand and a cloth-covered tray in the other, staring at his feet as he tried to look as though he was not listening.

"No. Orkney… Your Grace, the Earl of Orkney is dead also."

James stood silent as the words washed over him. Orkney. Orkney who had been as near to a father as he ever truly had. He brought Orkney's face to mind as he had knelt that day in the Tower yard and had given his oath.

"It was a catarrh that went to his lungs. They say he went quickly. His son William inherited the title, but he is young. You cannot yet depend on his support."

James nodded numbly. "But the lad is safe? In his own lands and protected?"

"Aye. Even Murdoch is not fool enough to try to reach past their galleys. And it would be more effort that he would put forth." He paused, looking thoughtful. "Though I might not say the same of his brother, John. He is fat as a hog but not idle, as is Murdoch."

James sank down into his chair, mind flying from one thought to another. "Without the old man to oppose it, Murdoch might be pressured to allow my ransom. The problem is as much convincing King Henry of it."

"Last year, he agreed to giving you parole in return for hostages, so mayhap he is nae so hostile to the idea."

Snorting a laugh through his nose, James shook his head. "Only my parole, not a true release. It would have been madness to agree in exchange for so many hostages of the highest degree." James realized Iain was straightening the table where he had laid out the wine and a platter of soft white cheese, bread and dried sausage that gave off a spicy scent. "I'll call you if we have need of aught, Iain."

"The earl had another concern to bring up with you." Douglas went over to pour two cups of wine and turned, frowning at James. "We were bothered over this proclamation of treason. You truly signed such a thing?"

"I thought I had little choice at the time." James scrubbed his hand over his face with a hollow feeling in his chest. "You know that he executed the Scots at Melun? The proclamation was his excuse. One I am shamed that I gave him. It was under duress, but I sore regret it." He snorted what he meant to be a laugh, though he was sure it hadn't sounded like one. "The earl surely does not intend to obey it."

"No, certes not. Nor does Buchan with his thousands of men." He handed James a cup of wine and sat down to take a drink.

"What Henry was willing to do, I cannot say. I should have forced his hand to see. Never have I regretted an action more." James swirled the wine in his cup as he thought of exactly how much dire force Henry of Monmouth would use to achieve an end. "I'll ask you to carry a letter to Archie Tyneman for me. The earl needs to know how things are with me. But— How badly do things stand? At home?"

"His father could not control Murdoch's sons, and he, even less. They pillage at will. He enforces no laws. Taxes go uncollected, felons unpunished. They're grabbing everything they can. Governance of the realm in a' respects has ceased, for to enforce the law might cause ill feeling toward him. If anyone rules, it is the Earl of Mar, but he cares for nothing but his own lands. Murdoch won't raise a hand to keep the law or the peace, even less than the old man." Douglas shook his head. "Things are ill and worsening."

James tilted his wine cup to his mouth and drained it. He bounced it in his hand, thinking of throwing it, but instead slammed it down on the table so hard that the table shook. "You know wha' this is— Bringing me with his army— Arming me— Allowing me to fecht for him…"

"More than that curst proclamation, you mean?"

"He thinks he can convince me to swear fealty." James jumped to his feet and made a furious turn around the room. "He wants me to see wha' he will do to Scotland once he finishes with France, unless I bend a knee to him. More times than I could count he has sworn I'll not go free until I do."

"You truly think that's wha' he intends? But how can he think we would agree? Any more than we had Toom Tabard back when the English tried to force him upon us."

"I have no doubt of his intent, my lord. And if he can force France to accept himself, as he has, he is sure he can force Scotland to accept me as his vassal. I need advice from you and from the earls. We have some time. This defeating the Dauphin will not be fast, but we must have a plan for when it happens." He propped his hands on the window's surround and looked out at snow that had begun to fall, swirling in eddies in a darkening day. "We must save Scotland from Henry of Monmouth, but how?"

"Murdoch will not raise a hand to free me. He combines

the worst of idleness and greed. Archie Tyneman knows that you must be freed, though he has yet to convince Buchan of that. It is Wigtoun he left to work for your freedom whilst they aid the Dauphin. But we must free you. Somehow."

Douglas had no more of an answer than he did. James gave a heavy sigh. "I'll ready a letter for you. This war of Henry's is costly. More than I ever imagined. Mayhap we can tempt him with a large enough ransom."

CHAPTER 33

The crowds were cheering outside Westminster Abbey. James could hear them even within its great walls. The rabble loved Henry so much they were even willing to love a Frenchwoman for his sake. She belonged to their strong young king: the conqueror of their ancient foe. They weren't worried anent what the conquest had cost them or how much more it would cost to complete it.

James wiped a drop of sweat from the back of his neck. In spite of the frigid February, the abbey, now filled with hundreds of nobles, was stifling. He licked his dry lips, wishing he'd broken his fast and drunk wine or even some ale before they started their long trek. The streets of London, were draped in long pennons of velvet and silk and crowded with screaming onlookers.

The soon-to-be queen-consort looked beautiful in her magnificent gown, white velvet with lions and fleurs-de-lis formed from pearls and rubies. An ermine and red velvet cloak stretched out twenty feet behind her, the end carried by three ladies in waiting. James caught his breath when he recognized Joan de Beaufort. When they reached the front, between the other ladies in waiting, Joan glided to stand at the side of the nave, an enigmatic smile on her lips.

The king looked as severe as his queen looked lovely. He wore a doublet of dark brown velvet, the sleeves slashed with crimson, and the heavy gold chain of the Order of the Garter draped about his shoulders. The crown was a heavy weight on his erect and proud head, and he stood to the side as the archbishop droned a prayer.

A choir was intoning hymns, and the Archbishop of Canterbury in his high gold miter had Catherine recite the traditional oath as he solemnly celebrated the High Mass aided by Bishop Beaufort and a Papal legate, and she knelt when he offered her the Holy Eucharist.

James leaned forward to see past Henry Percy. The archbishop placed the heavy crown onto the queen's golden curls. A hot flash of anger went through James. This girl was offered what he was denied—wrongly denied. He tamped it down hard. He had better things to think of just now.

King Henry stepped to stand beside his queen. "I present you my wife, Catherine, Queen of England," he said in a resounding voice.

When Catherine curtsied to him, almost to the ground, he lifted her hand to kiss, and light shining through the stained glass cast jeweled patterns around them, rebounded off gleaming brass and lit motes of dust that swayed in the air like heaven's own angels.

Thanks be to the Blessed Virgin. Now let us go to the feast, and I shall somehow seek Lady Joan out. The feast was to be huge. The king had made the strange pronouncement that James would be seated next to the queen, but that would not prevent him from escaping for the hunt. His prey was too sweet to miss such a chance, though he feared the prey was he, and he was already captured.

The king's brothers, Thomas of Clarence and John of

Bedford, led the procession from the Abbey in shining armor and scarlet cloaks. Then came the king and queen, her long cloak still carried by her ladies-in-waiting, followed by Humphrey Stafford, the Lord High Constable of England, the Duke of Exeter, and then the numerous Beaufort uncles and cousins.

As James reached the high arched doors of the abbey, the noise of cheering was thunderous. He stepped out into the icy February air, and Henry Percy said, "I thought it would never end."

"Impressive, I suppose," James replied, rubbing his growling stomach. "The main lack was food and drink. It has been a deal of time since last night's supper."

Percy grinned. "You always did like a good meal, James."

As they made the long, slow trek to Windsor Castle, they rode through narrow streets lined with commons shouting Catherine's name. She brought their king home, so she was their darling. Percy said something to him, but the words were lost in the tumult. When James shouted to ask what he'd said, Percy gave a helpless shrug, so they passed the rest of the trip in silence whilst their ears rang with the uproar.

When the long train clattered into the bailey yard of the castle, James jumped from the saddle and tossed his reins to one of the dozens of stable boys scrambling to lead away the horses. He heard Catherine laughing as King Henry swept her from her saddle, and a wave of jealousy crept through him. He did not want the queen, but Henry had everything that he did not. So, he must make do—for now—with what he could reach for himself. He looked around, but he didn't see Lady Joan in the crowd, so scowling, he went to join the crush making their way through the doors into the great hall.

Pages in royal livery were delivering guests to their places at the long tables as the heralds called out their names and ranks. One solemnly escorted James to his place on the dais next to the seats of honor. There were some wondering looks, but he received courteous bows and friendly enough smiles from the lords he had fought with in France.

"It is pleasant to be out of our armor for a while," Richard Beauchamp said when he stopped on his way to his place, though his black doublet and hose might still have been armor, they were so severe. "I believe our cavalcade leaves for Nottingham tomorrow, and even that will be better than sitting in the mud in a siege." Lord Richard gave a gruff smile. "Though they were your first sieges, so mayhap you didn't mind."

"I grew tired enough of armor, my lord," James said, "but I —I should say that I learned a great deal. More than I ever thought possible."

"War is like that, even sieges." The knight nodded sagely. "Now excuse me, it is time that I was in my place."

Above in the gallery, musicians with harps and lutes and trumpets and sacbuts and flutes and drums were already playing. But they ceased when the heralds announced the king and queen. Catherine had, sensibly, changed from her coronation robes into a gown of blue samite cut low to reveal the tops of her breasts and a pointed headdress with wispy veils that flowed down her back. James smiled at the English putting their heads together to whisper over the new styles of her French attire.

Trumpets blared whilst the pair strolled to the seats of honor, smiling and greeting their guests as they went. When they reached their places, Catherine gave James her hands to kiss as he bowed low over them and then kissed him on each cheek. The king was greeting his brothers, only two of them, since Thomas of Clarence was still in France leading the English army. The king's brothers pounded James on the back, and even Bishop Beaumont's smile was less oily than usual. Philip of Bourgogne greeted him the French way with a kiss on each cheek. James spotted Charles d'Orleans at a far end of the table, being ignored and looking down his nose at the Burgundian. James nodded to his old friend from the Tower, and Charles gave him a wry smile. No doubt the planning was to keep those two enemies well away from each other.

The Archbishop of Canterbury made the usual prayers, and the king toasted his new queen. Once they had all drunk and cheered, the feast truly began. James sipped at his wine, more interested in finding Joan amongst the crowd. And there was Joan, sitting at the far end of the table on the right. She leaned forward to speak to a nobleman James did not recognize. Her beauty had only increased in the year that James had been in France, as had her delight in the merriment around her. James watched as she laughed at some quip that the man made. She gave her same enigmatic smile when he offered her a drink from his cup, and a flame of jealousy coiled through James.

More courses were served, and James ate them but couldn't have said what they were. Then Joan turned and looked at him, her gaze level. She cocked her head like a beautiful little bird examining who knew what? But her eyes were on him, and her smile was the same: small and mysterious.

Dishes and entertainments came in a dizzying profusion. Masked mummers tumbled and danced in circles. The king's jester chased a squealing piglet around the room, beating it with an air-filled bladder and calling it the Dauphin Charles. The dozens of musicians in the gallery played familiar airs. But none of it held James like Joan's smile. She would look away, but then her eyes would turn to him again. He couldn't help his wide smile when her companion at the table had to speak to her before she took a sliver of swan from his knife.

A new line to the poem he had written to her so long ago came into his mind, full blown:

BUT A' the world to witness this we call,
  That strewn it has so plainly over all
  With new, fresh, sweet, and tender green,
  Our life, our desire, our ruler and queen.

AT LAST, the king commanded the lower tables removed for dancing. Shouts of delight went up, and servants scurried, carrying the trestle tables away as the guests gathered in clumps along the walls, chattering and laughing. With nods and smiles, James eased himself through the crowd, Joan's golden head visible even in the press. The musicians in the gallery struck up a lively air, and King Henry took the queen in his arms, whirling her until she threw back her head, laughing, and cried that she was dizzy.

But James had reached Joan. She blushed when he took her hand and bent over it, but he turned it and kissed the inside of her wrist.

"My lord," she said so softly he could barely hear her over the din.

He straightened but kept her hand as he looked around. "Can you escape, my lady?" He nodded toward a side door behind the dais. "Would you escape? For a moment?"

She checked her sleeve and gave him a wide-eyed look. "My chamber is in that direction on the floor above, and I fear I forgot my handkerchief should I embarrass myself with a sneeze." Her mouth curved in a smile that made his heart stutter. She curtsied low and then started for the door but stopped long enough to whisper a word to her mother.

James turned to a lanky knight and said that the queen

219

looked very fine, and the king seemed fond. The man grunted and replied that what mattered was that she provide an heir. James shrugged and agreed that was important for a queen. By that time, James felt it was safe to follow Joan, hoping no one remembered his chamber was in the Round Tower. He slid through the shuffling crowd as more merry-makers made their way to the floor to join the raucous rounds of dance.

He opened the narrow door and slipped into the torchlit passage. The noise from the great hall faded as he proceeded past closed doors interspersed with niches, where statues stood. Up he went on the winding stair and emerged to walk slowly through the hall. He heard only his own footfalls in the silence until he reached the next stairway and a soft whisper of "My Lord" came out of the murk. "You came."

He laughed a little, feeling drunk. "Certes, I came, my lady. I would follow you… anywhere."

She gave him one of her secretive smiles and said, "Why? You know me not at all."

He took her hand and kissed the palm. Then he told her the story of a lonely young prisoner in a high tower and the day he fell in love with a beautiful goddess who saved him from desiring death.

She breathed out, "Oh."

He was stroking her wrist and could feel the pulse pound. He leaned over and kissed her mouth, tasting honey and berries in her breath, feeling the tremble of her body. Her lips moved under his, a proclamation, a promise. She pulled back and smiled into his eyes. Then laughing, she turned and hurried up the steps and around the bend in the stairway. James smiled as he walked down the hall to the great hall, wondering what Henry would do if he found out that he was courting his cousin. Shaking his head, he decided he didn't care.

CHAPTER 34

MARCH 1421

The van of their cavalcade had dismounted and set up pavilions by the time James reached the clearing. The party stretched for a mile, a hundred knights, two hundred men-at-arms and mounted archers. That did not count the king's own party and the captured nobles with their households, who followed like a prize to be shown. Henry and his queen rode surrounded by men-at-arms with King Henry's brothers by his side. Behind them, Joan cast James occasional glances from her mother's side. At the rear of the cavalcade lumbered a dozen wagons piled with chests of clothing and bedding for their stays in the cities where the king intended to display his French queen.

James had been kept near the royal party throughout, along with Philip de Bourgogne. Well to the rear of them rode Charles d'Orléans. The glares of either of the Frenchmen when one caught sight of the other would have scorched the hide from a boar. The hundreds of riders were still dismounting when James walked toward his own modest tent.

A hand landed on his arm, and he turned as Charles

smiled. "Is it going well, old friend?" the duke asked. He was clad in a leather doublet for travel and a fur cloak, his face, as always, clean shaven, but there was a sprinkling of white amongst his dark hair that had not been there when James left for France. "Muscled and dark from the sun. From the look of you, you spend much time fighting and little with your poetry."

"I've spent little time with the pen; I confess it." James tilted his head toward the flap of his tent. "Come within so we can talk."

Iain had lit a brazier to take the chill from the air, and he turned to take their cloaks. He poured out a measure of wine to heat, stirring in a dollop of honey and a sprinkle of cinnamon.

James tilted his head and looked at his old crony from the Tower. "They are treating you well?"

Charles shrugged. "Well enough, since they will never free me as long as King Henry lives. It is boring, as you know well, but gives me time to write I would have never had, so not all a loss. Hearing what is happening in France, though, that is hard."

"Is that hypocras heated?" James asked.

"Yes, Your Grace." Iain served the steaming drink in their plain cups, and Charles pulled off his leather gloves to take one.

He sat on a camp stool. "You have been with your lord long. He is fortunate in his servants."

"It is my duty."

"Iain followed me faithfully into battle. I am indeed fortunate in those who serve me. They sacrifice much."

James took a deep swallow of his drink and felt the warmth as it spread from his belly. Traveling in the winter, even in soft England, was no pleasure. "You were speaking of the news from France. I wonder if you heard how ill it truly is?"

"I heard that Paris fell to him like a ripe peach, ripe for the eating."

"I'm afeart I thought a harsher term, but you're right. Melun was another case entirely. Sire de Barbazan used every wile he knew, many I had never heard of, to hold the city. If Dauphin Charles had relieved it—"

Charles shook his head. "The Dauphin was once as brave as any man I knew. His device of a mailed fist was one he earned. And now look at him: a craven who huddles in fear of his enemies!" Charles drew his mouth into a thin line. "And Henry… Is he a ravening dog to throw into a cage a brave and honored knight such as Sire de Barbazan?"

"That was the least of it, Charles."

"And yet you fight for him."

"With him. There are worse men in the world from whom to learn warfare, my friend, and if I one day must fight against him, you may be sure I'll use the lessons he taught me. Some of his lessons, I swear, if I have the chance to cause it, he will rue. He is a harsh tutor, I tell you. It is a strange thing to fight beside a man and hope that he fails."

"If there is any comfort to be had, it is that Orleans will not fall like a peach into his hands, however craven the Dauphin has become." Philip put his wine cup down. "You saw his father, the king. Mayhap we should not be surprised that his son cannot hold the realm. And to be called a bastard by his own father!"

"Is it true? The stories that some tell of Queen Isabeau did not seem to match the woman I met."

"Lies by people who hate her. She rules in the king's stead. Or did, which angered many. Though her decisions have made me hate her as well. She turned against her own son and the rightful heir." Charles ground his teeth. "If I were there, it would not be so."

"The Earl of Buchan is there, and the Earl of Wigtoun. They are not men who will take defeat lightly or be easy to defeat. Though many Scots died at Agincourt, and Henry hanged everyone who surrendered at Melun." James snorted. "If he thought that would change their minds about standing with the Dauphin, he does not know my people. We can be a thrawn people, and threats only make us more so. It only made sure that they stayed."

"I hope you're right."

"Aye. As do I." James twitched a smile. There was a time not so very long ago when he would not have understood much of what he had learned. Now he almost wished that he didn't. Innocence seemed sweet. "Moreover, he is in need of money and men. Keeping an army so long in the field is expensive, it seems. And even when you win, you lose men. The bloody flux may have cost him as many as the siege, and the siege cost enough. We left hundreds, perhaps thousands in graves—which is the reason for this mummers' show."

"True," his old comrade in imprisonment said. "I have no doubt that he needs both men and gold. But the English love him. I think he will be given what he needs."

James grunted. He couldn't argue that Charles was wrong.

"And his queen. They will love her as long as she gives him a son."

James twirled the dregs of his drink in the cup. "This lingering to raise money and men puts him in her bed, so at last there is a chance he will give her that son. Whilst in France, he barely went near her. Whether that bodes good or ill for the two of us, I do not ken."

James talked with his old crony for an hour before the Duc d'Orleans took his leave. When he was gone, James donned his heavy fur cloak and went to walk in the dark and breathe in the sweet scent of pines.

He loved being away from castles. They made him think of being locked up, unable to win free. They would never be dear. Few things were as fine as breathing the open air, but the men looked much less happy. They huddled around cook fires, grumbling about the cold. A man-at-arms trudged a path around the picket line, his hands tucked under his arms. The nobles were in their tents with braziers burning, and if they weren't warm, they were at least less miserable. In the trees, an owl hooted, and the gusting wind made the branches creak and whisper.

When James circled back to his own tent, he found Sir John Water talking to a guard.

"I cannot rest," James told him. He picked up his shield that was propped against his tent. "Come work out your sword wi' me."

"We've never faced each other," Sir John said with a wary look, but he slid his arm through the loops of his own shield and followed when James turned. A sentry challenged James as they walked from the camp. Sir John gave him a gruff reprimand. They walked along the rutted road until they found a level spot.

"You're good with a blade," Sir John said as he drew his sword, "but I have years in the business of fighting behind me."

James used his sword to salute, and Sir John moved in to attack, swinging for James's belly. James caught the stroke on his shield and answered with a counter-stroke that Sir John caught. James broke off with a step back. They were still feeling each other out, and he smiled. He took the lead this time with a downward strike. Sir John met it and they traded blows, steel ringing on steel. Each blow was blocked and slid into a new attack, swords slashing from side to side, flickering in the moonlight. Then in a move so fast, James did not see it coming, Sir John thrust his sword through James's defense. James jumped back as the point of the blade bit into his arm.

"Yield?" Sir John taunted.

"Hell mend you," James growled as he came in with a sweeping side cut. Sir John smacked it away and made a vicious downward blow. James deflected it with his shield. Sir John followed up fast, sliding his blade down James's until their hilts locked. James was the first to move, and the knight tried to slam his face with his hilt. James backpedaled, drawing the knight toward him. For a second, he was open, and James slammed with his shield into his forehead. The knight's face went slack as he fell.

Sir John was on his back. In the moonlight, his eyes looked dazed, blank. James put his sword at the man's throat and pricked it. A drop of blood welled up black in the faint light. Sir John blinked and his eyes widened. James could press home here on the road with only his guard dog, who would be dead. He stared down, his heart thundering like a horse at the gallop. He watched the drop of blood run down Sir John's neck, and then he stepped back.

He snorted a breath. No horse. No coin. And a man dead who only did his duty. He offered Sir John his hand, and the man took it to be jerked to his feet.

"I thought I was a dead man." Sir John rubbed his throat and looked at his fingers smeared with blood.

James cuffed him on the shoulder, his arm stinging where it had been nicked. "Not today."

The next day of their journey chilled James through. The wind swirled dead leaves around the legs of their horses and creaked the branches in the trees. Even in his heavy fur cloak, James could feel the icy northern kiss. Joan hunched on her horse, next to her dignified mother, whose golden hair was streaked with silver, and James thought he saw how she would look someday as a matron.

He spurred to trot up beside her. "This is cold too much for you, my lady," he said. He unfastened his cloak. "Let me put this about you."

Joan smiled at him as she shivered. "My lord, thank you. I should have brought a heavier cloak for riding, but I am not such a frail thing that I cannot live through a cold north wind."

As her mother turned her gaze on them, mouth thinning, James swung off his cloak to wrap around her and smiled when color flushed her cheeks.

CHAPTER 35

MARCH 1421

"How long is Henry going to drag us about the kingdom, I wonder?" James said. Already it had been more than a month of constantly moving from Bristol to Leicester to Coventry, and yesterday it had been late afternoon when they had sighted Middleham Castle rising over huge oaks bright green with the first leaves of spring and hills awash with bluebells.

With the castle so crowded, the outer bailey had been given over to guards and some of the guests to raise tents and pavilions. In his tent near the entry to the keep, James fastened the brooch that held his cloak, a brass lion rampant that would almost pass for gold. Iain straightened the wrinkles it had from being folded in a chest and nodded that he was done.

Lyon snorted and looked up from the table, where he was writing a letter for James asking Perth to send funds. "Until he's wrung every pence from every lord that he can."

Only part of the time had the queen and her ladies-in-waiting journeyed with them. The king had sent them on side trips to Hertford and Bedford. But for much of the past month the queen, with Joan at her side, had ridden with the king. The very thought of the nights Joan had slipped her hand into his for the dance made his heart beat fast. That she slipped her hand into his so readily, looked around for him after the feasts and that color rushed to her face when their eyes met, that made him hope for more than he ever had before in his miserable life.

A page appeared at the door saying that the feast would begin soon, and James sighed. Even freer than he had once been, though Sir John was never far and gave him looks as wary as a snarling dog, James had not learned to love castles. But he followed the lad up the steps to the towering slate-roofed keep. Outside its massive door, guards in the red livery of the king stood with halberds in hand, but the doors were flung open, and the usual crush of nobles and royals were streaming through. The floor was strewn with fresh rushes mixed with lavender that gave up its sent when they trod on it. Long trestle tables draped in white filled the room. A fire crackled on the hearth. Everyone seemed merry. The winter winds had eased, and they had shed heavy furs and smothering cloaks for colorful silks. Henry Percy had joined them, since it was near enough that he could leave his duties holding the north border. He grinned at James across the vaulted hall. Humphrey of Gloucester guffawed at some jape by Jack of Suffolk. Joan was bright-eyed as she smiled faintly and listened to her elegant mother, who seemed to be lecturing her. The queen and king swept in with only a blare of trumpets, the queen plump and blooming.

James was seated, as he often was, by the queen, but Joan had never before taken a place on his right. He saw her mouth twitch as he took her hands and kissed her on each cheek. She used a scent of rosewater that well became her. James was glad, as always, that Bishop Beaufort was not long-winded in his blessings. The king's fool soon somersaulted into the hall. The servants carried out a huge platter with a quarter of stag cooked with parsley and vinegar and giving off a strong scent of ginger.

As James offered Joan his wine cup, she murmured, "My lord, have you ever desired just a bit of cheese in a quiet corner?"

"I have been too much alone to desire that." He covered her fingers with his hand when he took back his wine cup. "But I often desire someone to share one wi' me, and then it might be a pleasant thing."

"Secret corners are hard to find in a castle so crowded." She gave him one of her puzzling smiles, her lips closed, but sweetly curved. Then she lowered her eyes. "Though I know a secret that is not a place."

He raised his eyebrows as she toyed with the dove pie in front of her and whispered, "The queen is with child."

"Och, so an heir..." James thought that over. An heir to the throne was important news.

Her laugh was low and throaty. "It is not a thing one can keep secret long."

"The king will be pleased." But he was weary with thinking of Henry of Monmouth, so he lowered his voice and leaned close as he offered her a sliver of meat from his knife. "There is a garden lined wi' willows that I walked through today. The ground is deep with bluebells. In the evening, it would remind me of a garden at Windsor. If I could, I would walk with a lady I saw there."

"Lord James, that lady would walk with you." When she smiled and her lips parted, his heart did something queer in his chest, as though it stopped and restarted. "If you asked her."

A shout at the door turned both of their heads. A courier brushed by the heralds. The hall fell silent as he hurried to throw himself on his knees. On the breast of his soiled surcoat was the lion device with a label of three points that belonged to Thomas, Duke of Clarence.

"He is dead, Your Grace," the courier said in a voice that dragged with exhaustion. "Duke Thomas fell in battle to the Scots."

King Henry froze for a moment, his mouth open and the color slowly receding like a tide. "My brother..." he said and shook his head, as though stunned by a blow. "Where? What of his army?"

"Near Vieil-Baugé, Your Grace. There was great slaughter, but the Earl of Salisbury saved some few."

"How could such a thing happen?" the Earl of Suffolk wailed. "His Grace left ample men to hold Normandy. The duke was to lead a chevauchée. All the reports said it was progressing well, burning and destroying in Anjou and Maine."

It would have been worse if he had left you in command, James thought. He took a drink of his wine to hide a twitch of his lips. It would slow the English advance, but Henry would not be in a mood to show any mercy, if he ever was. How this would help the Scots or himself would take some thought to untwist. Only when he heard a soft moan from Joan did he remember that Thomas of Lancaster was her stepfather. He wanted to shake his head at himself for not thinking, but he took her hand and pressed the back to his lips.

"My mother..." she said. She released his hand and hurried to kneel at the side of her sobbing mother.

"The Scots, along with some of the French troops, blocked his progress. They agreed to a truce for Easter, but Duke Thomas attacked before it began."

The king rose. "This is no matter to discuss at table." He glanced at his cousin with her mother's head on her shoulder. "Take your mother to her chamber and see to her, my lady. I shall see all my commanders in the privy chamber. And you will give us all that you know anent this monstrous act by our enemies."

James watched as Joan walked away, her arm around her mother's waist, although by this time her mother had regained her control, pressing her hand to her mouth. He wasn't sure that he would be welcome, but he could at least offer to do anything he might. So, he had started to follow when a page tugged on his sleeve. "My lord, the king sent me to bring you."

James puffed out his cheeks, blew a long breath and followed the lad. When the page closed the door behind James, King Henry was sitting silent with his wine untouched before him, his face stony and unmoving. The only noise in the room was the crack of a log splintering in the fire on the hearth and John of Bedford tapping his fingers on the table. When James took his place, Henry nodded to his brother to proceed.

"You said the Scots had blocked the way?" Bedford prompted.

The courier shifted from one foot to the other and nervously licked his lips. "Mayhap his lordship didn't realize how big their army was." He shrugged, looking at his feet. "The archers were scattered and the army in no order, but he commanded an attack. John Holland and Gilbert de Umfraville advised that he wait, but he sent the Earl of Salisbury to round up all the archers and bring them after him. The... The duke..."

The king leaned forward on his elbows, his face grim and dour. "Proceed."

"I'm not sure how many men he had. Less than half of our army and near no archers. But he charged the bridge, where they held the way to their main force. The Scots were rallying on the other side. If he could have reached them before they formed…" He was blinking nervously, obviously too fearful to look at any of the royalty around him. "He tried to cross. There were a hundred Scottish archers cutting our men down, and half a hundred knights and men-at-arms held the bridge.

"But he fought his way across, Your Grace. No one would say he didn't fight. Then we faced the main body of the Scottish army. They were dismounted, and their archers had the height of a hill. He was still mounted, and one of the Douglas men met him with his lance and unhorsed him. Then… there was no reaching him, Your Grace. They swarmed him. One held his helm aloft on a pike and it became a rout. The army was cut down as they fled. De Umfraville was killed. John Holland captured. Edward Beaumont as well, and the Earl of Somerset. Captured. It… it was a disaster."

Henry flicked a glance at James but didn't speak to him. He just nodded to the courier. "What of Salisbury? The archers?"

"He reached the battle too late to do aught except cover the army's retreat and retrieve your brother's body, sire."

"God's blood!" Humphrey of Gloucester said.

"Salisbury said to give Your Grace his oath that he would have revenge and would burn all of Baugé."

"Damn him." John of Bedford sounded more angry than grieved. "Was Thomas drunk, do you suppose?"

King Henry formed his hands into a steeple beneath his chin. Under his golden coronet, his face was so wooden it might have been that of a statue, but James could see his eyelids twitch as he listened.

"How could this happen?" Young Suffolk moaned again. "The king's brother dead. Our army shattered!"

John of Bedford glared at him. "We know how it happened, Jack of Naples." Suffolk slammed his cup down on the table at the hated sobriquet but subsided when Bedford glowered back at him. "My brother was a fool, a kindly fool but a fool, and was probably drunk at the time. That does not matter now. So, I will thank you to shut up."

"It might be a good time for a truce," Beauchamp said. "We could offer a trade of prisoners as they took so many. We could trade Sire de Barbazan for Beaumont, John Holland, and the others."

King Henry rose to his feet. "They killed my brother," he said in a low, cold voice. "Prepare to depart at daybreak in two days. We are for London and then for France."

James shouted for Dougal and Iain as he hurried into the tent. "Dougal, write a letter for me to the Earl of Douglas." He jerked off his cloak and flung it onto his bed. Iain had awaited his return and watched his king pace, picking up the cloak to fold it. "You and Iain will leave at first light for Scotland to carry it. And one to Bishop Wardlaw as well."

Dougal sat down at the table and pulled a parchment in front of him. "What should the letter say, Your Grace?"

James took another turn around the crowded tent, kicked a stool out of his way, and stopped, arms crossed. "That the Earl of Buchan had a great victory at Baugé. That it changes the possibility of my ransom, which I would discuss with him, and that it cannot be said in a letter. Pray that the earl use your safe conduct to join me in London at his best speed before I leave once more for France."

Lyon was hopping to take off a boot without sitting down, which he couldn't whilst James stood. James growled at him, "Oh, sit down, man."

When Lyon dropped onto a stool and levered off his boot, he said, "You think he will come? He hasn't been eager to return to England since years ago when he was a captive."

"Aye, I do. He has been speaking kindly of helping me and has reason and more for anger at Albany. Forbye, Albany's brother of Buchan winning at Baugé could tilt the power, could weaken the Douglas. A' the more reason to help me."

The scratching of Dougal's pen paused for a moment as he said, "But Douglas's son, Wigtoun, was at Baugé at well."

James laughed. "It wouldn't be the first time Archibald Tyneman was on both sides of a battle."

CHAPTER 36

MAY 1421

The fact was, James was hungry, and his knees ached after a night of fasting and praying. He was glad that the whole ceremony would soon be over, but being knighted by Henry of Monmouth was a mixed blessing. Whilst it said to many he was a true and valuable knight, it came alarmingly close to making him seem Henry's vassal. James shifted on his knees and glanced out of the corner of his eye. George de Neville knelt beside him, and beyond in the chapel, a dozen men awaited dubbing.

When the doors were thrown open, a flourish of trumpets blared, and a herald intoned their names as they filed out of the chapel and through the long halls to the throne room.

Before them was the gilded throne with scarlet cushions, where sat King Henry, crowned and a sword across his knees. James walked to stand before a kneeler, the first in a line that stretched across the vast chamber. A hundred nobles at least filled the room, watching intently, for many of their sons and cousins were being knighted for battle. But Joan was still making a slower progress to London with the queen. James wished she were here to see, and he felt his face heat.

Light flooded in from the high windows, and motes swayed in the sunbeams, seeming to celebrate the day. He knelt and found his mouth dry as sand. He worked moisture into it and swallowed the stone that lodged in his throat.

The trumpets flourished, and Henry rose and strode to James. Bracing himself, James waited. The bruising clout on his shoulder rocked James. Henry lifted the blade and slammed the flat into his other shoulder. "Avance, Chevalier au nom de Dieu," he pronounced. James rose, and the movement sent hot twinges through both shoulders. He held a laugh behind his lips. He would have purple bruises tomorrow, but his knighthood was worth it. A squire handed Henry a pair of golden spurs that the king thrust into James's hands and turned go to where George de Neville knelt.

There should have been a great feast after the dubbing, but Henry had forbidden it. There was too much to be done, he had said. Messengers had been sent across the kingdom, and thousands of troops were gathering for Henry's push to punish the army that dared to kill his brother and take lands he had won with force of arms. He had no time to spare for frivolity. James clutched the spurs and waited for the dubbing to be completed, which Henry went about briskly, moving from one new knight to the next.

He was still mulling over why Henry had decided to include him in the honor. Though it was nearer to vassalage than he liked, it did not include the essential oath that he would have refused. All too often, the English king was a step ahead in his thinking. There was no doubt in his mind, however, whom his knighthood was meant to serve. Another flourish awoke James from his musing, and the ceremony was over.

Henry beamed as he handed the Master of Arms his

sword and came to grip James by the shoulder. "I have word that the Earl of Douglas is in the city."

"You are better informed than I, sire. I had nae been told."

Henry gave him a push toward the doorway. "I'd a word with you, Sir James. Since the earl is here, I have a bargain for the two of you to think on."

He urged James along to his privy chamber and a guard closed the door behind them. Henry removed his crown. "It weighs on me," he said as he laid it aside.

James noticed for the first time as the king took his chair that Henry had a little gray mixed in with his brown hair above where it was shorn on the sides.

"Albany... I hoped to deal with him." Henry shook his head. "That is not to be. He lets Buchan do whatever he pleases in France, whilst his own sons and grandsons rampage about your kingdom. What a family. Not a coward like Albany, though, sending his brother to do his dirty work. But the Douglas, Tyneman, you Scots call him, is another matter. I think he may be brought to our side, convinced, if not to aid us in France, at least not to oppose us."

James raised an eyebrow. "Our side?"

"If not identical, we have interests in common. Mine, to defeat the false Dauphin and the Scots who aid him, Scots who side with your enemy. Yours, to return to Scotland to be crowned and draw the fangs of Albany." Henry took his place at the head of the polished oak table.

James shook his head. "How does one help the other?"

"I know that you have exchanged letters with the Douglas about supporting you against Albany. He might help with arranging hostages to exchange for you." Henry waved a hand for James to sit. "Merely a parole for a year, as we proposed before, but I believe that he will do so if I aid you in that."

James felt color flood his face. How had Henry learned

the content of private letters to the Earl of Douglas? He bit his lip and leaned back in his chair. But it was true that Douglas did seem inclined to come over to his side. "You would aid me? Why? And how?"

"To cease Scottish support for the Armagnacs. Douglas is the most powerful man in Scotland, more so than the so-called regent. With his men, you can safely return to Scotland, and I can make it so that he does back you."

James narrowed his eyes as he examined Henry's face. There was more to this offer than he could see on the surface, as always. There was a scratch at the door, and when Henry called out permission, a herald opened it to say that Archibald Douglas, Earl of Douglas, Lord of Annandale and Galloway was without.

The Douglases of that ilk had long been called the 'Black' for good reason. The earl's hair might once have been as black as night, though now it was threaded through with gray. His eyes were chips of obsidian, and his skin dark as old leather, tan and creased. He was still muscled beneath a softening of age. He bowed courteously to King Henry, but he looked James up and down. With a satisfied nod, he strode to him, grunting as he went heavily to one knee. He took James's hand and bowed over it. "Your Grace."

"My lord," James said. "It pleases me to meet you—at last."

The Earl of Douglas levered himself to his feet. "I have longed for this day, Your Grace."

James thought that he could have achieved it, had he longed for it so much, but this wasn't the time to mention that.

When Henry gave him permission to sit, the Douglas took a place as he inclined his head to James. "Hearing you were dubbed by the finest knight in a' Christendom, sire, was braw news."

"And acknowledging that I am the finest fighter should

239

mean you know how fruitless it is to keep sending armies to fight me in France," Henry snapped. "Nor, I think, can Scotland afford to have me as an enemy."

Archibald Douglas gave the king a bland look. "Certes, I cannot, Your Grace. I have never desired to be at enmity with you. But you hold our king prisoner, so I cannot count you as friend."

"And have treated him well. Fed and clothed him. Educated and armed him when the Duke of Albany seized his regalities. Protected him when those in his own kingdom would not." Henry slapped his hand down on the table. "I say that makes me more his friend than his own people and should make me yours."

"You could have also sent him home long since, had your demands not been beyond anything. Though they say the king your father made you swear to do so."

King Henry's eyes flared with temper.

James felt a bit like a bone being yanked between two growling dogs. "What His Grace says is true, at least in part. I was indeed fed and clothed and educated. And gently treated as a royal prisoner should be. But surely what concerns us is his proposal for my return home." He tilted his head as he looked thoughtfully at Douglas. Had he been sending Henry every word that passed between them, or was it someone in his household? "Do you know the terms of what he proposes? I do not."

"No. But I would like to hear."

Henry pulled toward him a stack of parchments, shuffled through them and took one out before he spoke. "Lord Douglas, I offer you a generous annuity: two hundred pounds." He glanced at James. "With the permission of your king. If you undertake to serve me against all men excepting him and bring me two hundred knights and squires and two hundred mounted bowmen to serve me in France. And I will pay their fees and for their equipage."

Douglas wound his thick fingers together as he looked from Henry to James and back again. "I would be fighting Albany's brother, my own good-son. And my own son, the Earl of Wigtoun, is there."

Henry gave him a cold smile. "Do you care?"

Douglas gave a harsh bark of laughter. "Buchan. No. But I would nae do battle against my own heir."

Henry nodded. "I would not expect it, but there are many fights to be had. I would use your force elsewhere. I agree that, if your son is there, your men should retire. That is agreed."

"Reasonable. But two hundred pounds is nae much for so large a change in alliance. I am nae beggar at yon door. To be honest, Your Grace, it would take more than that."

James considered his fingernails where his hands rested on the table. But the next words lifted his gaze.

"And your king to be released for a year when we return from France, if within three months of our return certain hostages are sent to me here."

"What hostages?" James demanded.

Henry slid the parchment under his hand across the table. "These."

James started reading and held back a snort. The first name on the list was Walter Stewart, Murdoch's eldest son and heir. Even if Murdoch would agree to his heir being hostage, the ungovernable Walter Stewart certainly would not. Next on the list was the Earl of Atholl, no friend to James. He ran his finger further down the list. Five earls. Four bishops. Ten other nobles. James stood and dropped the paper. Then he threw back his head and laughed.

Henry clasped his hand into a fist, and his face tightened.

James knew that laughing at him was dangerous, fool-hardy, but he truly couldn't help it.

Douglas took the list and, after a moment, coughed.

"Enough!" Henry snarled.

James finally swallowed down his laughter, but he shook his head. He would force out an apology, however futile the list was. "Forgive me, Your Grace. But you think Murdoch would send his heir as a hostage—for me? I vow that you know he would not."

"Wait, sire," Douglas put in. "Let us consider. Things might change before you return from France. Who knows how long that would be or what might occur before then? Mayhap we should nae be hasty in refusing His Grace of England."

James tapped a finger on the top edge of the chair. Archie Tyneman was known as a wily old fox, a description James had to admit did not apply to himself. "And if we cannot fulfill the terms?"

"Then according to the indenture, as I understand, you would not be freed, but would be no worse than now."

Henry grunted in assent, and James was sure a smirk touched his mouth for a moment. So, Henry thought he was putting one over on James and the Douglas? For a moment to consider, James reached for the list and pretended to look at the names as he thought through what the Douglas had said. Henry would tie up the Douglas and be sure that the earl didn't join both Buchan, his good-son, and his son with the Dauphin's forces in France.

James doubted Henry would trust Douglas enough to actually use his men in battle. He wouldn't, were he in Henry's place. And if the indenture didn't release James, it would cost Henry nothing. James knew the indenture would never be fulfilled. But the Earl of Douglas was willing to agree, so it must be because he didn't want to join Buchan and his son. Giving the Douglas what he wanted might well bring him firmly onto James's side in the battle with Albany. And James needed him. James caught the man's gaze, and a wry smile passed between them.

James nodded. "Aye. I will agree to it."

CHAPTER 37

AUGUST 1421

For miles behind they had left a smoking ruin. Torches tossed into June ripe fields, farmhouses set aflame. The smell of war, James decided, was not one he would learn to relish. When he and Humphrey of Gloucester, with their five hundred men in long columns and their wagons behind, reached the city walls, the June sun was high in the sky, and the gates were barred. A crossbow quarrel whispered into the ground before them.

James pulled up his horse, sweat dripping down his sides beneath his armor. Dreaux was a small city, but red tile roofs beyond the gate made it look a place he would enjoy a cup of wine and a lass in his lap. Or a certain lass he had not seen since they were at Middleham in the spring. A pity that, instead, James was here as an enemy.

Beside him, Humphrey scratched at his chin, cheek plates on his visor folded back, and sighed. "It was too much to hope that they would be sensible."

"Unfurl the white flag," James said to John. He shrugged at duke. "I'll ride to the gate and see if they will surrender the city."

"They're fools if they don't."

"Men often are, it seems to me."

Iain of Alway looked alarmed. "Your Grace, they've fired—"

"Only crossbow bolts. It might not pierce plate armor, and I'll keep my visor down. And mayhap they won't fire on my white flag." He had to hope they wouldn't fire on a herald as well, who was in lighter armor.

A herald wearing a surcoat marked with Humphrey of Gloucester's lion device with its blue border, holding the white flag atop a tall staff, rode beside him. James drew up a few yards from the closed gate and craned his neck to look up into the barbican atop it. "I would speak to your governor," he shouted in French.

A crossbowman poked his head out and ducked back in.

James shifted, and his saddle creaked. He chewed his lip as he waited. Perhaps Humphrey should have done this. He had more experience at war, though less than his brothers, but James wasn't going to go back to Henry and tell him his brother took a quarrel through the throat.

At last, a face poked out, gray-haired and craggy. James couldn't see much of the man, but he didn't look like any great knight. He took a breath. "In the name of Henry, King of England and Regent of France, I demand that you open the gates."

"I've heard what he did to Sire de Barbazan and the others at Melun after they surrendered. What he did before at Rouen. I'll not open my gates to treacherous English. If you want my city, you shall have to take it."

"My word of honor. Open your gates, and I'll grant you and your men your lives. The nobles will be held for ransom, yes. The rest can go where they will. They can stay under the governance of the English or flee south and find where the Dauphin has fled. My word as a knight."

245

"Your word of honor? As a knight?" The man pursed his lips and spat. "That on English honor and your word. I know better than to trust it. I had a cousin at Melun who did no more than help friends escape and died for it." He made a sound of disgust. "Honor."

"Do you want to die, you and your men? The Dauphin has retreated, and the Scots. They'll nae come to your aid. You see the size of our army. Open the gates and save your own lives."

"In twenty breaths, my men will no longer hold their fire." The man turned and was gone.

James jerked his horse's head about, but he refused to set it to a gallop and hoped the man's threat was a bluff. He felt a twitch in the middle of his back, but he was out of range when he heard the thud of a quarrel hitting the road behind him.

Humphrey met him standing in the road, and Iain held his bridle whilst he dismounted. "Do I need to ask how it went?"

"The crossbowman missed, so it could have been worse." James grimaced. "So now we'll have to take it by force." He turned and, arms akimbo, examined the walls. "They're nae so high. Ladders should do, don't you think, my lord? A city this size cannot have many defenders."

"We'll make camp."

"We had better put outriders on the roads as scouts," James said. "If the Armagnacs decide to stop retreating and come to their aid, I want to know it before they're on top of us." Duke Thomas's death was much on all their minds.

"They'll expect an attack tonight, but we'll let them stew for a bit; we shall rest for a day or two and put the men to building ladders. They may decide we're going to starve them out and relax their guard."

James nodded slowly. The duke had taken part in more

sieges than he, and it sounded like a good plan. But it would come down to bloody sword work in the end. So, James pointed out a spot on a hill for his pavilion and Duke Humphrey's, whilst the duke sent men to digging a latrine ditch and setting out a picket line for the horses. The oak woods nearby rang to axes for campfires. Sergeants sent out sentries, and well before nightfall they were encamped before the city they had been sent to take for the English king, whilst he was besieging the castle of Beaugency.

Sieges were boring, yet beneath the tedium was always a prickling at the back of the neck from being watched by enemies close at hand and twitching of fingers that waited to hold a blade. For two days, ladders were hammered together just out of sight of the walls. The camp was alive with the whish-whish of blades across whetstones and smelt of armor being polished. James paced to stare at the stubbornly closed gate. On the fourth day, the sky was lightening with streaks of pink and gold to the east, and faint stars spread across deep blue firmament to the west. James had checked and re-checked who would carry the ladders and who would be with him first over the wall. Half their force would hold back and charge when James opened the gate.

Iain of Alway was chewing his lip nervously, and James said, "Guard my back. That is your only task."

"Aye." Iain's Adam's apple bobbed as he swallowed. "I will, Your Grace."

Their men massed in front of the camp. "Up and over the walls, before they gather more men," he shouted. "The city is ours!"

The ground was hard in high summer's heat. The land had been cleared of trees near the walls long ago, and only a few stumps marred the way. James's heart pounded in his chest, and his skin was cooled with sweat though the sun wasn't yet up as he held his sword high over his head.

Duke Humphrey mounted his horse and nodded.

James yelled, "Attack!" as he brought his blade down to point at the wall.

He ran.

"For St. George," a sergeant shouted.

"For King Henry and St. George," another picked up the cry.

Their feet thudded on the hard ground. Beside James loped a man-at-arms, nameless and anonymous in the half-dark, over his shoulder, the top of a ladder. On the other side, an archer carried his longbow.

A crossbow twanged, and someone screamed, but it was still too dark for good bow work. Now they all shouted war cries as they pounded forward. James saved his breath for the fighting. Another man screamed as he fell to a crossbowman.

A horn blew an alarm, thin and lonely up on the wall. The light from a brazier flickered in the tower.

Suddenly, they were at the wall, and the man-at-arms grunted, hoisting the ladder. There was a clatter as others of the twenty hit the stone embattlement. James pushed the man-at-arms aside and climbed, one-handed, cursing under his breath that it was clumsy, but at the top he threw himself over and rolled to his knees, somehow not losing the blade. A dozen silhouettes swarmed beside him as the others climbed onto the parapet. He bellowed a command to hurry. Next time, if there was a next time, James thought, he would use—

But then there was no more time for thinking. A guard threw down his crossbow and fumbled for his sword. James thrust from his knees. It was a bad position to thrust from, but it went through mail and muscle. The man gripped the blade with both hands as James jerked it free and wrenched himself to his feet. He started to finish the man and then realized he was already dead. James kicked the body out of the way, and it tumbled from the parapet walk onto the ground.

"Clear the parapet!" James shouted and ran for the barbican.

"Pour la ville! Dreux!" a voice rang out.

Two guards came bursting from the door of the barbican, side by side, swords in their hands. James ducked a wild slash from one as he hacked across the others' leg, laying it bare to the bone. Then the guard shrieked. As he went down, arms flailing, James spun to face the second man with his sword raised. Iain scythed his sword in a wide swing and raked the guard deep across the throat.

James slapped his shoulder and shouted, "Come wi' me!" He raced down the narrow stairs with his squire at his back. A crossbowman poked his head out from behind a building and got a quarrel off before he ducked back again. James heard shouts and fighting behind on the parapet. When the crossbowman reappeared, he got another quarrel off before an arrow took him in the chest. He fell backwards and was still.

Then a dozen men-at-arms boiled out from a turn in the street. James heard the sergeant shout. Down the stairs, the English troops poured, blades in hand. A couple of arrows arched in the air.

James shouted, "Help me with this gate." It was a simple one, iron studded, thick as a man's arm is long, wide enough for a large wagon and fastened with two massive oak bars. They heaved together to lift the first. Another quarrel thudded above their heads as the bar crashed to the ground. James grunted as he hefted one end of the second while Iain hauled the first out of the way. James grabbed the hasp and began to pull the gate open. Shouts came from outside, and men-at-arms ran to push from the other side until the gates of Dreux were wide open.

Shouting, "For St. George and King Henry!" Humphrey of Gloucester thundered past him, his crimson, gold and blue banner rippling overhead as he raced toward the fight. A hundred knights and men-at-arms rode behind him, dawn's light flashing off their armor. The guards and some knights and a few merchants were shouting, "Yield! Mercy!" as they threw down their swords and pikes.

James leaned back against the thick edge of the open gate and stripped off his helm. The cool morning breeze caught his sweat-drenched hair and moved it around his neck. He tilted his head back and closed his eyes before he straightened.

Whilst Duke Humphrey's men were gathering up the prisoners, he went looking for their wounded and dead. He turned over bodies, but they did not wear the English devices. But one he found with a quarrel through his chest in a pool of blood. Another had been thrown from the parapet and lay with his head at a hideous angle. Their sergeant sat on the bottom step of the stairs to the parapet walk, wrapping a strip torn from his surcoat around his bleeding arm.

When James climbed the stairs, he found Sir John face down at the top, one of the knight's squires kneeling beside him. James squatted and turned him onto his back. He blinked away a burning behind his eyes. He'd become strangely fond of his guard dog.

For charging a city's walls, they had done well with so few deaths. He left the squire to look after the body, sent his own squire for his horse and went to join Duke Humphrey. The duke was standing beside his courser as his squire stripped off his gauntlets and their men stripped the prisoners, herded together and hands bound, of their armor and weapons.

"A fine attack," the duke said when he saw James. "You did well."

James nodded his thanks. "How many prisoners?"

"Twenty, though we must search the city to be certain none have hidden." His mouth had an angry twist. "Five are Scots. Two are English. Those will hang by the king's orders."

"The Scots are not his subjects. You have no right to hang them." James pulled off his gauntlets and threw them hard on the ground. "Do what you will with the English, but the Scots are mine to deal with. They only fought as their liege lord commanded. I'll nae have them hang."

He looked at the duke, face set and ready to fight the matter to a finish, but Duke Humphrey sighed. "My royal brother would take that very ill."

"Then he must."

"You earned the right, I suppose. Though I won't take the raking for you when he hears." The duke turned his head and shouted to a tall, lanky sergeant, "Release the Scots to Lord James."

CHAPTER 38

SEPTEMBER 1421

wo men-at-arms rode beside James and fifty more behind as they passed though the charred desolation of the Loire valley. Lord Humphrey had turned aside with their main force at his brother's command to proceed to Rougemont, but James followed the blue-green ribbon of the river Loire. Farmhouses were blackened shells, and the carcasses of dogs and cattle rotted under living blankets of feeding ravens. Occasionally, smoke still drifted from the fields. His escort seemed lost without their leader, but if anything, their confusion led them to keep him under closer watch. They were never more than a step from his side.

They crossed the long stone bridge to Beaugency, the river splashing below, and it was midday when they rode into sight of the castle towering over the Loire like a steep gray mountain. Its granite walls might have existed forever, so massive did they seem, higher and thicker than even the Tower of London. This apple will not fall easily into Henry's lap, James thought.

The vast English camp lay just out of bowshot from its walls. Men swarmed over the skeleton of a tall trebuchet they were building beside three others already completed. As he watched, the arm on one was pulled back, and it released a stone that sailed over the wall. Even from the road, James heard the crash.

Behind the trebuchets, thousands of tents and campfires and pavilions were spread out in neat array. On one side were picket lines of horses, and nearer, lines of empty wagons awaiting a move to another siege or battle; and all around the perimeter, sentries stood watch. His brother's defeat had made Henry even more wary than usual. It had them all.

On the ramparts between the merlons, James could make out movements as men watched. High above fluttered the blue and gold banner of the Dauphin Charles, though James was sure it was only defiance and the prince was not there.

As they rode between the tents, James could feel eyes on his back, though perhaps it was his imagination that they were hostile. But James had sent a message ahead, as had Duke Humphrey, about the capture of Dreux. How angry Henry was that the Scots had been freed, James had no way to guess. He wasn't sure he wanted to.

"Your Grace," Iain said, "where should we pitch your tent?"

James grimaced. Without knowing how he would be greeted, he wasn't sure if it should be. But Henry wouldn't pack him off to the Tower of London before tomorrow, so he pointed to the edge of the camp. "There. And find us some food. I'm weary and may be more so after I call on King Henry."

He turned his horse's head and swung from the saddle beneath the huge Plantagenet banner that flew about King Henry's pavilion. He raised an eyebrow at the blank look of the guards at the flap and said, "Tell His Grace that Lord James awaits."

The man gave him a stony look under his helm, which spoke a great deal, but James crossed his arms, studying the scurrying clouds in the August sky as he waited. When the guard returned, he said that Henry would see him shortly and to wait. James turned his head to conceal a wry smile. He was to be humiliated as part of his punishment for sparing the Scots, but he had suffered worse in his day.

He tried to think of a new line for the poem he was writing for Lady Joan, but the camp rang to the hammering on the new trebuchet and the periodic crash of a stone being thrown. It droned with men talking, cursing, and laughing as they waited for something to happen. He shifted his feet and wished for a chair. The morning's ride, after so many others, had been long. His body ached from the weight of his armor. At last, he crouched and picked up a twig to scrawl in the dust.

A squire threw back the flap and peered around before he noticed James where he was scratching a line of Chaucer's Knight's Tale into the dirt:

AND THEREFORE, AT THE KING'S COURT, MY BROTHER,
EACH MAN FOR HIMSELF, THERE IS NONE OTHER.

"LORD JAMES, His Grace requires your presence."

James threw down the twig and strode into the pavilion behind the squire, who went to stand quietly in a corner.

He bowed and smiled crookedly. "Your Grace."

"Lord James. You expressly disobeyed my command and violated your own edict with your actions at Dreux." The English king had not raised his voice, but James could see anger seething in his eyes. "I do not tolerate disobedience in my commanders."

"You had no right to give me commands concerning the

Scots," James said quietly. "If I am their king, then only I may command. If I am not, my edict has no weight."

"You are my prisoner. My pensioner. And were my commander. Obedience is what I expect and what I shall have."

James bowed slightly. "And you shall have it, sire. Except where it affects my own realm."

King Henry rose abruptly. "You no longer have my trust, Lord James. No longer. So, I now set you to a task and with such guardians that trust is not needed." He glared at the squire. "Pour me a cup of wine." The king took the wine cup and swirled it thoughtfully before he took a deep drink. "The queen will give me a son within a few months. As soon as they are strong enough to travel, I shall have them brought to Rouen. You will go there and set up a household and prepare a household for the queen. One of my clerks, a John Waterton, will provide you with funds and help oversee the task. And you shall—" Henry glared at him. "—have a new keeper and more bodyguards to be most straightly watched."

James almost smiled at the king's certainty he would have a son. But then, with King Henry's good luck, he probably would. Biting the inside of his cheek, he kept his face still and wooden. In truth, it was better than he had expected, but smiling would hardly be wise, so he said, "Might I ask who this new keeper is?"

"Sir William Meryng." Henry glowered at him, his lips tight and scar white against his dark face. "I have given him four squires and ten archers for your guard, and he will attend you beginning today."

"As you command, sire."

James walked slowly to his tent and ducked within to where Lyon was pouring wine and Dougal was slicing a haunch of beef. Iain knelt to unfasten his cuirass. His chest was dripping with sweat, so James dipped a cloth in the basin and sponged himself clean. It felt good after the long, hot, weary ride.

"We may enjoy Rouen, I suppose," he said. And in truth, unlike the English king, James did not love war. Henry said war without burning was like sausage without mustard, but James was sure he could live without either.

CHAPTER 39

MAY 1422

*J*ames had somehow missed the feast. He had seen that he was outside the city riding with Sir William and his constant escort, inspecting the tent city that housed the five hundred men the king had brought with him to meet his queen at Rouen. The king's face had been grim when he learned she had not brought his son, but she pleaded the infant's youth. The king surely did not want to expose him to the rigors of a sea voyage when he had only six months.

The royal hall had been scented with roast venison and spices, but James was sure they could find a meal at one of the hundreds of cook fires. Iain had shaved his cheeks close and brushed the blue doublet he had worn to be dubbed, a gift from King Henry. And the letter he had left in Lady Joan's room would, he could only pray, bring her to the little garden tucked behind an old lady's solar, no longer used. He had seen for a moment her golden head as the hall had swarmed with the queen's court all in all colors when the king strode in, his steel armor burnished, decorated with gold scrollwork. James knelt and kissed the queen's hand before fleeing.

Sir William was a tough old knight, big and bristly and stubborn in following his king's command to keep James under close guard, but not unkindly. He laughed when they walked between the cook fires as the afternoon darkened toward a soft May night. "You did well, Lord James, escaping another feast, sitting until our arses were numb."

James slapped his back and grinned. "That I did." They kicked up puffs of dust in the ground broken by a thousand feet. The sound of drunken laughter came from one of the larger tents. Apparently, the king had loosened the stricture on drunkenness, at least for the night, or they dared punishment. A smell of shite blew from the picket lines just to the north. The arrival of the King of Scots was noticed. A circle of men casting a die stopped to watch him. A whore, whom he recognized from the town, taking a coin from the first of several men in a line, grinned at him and called out that her sisters were still in the town. With a smile, James replied that they would have to find new custom.

"Lord James," someone yelled after him. When he turned, a sergeant who had gone over the wall with him at Dreux offered him half a rabbit that sizzled over his fire. James split it in two, handed quarter to Sir William, and squatted by the fire. "Have you seen him?" the sergeant asked. "The new prince?"

His mouth full of the dripping meat, James wiped his lips on his arm and swallowed. "Still in England. It would be a rough crossing for a bairn. Nae doubt his mother knew best to leave him home."

Sir William nodded. "Aye, but it would have been good for the king to see the boy." He gave James a frowning look, and James nodded. No one spoke about the dark circles under the king's eyes, his thin face, or that he had winced from a sudden pain when he dismounted. But Henry of Monmouth was too young to ail. It must have only been weariness from a long siege.

Juices ran down the sergeant's face as he stuffed a hunk of rabbit in his mouth, and he said around the meat, "I'm right glad to be in the king's train. It's taking a rest for me." He took a cautious look around before he said, "The siege was bad enough. Men died like flies from the flux, and the be-damned French fought like very hell-spawn devils." He gave a sheepish look. "It shames me, but I cannot take pleasure in drowning even my enemies when they yield." He gave James a pointed look.

James grunted. The man had cut the prisoners loose when James forgave them for fighting against him. James loosened the wineskin he had tied to his belt and offered it to the sergeant, who thanked him kindly and took a long pull. They passed it between the three of them to wash down the rabbit, until Sir William drained the last drop as the sun melted into the hills, sending streams of orange and red across the darkling sky.

James wished the sergeant good luck and trailed by the squires and archers started back toward the gray stone keep of Rouen Castle, where, since the king's command, James had kept his household. "A pity there was nae enough wine to share wi' the squires," James observed, loudly enough that his voice carried to the guard.

"We are not lackeys to haul about a tun of wine for the squires," Sir William said.

At the stairs to the tower up to James's chamber, he sketched a bow and left as one of the squires followed to keep watch outside the door.

When they reached it, James gave the spotty, plump squire a kind look. "Alart, they call you? You didn't have even a mouthful of the wine. Come in, and we'll share a cup wi' you." When he gave James a worried, hopeful look, James said, "You'll be standing guard, only within the room."

James felt a bit sorry that the wine wasn't watered, as the lad no doubt was used to, and it was richer than anything a squire would be allowed. James stretched out his legs and refilled Alart's wine cup, sipping at his own, and refilled it again whilst the lad blethered on about being knighted and the adventures he would have until his head dropped onto the table and his snores grated in the night air. Iain chuckled, and James said, "Look after him. He's nae likely to awake, but if he does, give him some more wine or knock him on the head." He winced. "Nae too hard, though."

James put a light summer cloak around his shoulders, held a taper to one of the torches, and made his way down the stairs. At the hall to the king's quarters, a guard saluted as he passed. Down he went to the ground floor and to the old tower and to a narrow side door. He snuffed the taper and stepped out into a garden. The ground blanketed in prim-roses and crowned with a circle of tall beeches. He bent to break off a branch of the sweet-smelling wildflowers and waited in the deep shade of the trees.

When the door opened, she stepped out and walked slowly into the midst of the flowers. Silhouetted against the moonlight, her hair was a golden halo. She lifted her face to the moon and seemed to be listening, perhaps for his foot-steps or just for the rustle of the wind in the leaves.

James moved toward her. She jerked her head at the sound of a twig snapping beneath his foot. "You came," he said and felt foolish.

"As did you, my lord." She tilted her head, serious, inquiring like the nightingale the first day he saw her and waited until he came close, and then she lowered her eyes.

With his fingertips he stroked the side of her neck and leaned his forehead against hers. "Joan." His voice was thick.

"Be my lady. My queen." She looked up at that, showing James the mysterious smile he had come to love. "I love you," he confessed.

She put a hand on his chest, and he pulled her into his arms, burying his face in her hair.

"I love the softness of your skin. I love your golden hair. I love your mouth and the way you smile at me."

"Much to love," she whispered. "Or little. There is more to me than my soft skin."

He kissed her. "You have a strength that I think mayhap only I can see. A sweetness that everyone sees. And sometimes, when we talk, you laugh. Did I say that I love your laugh? My sweet... My goddess."

She chuckled then, low and throaty. "You are a poet, my lord. Everyone knows so. I am no goddess."

"Just my lady, then? My queen, if I gain my crown? Come with to Scotland. Be with me." He kissed her mouth. She kissed him back and twined her arms around his neck. He turned her and pressed her back against the beech tree, leaning into her so that he felt her body beneath the silk that she wore. When he broke off, she was breathing fast.

"Your lady," she whispered. "You Grace, I would be your lady."

He kissed her again deeply and whispered against her ear, "Promise yourself to me. I have nae ring for you, but I faithfully promise to marry you in times meet and fitting."

She made a sound, not quite laugh nor sob, and said in a choked voice. "I promise."

"Then lie with me? Now? My own Lady Joan."

"The earth will be hard..." Her voice wavered.

"Aye. Earth is as hard as life, but the primroses will ease it."

She looked up at him thoughtfully. Her eyes gleamed in the moonlight, and he waited. "I will."

She loosed her cloak from her shoulders and unfastened her gown, not hurrying, until it was a pool of silk around her feet. James's hands shook as he shed his clothes, dropping them in piles.

Her skin glowed ivory in the moonlight. He drank in her proud, straight body. She stretched out a hand and touched the scar on his arm, stroked it lightly, but her glance was wily and coquettish. "When you looked at me across the dance floor that first night, were you thinking of this?"

"Aye. You could tell?"

"I could."

He took the hand that stroked his arm and kissed her palm and her wrist. "I was afeart so."

She laughed and slipped the other arm around his neck. "Truly?"

There were no more words. He stroked her soft, round breasts and pulled her against him. They sank into the bed of primroses to learn of each other's bodies, pleased and pleasing. She wrapped her arms around him and welcomed him. The world narrowed down to the two of them. Slow and delicious, the surge of fire built. She called out, "James!" in a kind of convulsion, and James went up in a burst, heat rushing through him. A swooping wave threw James forward. He shuddered—thoughts, strength, all faculties gone—everything boiled up and out and into his lady.

For a moment they trembled together, moist skin and breathy sounds mingling. Then she held him, and her embrace poured through the cracks, healing hurts he had not even known he had suffered. Murmuring comforting words that made him smile into her hair, she rocked him in her arms as they caught their breaths. So young—innocent. How could she know the ease he needed better than he did himself?

He pillowed his face into her thick hair and breathed in

her scent. The pulse in his throat matched the one he felt in her. Hearts beating together. James for once had no words.

After a long calm, she said, "The king would be furious. To promise myself without his leave." She clicked her tongue against her teeth. "And to a king who is his prisoner."

"He must nae yet ken. He might turn his anger on you. But when I return to England from France…" He reached for his cloak and pulled it over them. "Shall I tell you what has been said about my return to Scotland…"

CHAPTER 40

AUGUST 1422

*H*e was standing in the high window of his chamber in the Tower of London, where he had passed many hours through the years. The yard below was empty, and snow blew against the panes.

"Iain," he said, and no one answered. When he turned, there was no one there. "Dougal," he called and went to the door. He pulled and it wouldn't open. He pounded on it. "The door should not be locked against me!"

"My liege," a voice said, and James recognized Orkney's voice. He let out a sigh of relief and turned. "My liege," Orkney said again, kneeling, and when he looked up, James saw the empty eyes of a skeleton.

He jerked away and grabbed the edge of his mattress to keep from tumbling out of bed. His heart was thumping in his chest, and someone was pounding on the door. The room was pitch-black, and Iain was mumbling in his pallet as he awoke.

"Lord James!" the squire on guard called.

"What?" James said, throwing aside his blanket and staggering to his feet. "Wait."

Iain cursed softly, and there was the sound of a flint struck, and candlelight flickered as he stumbled to the door. "It's the middle of the night, man. Wha' do you want?"

A page stood behind the guard, his face pale, wringing his hands. The squire-guard said, "There is urgent news from Vincennes. The queen requires his presence."

James swallowed. They had news three weeks before that the king was so ill he had been forced to turn back to Vincennes from joining the battle at Cosne-sur-Loire.

"I must dress," James said.

Iain pulled out a blue silk doublet and tights, and shortly James followed the page through the dark halls, where only a few torches flickered in their sconces. The royal apartments were on the far side of the castle. A knight stood guard at the door, and the page announced, "Lord James Stewart, son of the late King of Scots."

Within, in the anteroom, a fire blazed on the hearth, filling the room with a glow, and candles burned on the table where a letter lay abandoned. Queen Catherine sat in a large chair, the blonde, sturdy Lady Jacqueline de Bavière kneeling beside her, stroking her hand. Joan patted the queen's loose, tousled hair. A priest stood by the windows with a breviary in his hands, and a servant brought a goblet of wine that Lady Jacqueline placed into the queen's hands.

"Lord James!" the queen exclaimed. "You must tell me. Explain to me. The king, he has sent for you."

"For me?" James shook his head, wondering if he was still asleep and dreaming. The king had barely acknowledged him in more than a year. "The page said news. What news? What has happened?"

The queen shoved the wine into Lady Jacqueline's hands, as she pressed a palm to her mouth. Her eyes were red and swollen. She uttered a choked moan. "The letter said he is receiving the Extreme Unction. That he is calling all the nobles to his side before he dies. But he does not call for me."

James had no idea what to say. Perhaps something had happened between them, and the king was angry with her. That she had not brought his son when he commanded? Henry could become enraged when he was disobeyed, of that James had enough experience.

He looked at Joan and made a tiny shrug.

She put her arms around the queen and said, "You mustn't upset yourself. It must be that he does not want to endanger you. Who knows what this illness might be that has seized him?"

"If he commands me, I should prepare to go straight away," James said in as soothing a voice as he knew. "I'll find out why he doesn't send for you, if I can. Mayhap when he is better…"

Joan gave him an incredulous look over the queen's head. They both knew if the king had received the Extreme Unction that he did not expect to live.

"With your leave, Your Grace, I should go."

But the queen was crying into Joan's shoulder, so James bowed and strode out the door almost at a run.

In two hours, a score of men-at-arms awaited him in the castle's bailey yard. Sir William Meryng, along with his four squires and ten archers, joined them.

His courser with such beautiful lines James thought he must be as fast as the wind would speed the journey. Iain held the bridle while James mounted, considering how much he had changed from the lanky lad he had been when he had joined James all those years ago.

The streets were empty as they rode through the city. A wagon was being unloaded of barrels at a warehouse, two men grunting as they carried the load on their shoulders. In a shadowy alley, someone moaned. As they passed through the city gates, the Angelus pealed at the cathedral, and church bells joined in across the city. Pale threads of dawn were stealing into the sky, chasing back the stars.

They rode through the day cantering and then slowing to a walk only to canter again, stopping at streams when they must to water the horses and let them cool. When the sun was at its zenith, James insisted they stop long enough for the horses to rest, whilst the men sat beneath a stand of chestnuts and cut up hard sausage from their saddlebags, before they rode on. No one spoke the long day. What was there to say, except the young and strong King Henry could not be dying.

That night, they made camp beside the River Seine. They hadn't brought wagons or pack horses that would have slowed them, so they gathered deadwood and huddled around campfires. James set sentries and a watch on the picketed horses, even though an attack was unlikely, but there were gangs of bandits, and he didn't intend to take any chances.

Come morning, it was another bright, sweltering day. James kept the column at a good pace southeast along the Seine. The signs of recent war were everywhere. Fields that should have been full of ripening summer grain were choked with weeds. They passed groups of merchants' wagons, whose guards looked at them, eyes full of suspicion. Yet the world grew dazzling, and they rode beside water that rippled, gleaming with bright sunlight.

In the early afternoon, the tall, square keep of Vincennes rose before them at last, around it five towers and thick, sandstone walls. James drew up before the gate and his name soon opened it before them.

James passed knights whispering in the hallway, hands twitching with nerves or with fear. Two priests knelt in the hallway, mumbling prayers. A squire opened the door and motioned James in. The lack of ceremony made a chill go through him.

John of Bedford was thin, his face drawn and eyes sunken, as though he hadn't slept in weeks. James saw him and knew it was as bad as he had been told. Richard Beauchamp paced back and forth in front of a window, his hands clasped behind his back and his head bowed. Thomas Beaufort sat in a chair by the hearth, where a fire blazed, despite the day's heat, his elbows on his knees and hands plunged into his scant hair. A brazier in the corner gave off a sweet scent that didn't cover the stench of shit and sickness.

"My lord," James said quietly.

James couldn't see beyond the bed's heavy draperies. A plump physician in a rich robe bent over the bed, a cup and spoon in his hands. After a moment, he turned and said, "I gave him just a spoon of the syrup of poppy for his pain, my lords, but I dare not give him more."

"Is that James?" King Henry said in a thin voice.

James bit his lip so hard that he tasted blood to hold in his gasp at the skeleton that lay under piles of blankets. Henry was shaking with fever, and his cheeks, where the bones jutted out under nothing but skin, were brightly flushed.

James dropped to one knee beside the bed. "Your Grace," he whispered.

"Damn you," Henry croaked with a blaze of his old fierceness. "Now you will never swear fealty to me."

James twitched a wry smile. "I never would have. You ken that, sire."

Henry flinched with pain as he nodded. "I have confessed. Received Extreme Unction. But I must know, James, so I can confess it. Have I wronged you? I swore..." His face contorted, and he drew a deep breath. "I swore to my father on his death bed that I would free you. But you were still young. Too young. Did I wrong you? Wrong my father?"

James bowed his head for a moment. The man was dying. Perhaps it would be a kindness to lie, but he should confess it. Go to God with a cleansed soul, if that were truly possible.

He raised his eyes and met Henry's gaze. He nodded. "Your wronged me, Your Grace." He tried to make his voice gentle but heard the shard of hard anger within it. "You broke a most sacred oath to a man dying, your own father. And wronged me most cruelly."

The king's thin face twisted in a grotesque smile. "Always honest, James. I thank you."

James stood and looked down, shaking his head. Not a word about righting the wrong. The king's eyes closed, and he turned his head away, sagging into the pillows.

After a moment, James left the bedside. "How long has he been like this?" James asked John of Bedford.

The duke shook his head. "He has grown worse daily for two months. Were my brother not so strong…" His voice broke.

"Should we remain? Or return to Rouen? The queen was distraught."

"I want you here, so if he calls for you again…" His Adam's apple worked as he swallowed, and his voice was thick. "But it will not be long, all the physicians say."

Outside the door, James wavered on his feet, exhausted, and realized he had nowhere to lay his head. He needed to find the seneschal and arrange rooms for himself and his men. And sleep. His belly was empty, but all he wanted was sleep.

By the time a servant led him and Iain to a tiny room in the east tower, the castle was full to overflowing, and he was lucky to be given it. He was numb with weariness and felt nothing as he threw himself onto the bed.

James opened his eyes, awake. The room was gray with moonlight. Wide awake. Shouts. "The king is dead." Strange that no one shouted the second part. Feet pounded, running, and another voice shouted, "The king is dead."

Iain snored, rolled in a blanket in a corner.

James rose, shoved his feet into boots that Iain must have removed whilst he slept and went into the hall, down the stairs. The keep was dark as James strode across the inner bailey. The full moon hovered over the tower. On the parapet walk, the guards stood still, frozen by shock.

A squire cried in the hallway, sobbing, face buried in his hands.

A knight ran up the stairs shouting, "The dukes must be told! Why haven't the dukes been called?"

The guard at the door of the king's bedroom just looked at him blankly. Within, the only light was the red flicker from the hearth. The panicked physician was clasping himself and rocking as he said, "We told them he could not be saved."

James picked up Henry's hand, and already it felt cold. He smiled in the near-darkness, standing beside the dead king. It didn't feel like a nice smile, more like a sneer of bitter joy, and James was glad no one could see it.

HISTORICAL NOTES

In the writing of this novel, I have stayed as close as possible to known historical events. For the purpose of storytelling, however, I did change the location or date of a few happenings. King James's attempted escape occurred at Windsor Castle rather than Raby Castle, and his stay at Raby was slightly earlier than in the novel. I was careful however not to alter the occurrences in any substantive way.

King Henry V's executions of prisoners were, if anything, more extensive than I described and were brutal even by medieval standards. While some of the battles, especially those in the tunnels under the walls of Melun, may seem strange to modern readers, they did happen and were described by chroniclers of the period. As for the nature of King James I of Scotland, his love of both athletics and poetry were well documented as was his participation in the war in France.

For anyone who would like to do a little reading on the main characters of the novel, I recommend *James I, King of Scots* by E. W. M. Balfour-Melville. King James's semi-autobiographical poem *The Kingis Quair* is available online. Those only skim the surface of the topic of the reign of King James I, but much of the information is about events not included in this novel. They will be in *A King Uncaged*.

LIST OF PRINCIPAL HISTORICAL CHARACTERS

James Stewart—Youngest son of Scotland's King Robert III, Earl of Carrick, and Prince of Scotland. Heir to the throne. Later James I, King of Scots

Joan de Beaufort—daughter of John Beaufort, 1st Earl of Somerset and Margaret Holland and a half-niece of King Henry IV of England, eventual wife of James I of Scotland and Queen of Scots.

Robert III—King of Scots, son of King Robert II

Robert Stewart—Duke of Albany, younger half-brother of King Robert III. Governor of Scotland

Archibald Douglas—Earl of Douglas, known as Archie Tyneman

Henry Percy—Eventual Earl of Northumberland, son of Henry Hotspur

Henry Wardlaw—Bishop of St. Andrews, primate of Scotland

Sir Henry Sinclair—Earl of Orkney

Sir David Fleming of Cumbernault—Chancellor of King Robert III

Sir Robert Lauder of Edrington—Lord of Bass Rock Castle

Robert Lauder—Son of Sir Robert Lauder

William Giffard—Esquire of James Stewart

Hugh-Atte-Fen—English pirate

King Henry IV—King of England

Thomas Rempston—Constable of the Tower of London

Gruffudd Glendwr—Prisoner in the Tower of London, son of Owen ab Glendwr, rightful Prince of Wales

Murdoch Stewart—Earl of Fife, eldest son and heir of the Duke of Albany

John Lyon—Priest and secretary to James Stewart

Dougal Drummand—Priest and confessor to James Stewart

Henry of Monmonth—Son of Henry IV, Prince of Wales and eventual King of England

Sir Richard Gray—Lord of Codenore, High Chamerlain of England, one of the keepers of James Stewart

Charles—Duc d'Orléans and Valois, brother of King Charles of France, accomplished poet

Henry Beaufort—Bishop of Winchester, Chancellor of England, illegitimate son of John of Gaunt, uncle of Joanna Beaufort

Sir William Douglas of Drumlanrig—Scottish baron and ally of King James

Queen Isabella of France—Married to the mad King Charles VI of France

King Charles VI—King of France, known as both 'the beloved' and 'the mad'

Catherine of Valoi—Princess of France, daughter of Charles and Isabella, wife of Henry V of England and eventual Queen of England

Iain of Alway—Member of the household of King James.

(His name was actually John of Alway. I altered the name for the novel because of a superfluity of Johns)

Thomas of Lancaster—Duke of Clarence, son of Henry IV of England

John of Lancaster—Duke of Bedford, son of Henry IV of England

Humphrey—Duke of Gloucester, son of Henry IV of England

GLOSSARY

- **Afeart**—(Scots) Afraid.
- **Ain**—(*Scots*) Own.
- **Aright**—In a proper manner; correctly.
- **Auld**—(*Scots*) Old
- **Aye**—Yes.
- **Bailey**—An enclosed courtyard within the walls of a castle.
- **Bairn**—(*Scots*) Child.
- **Bannock**—(*Scots*) Flat, unleavened bread made of oatmeal or barley flour, generally cooked on a flat metal sheet.
- **Barbican**—A tower or other fortification, especially one at a gate or drawbridge.
- **Battlement**—A parapet in which rectangular gaps occur at intervals to allow for firing arrows.
- **Bedecked**—To adorn or ornament in a showy fashion.
- **Betimes**—On occasion.
- **Bracken**—Weedy fern.
- **Brae**—(*Scots*)**,** Hill or slope.

- **Braeside**—(*Scots*), Hillside.
- **Barmy**—Daft.
- **Braw**—(*Scots*), Fine or excellent.
- **Buffet**—A blow or cuff with or as if with the hand.
- **Burn**—(*Scots*), a name for watercourses from large streams to small rivers.
- **Clàrsach**—A Celtic harp
- **Chivvied**—Harassed.
- **Cloying**—Causing distaste or disgust by supplying with too much of something originally pleasant.
- **Churl**—A peasant
- **Cot**—Small building.
- **Couched**—To lower a lance to a horizontal position.
- **Courser**—A swift, strong horse, often used as a warhorse.
- **Crenel**—An open space or notch between two merlons in the battlement of a castle or city wall.
- **Crook**—Tool, such as a bishop's crosier or a shepherd's staff.
- **Curtain wall**—The defensive outer wall of a medieval castle.
- **Curst**—A past tense and a past participle of curse.
- **Defile**—A narrow gorge or pass.
- **Destrier**—the heaviest class of warhorse.
- **Din**—A jumble of loud, usually discordant sounds.
- **Dirk**—A long, straight-bladed dagger.
- **Dower**—the part or interest of a deceased man's real estate allotted by law to his widow for her lifetime, often applied to property brought to the marriage by the bride.
- **Empurple**—to make or become purple.
- **Erstwhile**—In the past, at a former time, formerly.

- **Ewer**—A pitcher, especially a decorative one with a base, an oval body, and a flaring spout.
- **Faggot**—A bundle of sticks or twigs, esp. when bound together and used as fuel.
- **Falchion**—A short, broad sword with a convex cutting edge and a sharp point.
- **Farrier**—One who shoes horses.
- **To fash (oneself)**— Feel upset or worried.
- **Fetlock**—A 'bump' and joint above and behind a horse's hoof.
- **Forbye**—Besides.
- **Ford**—A shallow crossing in a body of water, such as a river.
- **Garderobe**—A privy chamber
- **Gilded**—Cover with a thin layer of gold.
- **Girth**—Band around a horse's belly.
- **Git**—A bastard or fool.
- **Glen**—A small, secluded valley.
- **Gorse**—A spiny yellow-flowered European shrub common in Scotland.
- **Groat**—English silver coin worth four pence.
- **Hallo**—A variant of Hello.
- **Hart**—A male deer.
- **Hauberk**—A long armor tunic made of chain mail.
- **Haugh**—**(Scots)** A low-lying meadow in a river valley.
- **Hied**—to go quickly; hasten.
- **Hock**—the joint at the tarsus of a horse or similar animal, pointing backwards and corresponding to the human ankle.
- **Hodden-gray**—coarse homespun cloth produced in Scotland made by mixing black and white wools.
- **Holy Rude**—(*Scots*), The Holy Cross

- **Hoyden**—High-spirited; boisterous.
- **Jape**—Joke or quip.
- **Jesu**—Vocative form of Jesus.
- **Ken**—to know (a person or thing).
- **Kirtle**—A woman's dress typically worn over a chemise or smock.
- **Laying**—to engage energetically in an action.
- **Loch**—Lake, an arm of the sea, especially when narrow or partially landlocked..
- **Louring**—Lowering.
- **Lowed**—the characteristic sound uttered by cattle; a moo.
- **Malmsey**—A sweet fortified Madeira wine
- **Marischal**—The hereditary custodian of the Royal Regalia of Scotland and protector of the king's person.
- **Maudlin**—Effusively or tearfully sentimental.
- **Mawkish**—Excessively and objectionably sentimental.
- **Mercies**—Without any protection against; helpless before.
- **Merlon**—A solid portion between two crenels in a battlement or crenellated wall.
- **Midges**—A gnat-like fly found worldwide and frequently occurring in swarms near ponds and lakes, prevalent across Scotland.
- **Mien**—Bearing or manner, especially as it reveals an inner state of mind.
- **Mount**—Mountain or hill.
- **Murk**—Darkness or thick mist that makes it difficult to see.
- **Nae**—No, Not.
- **Nave**—The central approach to a church's high altar, the main body of the church.

- **Nock**—to fit an arrow to a bowstring.
- **Nook**—Hidden or secluded spot.
- **Outwith**—(*Scots*) Outside, beyond.
- **Palfrey**—An ordinary saddle horse, as opposed to a warhorse.
- **Pap**—Material lacking real value or substance.
- **Parapet**—A defensive wall, usually with a walk, above which the wall is chest to head high.
- **Pate**—Head or brain.
- **Pell-mell**—In a jumbled, confused manner, helter-skelter.
- **Perfidy**—The act or an instance of treachery.
- **Pillion**—Pad or cushion for an extra rider behind the saddle or riding on such a cushion.
- **Piebald**—Spotted or patched.
- **Privily**—Privately or secretly.
- **Quintain**—Object mounted on a post, used as a target in tilting exercises
- **Rood**—Crucifix.
- **Runnels**—A narrow channel.
- **Saddlebow**—The arched upper front part of a saddle.
- **Saltire**—An ordinary in the shape of a Saint Andrew's cross, when capitalized: the flag of Scotland. (a white saltire on a blue field)
- **Samite**—A heavy silk fabric, often interwoven with gold or silver.
- **Sassenach**—(Scots), An Englishman, derived from the Scots Gaelic Sasunnach meaning, originally, "Saxon."
- **Schiltron**—A formation of soldiers wielding outward-pointing pikes.
- **Seneschal**—A steward or major-domo
- **Shite**—Shit

- **Siller**—(Scots), Silver.
- **Sirrah**—Mister; fellow. Used as a contemptuous form of address.
- **Sleekit**—(Scots), Unctuous, sly, crafty.
- **Sumpter horse**—Pack animal.
- **Surcoat**—an outer tunic often worn over armor.
- **Tail**—A noble's following of guards.
- **Thralldom**—One, such as a slave or serf, who is held in bondage.
- **Tiddler**—A small fish such as a minnow
- **Tisane**—an herbal infusion drunk as a beverage or for its mildly medicinal effect.
- **Trailed**—to drag (the body, for example) wearily or heavily.
- **Trebuchet**—A medieval catapult-type siege engine for hurling heavy projectiles.
- **Trencher**—A plate or platter for food, often a thick slice of stale bread.
- **Trestle table**—A table made up of two or three trestle supports over which a tabletop is placed.
- **Trews**—Close-fitting trousers.
- **Tun**—Large cask for liquids, especially wine.
- **Villein**—A medieval peasant or tenant farmer
- **Wain**—Open farm wagon.
- **Wattles**—A fleshy, wrinkled, often brightly colored fold of skin hanging from the neck.
- **Westering**—to move westward.
- **Wheedling**—to use flattery or cajolery to achieve one's ends.
- **Whilst**—While.
- **Whisht**—An interjection to urge silence.
- **Wroth**—Angry.